We'll

Never

Tell

KAYLA   PERRIN

St. Martin's Paperbacks

This is a work of fiction. All of the characters, organizations, and events portrayed in this novel are either products of the author's imagination or are used fictitiously.

WE'LL NEVER TELL

Copyright © 2007 by Kayla Perrin.
Excerpt from *What's Done in Darkness* Copyright © 2015 by Kayla Perrin.

All rights reserved.

For information address St. Martin's Press, 175 Fifth Avenue, New York, NY 10010.

ISBN: 978-1-250-06945-0

Printed in the United States of America

St. Martin's Paperbacks edition / September 2015

St. Martin's Paperbacks are published by St. Martin's Press, 175 Fifth Avenue, New York, NY 10010.

10 9 8 7 6 5 4 3 2 1

This one's for my friends and fans in Buffalo:
Corbie Lavery—bookseller and friend
Sarah JM Kolberg—friend
Jennifer Parker—friend and book-fair chair
Annette Cole—faithful fan and friend
Angela Woodson-Brice—faithful fan and friend
And other friends and fans too many to name.

Thanks to all of you for your friendship and
continued support! You thought it'd be a great idea
for me to set a book in Buffalo, and
you were right.

And for Jonette Harper Stanley:
You went through quite an ordeal while pledging,
but you stood strong. You stood proud.
You exemplify the best aspects of sorority life.
Stay blessed, my friend.

Author's Note

While this story is a work of fiction, it is set at a real university—the University of Buffalo. However, because this is a fictional story, I took some liberties with the setting. At the University of Buffalo, there are no sorority and fraternity houses on campus. The university does not allow them. For the sake of the story I wanted to tell, I altered that fact in my book. So in this book you will find that the sorority and fraternity houses are located on campus, even though this is not the case in reality.

Acknowledgments

Writing a novel is not a simple task. It takes many hours, much sweat, and sometimes even tears. Contrary to the belief that an author completes a novel in total solitude, she actually needs to make contact with the outside world if she's going to write a realistic story—at least on occasion.

In my case, that contact came when I needed to research certain aspects of my story. I asked many questions, mostly of Sarah JM Kolberg, who lives in Buffalo and attended its university. She took me around the UB campus and answered my endless questions about the university and its students. She also showed me the Letchworth Woods that surround the campus and told me the story of a female student who was murdered there years ago. That, of course, got my creative juices flowing. Sarah, thanks for your patience and expertise. Your help while writing this book was invaluable!

I'd also like to thank Jonette Harper Stanley, who shared with me her unfortunate knowledge of the negative side of pledging. Thanks for letting me pick your brain, and thanks so much for your friendship.

Prologue

EVEN NOW, I'M not sure how it all happened.

I've tried to put the pieces together in my mind, to make sense of all the madness, but the pieces won't fit in a way that makes it any easier to explain.

How, after all, does one explain a murder?

What I can tell you is that it was a crime born of passion. I'm not saying that to justify anything. Wrong is wrong. But it's also true that some crimes wouldn't be committed if there weren't extenuating circumstances.

Love and jealousy.

Jealousy and hate.

Hate and murder.

It's amazing what a person is capable of. How love and jealousy can push you beyond limits you never imagined. How hate can take root inside you, like a seed of evil, growing bigger each day, consuming every part of you. Until you know that you'd do anything to rid yourself of the pain the hate brings, to be normal again, to be free of the burden.

Love and jealousy.
Jealousy and hate.
Hate and murder.
Hate can make you compromise your own moral code.
Even if that compromise means murder.

I

I SAW EVELYN coming from a mile away.

It was the scowl on her pretty face that caught my attention. She was known in our sorority house for her unpleasant demeanor, which had only gotten worse since her boyfriend up and dumped her at the beginning of the year, but even at a party like this, Evelyn let loose like the rest of us. So the fact that she was headed straight for me, looking as though someone had spit in her shot of tequila, had me alarmed.

She held my gaze as she cut through the crowd of partygoers at the Zeta Omega Beta fraternity party and, curious, I started toward her.

"Hey, Evelyn," I said loudly enough that she'd hear me over the pounding bass of the hip-hop that blared on the stereo. I was pretty sure I hadn't done anything to piss her off. We weren't close enough friends for that. "Great party, huh?"

"Come with me."

"Excu—"

She took me firmly by the arm and led me back in the direction from where she'd come.

"What is it?" I asked. "Did I do something?"

She didn't speak until she'd dragged me about fifty feet, to the entrance of the kitchen. "There." She pointed into the room. "*Shandra*. All. Over. Your. Man."

My eyes searched frantically through the throng of guys and girls milling about. And then I got the shock of my life. There was Shandra James, dressed in a slinky, barely-there red dress. She had a hand on Henry's chest in an intimate gesture, and her smiling face was upturned to his.

"Thought I'd let you know," Evelyn said. "I'd have a little chat with her if I were you. Before she steals your man like she did mine."

"Uh-huh," I mumbled, feeling sick as Evelyn walked away. I didn't have the heart to tell her that I'd already had a talk with Shandra about my fiancé just a couple of weeks before.

About two weeks before that, it became obvious to me that Shandra was attracted to my man. The way she'd look at him when he walked into a room. How she'd try to get close to him at a party. Head down to the field to see him after a football game. And I'd already heard the rumors about her last year when she was a freshman—how she went after guys for sport. The way she did with Evelyn's boyfriend. This year she was pledging my sorority—Alpha Sigma Pi, Incorporated. I wasn't thrilled about it, but it was to be expected since she was a legacy. Her mother and aunts held high positions on the sorority's national board.

Shandra had to know that Henry was my man, and for the most part I ignored her lustful looks at him, but when I found her down on the football field after a game, trying to get up close and personal with him, I knew I had to talk to her. I kept the talk upbeat rather than accusatory, even though I knew what she was up to. I impressed upon her that Henry was my longtime love and current fiancé, and how much he meant to me. Shandra said she understood, and as far as I knew, she had heeded my warning.

Until tonight, apparently.

I was too far away to hear what they were saying, but even a deaf person could figure it out. Shandra was no doubt telling Henry how hot she thought he was, how much she wanted him.

Fucking bitch. She kept angling her head, doing this "I'm so coy" act. And she was smiling and laughing as if Henry was the funniest person alive. Leaning in close to him, even as she took a long pull from her bottle of beer. And Henry—he stood there as though he didn't have the brains God gave him.

What the hell was wrong with him? As well as having a chat with Shandra about him, I'd made sure to tell Henry to be wary of *her*. It's not that I'm superparanoid, or even abnormally jealous, despite Shandra's drop-dead gorgeous looks. With honey brown skin, she was slim and had a booty like Beyoncé's, as well as the long, blond-brown hair Beyoncé sported. And I'd heard more than one guy compliment her bright hazel eyes. But the fact that most guys couldn't help gawking at her when she was in a room wasn't what bothered me about her. My issue with her where Henry was concerned was that she had a reputation in the sorority house—the kind guys appreciated but girls did not. Henry wasn't stupid. He had to know that about her even before I told him. And yet there he was, letting her slobber all over him like a bitch in heat.

I could hardly keep my anger under control as I watched them. This was a respectable fraternity party, not some low-life ghetto affair. But you wouldn't know it by the hoochie outfit Shandra was wearing. From all I knew about her, she came from a good southern family, and I doubted she had been a wild child while under her parents' care.

Not that she was the first person to turn into a freak at college—boozing all the time and having tons of sex—but she was definitely the worst I had seen. She was the kind of girl who thought because she was slim and gorgeous, she was entitled to everything her heart desired.

"I do *not* want to have to go over there, Henry," I muttered to myself. "*Walk away.*"

Shandra whispered something in Henry's ear, then laughed loudly. Henry laughed, too. Then suddenly Shandra was wobbling on her designer stiletto heels, and Henry was wrapping his arm around her waist to keep her from falling.

"One, two . . ." I waited for Henry to extricate himself from Shandra once again. But instead of moving away, Henry placed a hand on Shandra's shoulder as they shared a laugh.

"What's that bitch's problem?"

The question stopped me from marching across the kitchen and wrapping my hands around Shandra's neck. I turned to face Camille, found her standing there with Miranda. My two best friends. Lord, did I need them right then.

"That little heffa is all over your man like white on rice," Camille added, her thick arms crossed over her large bosom.

"Like she doesn't know you're engaged," Miranda said.

I scowled. "It's obvious she could not care less about that."

Not that I could fault the pledge's attraction to him— Henry was a definite pretty boy with his flawless dark skin, muscular body, and six-foot-one-inch frame—but I couldn't excuse Shandra's blatant disregard for our relationship. A relationship that dated back to high school. As soon as I laid eyes on him during my freshman year, I knew that Henry would be my husband someday.

"Damn, I hate when Henry drinks at these parties," I went on. "He can't hold his liquor. Look how he's swaying." But the words were as much to assure me of my fiancé's fidelity as they were for my friends.

"I hear you," Miranda concurred. She shook her head, her long black braids swaying from side to side.

"I mean, I'm standing right here, and if he were sober, he would have moved away from her by now. But he's got booze clouding his brain." It was the only excuse I had for Henry's blatant disrespect, and I was going to cling to it.

"Shandra's no fool," Camille said. "She knows what she's doing."

"I ought to knock some sense into her right here in front of everyone." I glanced down at my left hand and the two-carat rock Henry gave me when he proposed in the spring. A ring that all my sorors had fussed over in a sorority ritual when I announced my engagement. Now it felt like a dead weight on my finger.

"I can't stand this anymore." I started off. "I'm going over there."

"Whoa, whoa, whoa." Camille took hold of my arm before I could take more than a few steps. "Wait one second."

"Wait?" My insides were twisting, and my fingers had started to quiver from my anxiety. "Why the fuck should I wait?"

"Because you're better than that skank-ass ho," Camille answered.

"Yeah, and I'm gonna show her how much better I am."

"But if you march over there right now, you're gonna give her exactly what she wants—which is to get under your skin," Camille pointed out. "Don't you see how she's been glancing over here, checking for your reaction?"

I drew in a deep breath and stared at Shandra. True enough, when she glanced my way, she was smirking as if she knew she'd pissed me off.

"Damn that stupid whore." The last thing I wanted to do was give Shandra any type of leverage over me—like letting her know she'd gotten under my skin. "I still ought to smack her. She knows good and well that Henry is off-limits."

"And give her the sense of power she craves?" Miranda asked. "Uh-uh. She's a trifling, ghetto-minded whore."

I raised an eyebrow, staring at Miranda in shock. As petite and as cute as she must have been in kindergarten, she rarely said an unkind word about anyone. She was known in our sorority as Big Sister Hugs and Kisses because she always had a hug and kiss for everyone and always gave out encouragement.

Miranda shrugged nonchalantly. "I have to speak the truth. Just because her father is some big-time senator in Mississippi doesn't mean she's not ghetto. She'd love nothing more than for you to head over there and prove she's getting to you."

"Miranda's right," Camille agreed, running her fingers through her short black hair. "You know good and well that Henry isn't fool enough to fall for trash like her. When he sobers up, you give him a good talking-to. But I'm with Miranda. Don't let Shandra see she's bothering you."

Camille and Miranda had a way of calming me down when I was about to lose it. They were the two women I trusted with my life.

"Y'all are right," I conceded. "That's exactly what she wants—for me to cause a scene." So as much as it killed me, I would stay where I was and play like she wasn't getting to me.

"And until Henry comes to his senses, why don't you talk to Morgan?" Miranda suggested. Her eyebrows lifted hopefully, like the romantic she was. As far as I was concerned, she was a great catch for any guy, but she tended to scare them off by falling in love way too fast.

Which made me remember the current drama in her life. "Where's Damon?" I asked. "Is he still giving you the cold shoulder, or have you two worked things out?"

Miranda's quick roll of the eyes answered my question. "Don't change the subject. You know Morgan wants you. And he is one *fine* brother. Go spend some time with him. That'll give Henry something to think about."

"Tall, dark, and looks like Michael Jordan." Camille grinned. "What's not to like?"

Morgan. My stomach fluttered a little as I thought of him. He'd been a friend of mine for a couple of years and when I went through a mini-crisis right before Henry proposed, he was there for me in more ways than I can count. No one knew it, but Morgan and I came *very* close to sleeping together once during that time. Somehow we came to our senses before crossing the line.

We had still remained friends, for which I was glad, because I really liked his friendship. But I couldn't help thinking that Miranda was right, that maybe it was time I turned up the charm on Morgan, gave Henry a dose of his own medicine. At the very least, it would take my mind off how big a jerk my fiancé was right then.

"Where is he?" I asked.

"Right over there." Miranda turned and pointed a long red fingernail toward the area where the kegs of beer were set up. Earlier, people had taken turns chugging as much beer as they could through a fat straw.

The corners of my lips lifted as I checked Morgan out. Even dressed in black sweats, he looked hot. Yeah, it was time to turn up the charm where Morgan was concerned.

I was about to head over to him, but then I turned for one last glance at Henry. I reeled backward, feeling as though someone had kicked me in the gut. Shandra was on her tiptoes, her mouth pressed to Henry's cheek.

I couldn't help it—I saw red.

"Fuck that bitch."

I charged through the crowd. No way was I going to let Shandra and Henry make me look like a fool in front of my sorority sisters.

Shandra's shrill cackle pierced the air just as I neared her. I caught the bitch off guard by grabbing hold of her forearm and yanking her away from Henry.

The cackle faded and died. Shandra fought for balance, spilling her beer all over her front. Then she shot me a murderous look.

"What the—"

"I already talked to you once about Henry," I said, cutting her off. "I'm not going to talk to you again. Stay the hell away from my man!"

"Ph—"

"And you!" I whirled around to glare up at Henry before he could finish saying my name. "What are you doing? What are you thinking, letting this skank hang all over you?"

"Skank? Yo, bitch. Who you calling a skank?"

"You," I replied, both hands on my hips as I faced her. In her heels, she was eye level to my five-foot-eight height. "Everybody here knows you're a skank. A ho. A *puta*. You need to stay away from Henry. I'm not going to warn you again."

Shandra's eyes narrowed with hatred. I bet she wanted to slap me silly. Let her try. I was angry and humiliated and had something to prove. In fact, if it weren't for the fact that all eyes were suddenly on us, I probably would have lunged at her and beat her to a pulp.

Ultimately, Shandra glanced down at her wet dress, assessing the damage. She muttered under her breath as she walked away.

Wise choice, whore!

With her gone, I stared at Henry. His eyes were red and glazed, and I had to shake my head. After a beat I said, "Let's go."

"What?"

"We need to leave."

"C'mon, Phoebe," he whined.

"*Now*." I spoke quietly, but there was no mistaking my tone. I wasn't about to take any shit from him after how badly he'd behaved.

Henry, however, clearly wasn't about to be persuaded. "Phoebe, you needa relax," he told me, slurring his words. "You're goin' off like you some kinda jealous madwoman or somethin'."

"A *jealous madwoman?* Are you kidding me?"

"I leave now, I'm gonna look like a punk cuz my girl-friend's got issues. I'm ain't gonna look like a punk in fronta my friends."

"Oh, so now your friends are more important to you than your *fiancée?*" I was more than his girlfriend, and he had better remember that!

Henry casually sipped his draft beer. "Seriously, Phoebe. Calm down."

I wanted to tell him to go fuck himself, but I knew that he was partly right. I sensed that eyes were still on me, and I didn't want to make more of a scene than I already had. But still, it hurt me in a way I can't describe that he wouldn't leave with me.

"Will you please come with me?" I asked, trying a nicer tone.

"Uh-uh. But I'll meet ya later, okay?"

And then Henry walked away from me, and out of the kitchen.

I stood there in disbelief for a moment, then stomped off. Catching sight of Henry with a few of his buddies near the staircase, I huffed and headed for the door. When I got there, I glanced over my shoulder. Henry was laughing with his friends as if he didn't have a care in the world.

Or an angry fiancée to deal with.

I looked to the left, searching for Miranda and Camille. Instead, my eyes locked on Shandra's.

She grinned.

Oh, she was a bitch all right.

I turned and flew out the door.

2

I WAS FURIOUS. And embarrassed. And downright miserable.

I pounded down the steps of the fraternity house and sprinted across the front lawn. About a hundred feet down the road was my sorority house, which mercifully would be practically empty then since almost everyone was at the Zeta party.

But instead of heading there, I found myself running on past to Frontier Road, one of the roads that winds through the North Campus of the University of Buffalo. Thankfully, I was wearing low-heeled sheepskin boots that allowed me to run fairly comfortably. I liked to run and did so often. It was both a great form of exercise and a stress reliever.

I jogged along Frontier, headed for Hamilton Road, even though it was dark and anyone could be lurking in the shadows. And I do mean anyone. Five months before, in April, one of UB's students was strangled along the Ellicott Creek Bike Path in the Letchworth Woods that wrap around the campus, and so far the killer had not been found. I didn't know Carmen Young personally, but I had seen her around. I also knew that she'd applied to our sorority but that her application had been rejected. The word was, she wasn't attractive enough, and on top of that, she was too much of a nerd. The Alphas—whether model-thin or voluptuous—had a reputation for being attractive and cool.

Perhaps I was feeling a little reckless in an "I could not care less what happens to me" kind of way, because despite Carmen's murder, I almost wanted to turn right on Hamilton Road and follow it to the entrance of that very path. I pushed myself, sprinting as hard as I could. But as I crossed the road and my feet landed on the grass outside the trees, I could no longer breathe and I had to stop. I collapsed onto the ground, tears pouring out of my eyes.

I'm not sure how long I sat there, my knees pulled up to my chest, crying harder than I had in a long time. My grief had me irrational. Believe me, I was devastated at how Henry had hurt me. I gave that man my heart and soul, and I thought I had his.

My sobs choked me, and I started to cough. The thought hit me that the killer might approach me while I sat there helpless, but I couldn't bring myself to care. My grief had me not caring if I lived or died.

Or so I thought. Because when I heard a car approach, my heart slammed against my rib cage and I looked up. Headlights were coming in my direction. My heart calmed then as I figured that a killer would be lurking in the trees, not in a car. I wiped my tears and turned my head to avoid the headlights' glare. I thought the car would pass me, but instead it slowed down.

Great. Campus police.

I swiveled on my butt, turning away from the road. As I got to my feet, I heard the car door open. Just what I needed. More grief in the form of questioning from the cops.

If it was the cops. My God, what if it *was* the killer?

"Phoebe."

I didn't realize how afraid I was until I heard the sound of Morgan's voice. Slowly, I looked over my shoulder, saw him striding toward me. Lord, was I happy to see him. I ran the short distance to him and collapsed into his open arms.

"What the hell happened back there?" he asked me.

I buried my face in his chest and cried.

"And what are you doing out here alone? You know that girl was killed last semester."

"I know. . . ." And I did. I *should* have known better than to be wandering around the campus alone at that hour. I *should* have cared what happened to me. And yet, right then, I didn't. I was so miserable, I simply didn't care about anything. It was as though I had given Henry total power over me. Total power over my happiness.

It wasn't just what had happened with Shandra at the party. For the past few weeks, I'd felt that Henry was slipping away from me, a little at a time. His friends were more important. His studies were more important. We spent time together, but I didn't feel that we were connecting the way we used to.

Which scared me to death.

Morgan sighed loudly. "I hate what Henry does to you."

"He's drunk," I said. "He gets so stupid when he drinks."

Morgan didn't say anything for a moment. "Look, you want to go somewhere to talk?"

"I'm okay," I lied.

"You don't look okay. Why don't we go to that Borders across from the mall?"

"I'm fine."

Morgan placed a finger beneath my chin and urged my

face upward. "Phoebe. I'm not about to let you be alone. Not while Henry is back at the party like a big asshole, with Shandra on his lap."

"What?" I gasped.

"Yeah." Morgan stopped abruptly and turned. I looked beyond his shoulder to see headlights. This time I could see that the car in question *was* a campus police cruiser.

"Shit," Morgan mumbled.

The car slammed to a stop behind Morgan's black Mustang and an officer jumped out. As he walked forward, his eyes flitted between the two of us. He asked, "Everything okay here?"

"Yes," Morgan answered.

"Let the lady talk," the officer said. "Miss, are you okay?"

I nodded shakily. "I'm—I'm fine. I went for a walk. My friend saw me and stopped."

The officer eyed us both suspiciously while shining his flashlight in our faces. I squinted against the light's glare. "Honestly, Officer. I'm okay."

He lowered the flashlight and looked at Morgan. "You can't leave your car on the road like that."

"I'm sorry, sir," Morgan said. "I just wanted to make sure my friend was okay." He started walking toward his car, and I fell into step beside him.

"You've got a good friend," the officer went on. "It's not safe to be out here alone, especially at night."

"I know," I told him, my voice full of chagrin.

The officer didn't leave, not even when Morgan and I got into the car. Morgan glanced into the rearview mirror and said, "Great. He probably doesn't trust me."

"I'm sure he trusts you, or he wouldn't let me get into the car with you."

"Yeah, but he could be running my plate as we speak.

Noting me as a person of interest in Carmen Young's murder," Morgan added, but his tone said he wasn't serious.

"Yeah, right. Like anyone could think you capable of murder."

Morgan started to drive. "Why don't we just go to Borders? I can buy you one of those romance novels you're always reading, cheer you up."

"I don't think a romance is gonna cheer me up right now." Which was a shocking statement to hear coming out of my own mouth. I loved to read romances. Miranda had got me hooked on them.

"Then I'll buy you a coffee. I'm sure you could use one."

"You're right about that."

"The one with caramel, right?"

Despite my dismal mood, a small smile crept onto my face. At least someone cared about me right then. "I'm surprised you remember."

"Aw, come on." Morgan turned left onto John James Audubon Parkway, the road that circled the campus and would lead us toward the interstate. From there, it was a short drive to Borders. "You know better than that. I remember everything when it comes to you."

I had no doubt that he did. My brain might have denied it, but my heart knew that Morgan had feelings for me.

3

THE NEXT MORNING I woke up with a headache. I hadn't stayed out with Morgan too long the night before, only until midnight, when Borders closed. But when we returned to Greek Row, I went to the frat house with him instead of to my own room. I was determined to enjoy the last bit of the party.

Inside, Morgan took my hand and I let him hold it. As he led me through the crowd toward the stairs, a rush of attraction shot through me. I tried to ignore it. I always ignored the spark I felt when he looked at me, dismissing it as a purely physical attraction to a beautiful man. There was no way I wanted to act on a physical attraction when Henry and I had something deeper than that.

At least I thought we did.

I didn't see Henry as I headed upstairs with Morgan, but I secretly hoped he had spotted me. By that time, I was ready for some revenge.

Which is why I spent the night in Morgan's room.

Not because I wanted to sleep with him, though a big

part of me was tempted. But because I wanted Henry, when he finally sobered up, to wonder where the hell I was.

When I stepped into Morgan's room, however, I began to second-guess my motives. As I said, I knew there was a spark between us, and it would be oh so easy to cross the line. And with him knowing I was angry with Henry, why wouldn't he take advantage of the situation?

But there was no awkwardness between us once we got into his room. I told Morgan I was tired and, ever the gentleman, he gave me only a kiss on the forehead, then tucked me into his bed. He could have easily put the moves on me, but instead he made himself comfortable in a sleeping bag on the floor.

I thought about Morgan until I fell asleep. How he reminded me so much of the Henry I'd fallen for in high school. The Henry who was polite and thoughtful and totally into me. The Henry who had been my hero.

By the time morning came, my head was throbbing. And my stomach was twisted in a painful knot. I wondered what Henry was doing. If Shandra had wormed her way into his bed. I groaned, the thought making me nauseous.

"If you're gonna puke," Morgan said, looking up at me from the floor, "please don't do it on my bed."

"I'm okay," I told him.

"You sure?"

"I have a headache, but I'll live." I paused a beat. "How did *you* sleep?"

He rubbed the back of his neck but said, "I'm all right."

I sat up, ran my fingers through my shoulder-length hair, then threw off the covers. "I should probably get going."

"What?" Morgan glanced at the wall clock. "It's only five after six."

"I know, but . . ."

"But you're thinking about Henry."

I didn't respond. He was right on the money.

"God, Phoebe. Sometimes I don't understand why you even bother."

"I know you don't understand, but I love him."

Morgan dropped his head back onto his pillow. "Whatever."

"But I appreciate your being there for me."

"Yeah, sure. The nice guy finishes last."

"Morgan!" I climbed off the bed and knelt down beside him. I'd planned on playfully whacking him on the chest, but his musky scent caught me off guard. Instead of whacking him, I rested my fingers on his bare chest. And there was that surge of attraction again.

I swallowed. And thought of how comfortable I felt with Morgan. How easy things were between us. All I had to do was lean forward and kiss him on the lips and it would end the curiosity. I would finally know what it was like to make love to him.

Instead, I quietly sighed and gave him a soft kiss on the cheek. "You know that's not true."

"I do?"

"You should."

He slipped an arm around my waist. Tightened it and pulled me close. Lord, the attention was nice and, damn, he smelled so good.

"What am I, then?" he asked.

"You . . ." My fingers played over his chest. Yes, I was flirting with him but couldn't stop myself. "You are a sweetheart."

And then Morgan's lips touched mine, and something ignited between us. Something electric. Something overpowering. Something that made it impossible for me not to kiss him back.

The kiss was hot and hungry and went on and on. Morgan's hand slid under my dress, his warm fingers skimming my butt. The feeling jarred me like a douse of cold water in the face. I *wanted* to do this, but I couldn't. It wasn't right.

Moaning softly, I pulled away. "Morgan, I can't. I just . . ."

He released me. "Sorry."

I sat up, putting some much-needed space between us. "I do need to go."

Nodding, he sat up as well. "I'll see you later?"

"Of course."

I got to my feet, straightened my dress, and scooped up my Fendi clutch. Morgan made his way onto the bed.

When I got to the door, I glanced over my shoulder at him. Just looking at him made my heart thunder in my chest, and I couldn't help wondering if I should have just let nature take its course.

"Thanks again," I mumbled.

"Sure."

And this is where I made a really big mistake. Distracted by what had just happened with Morgan, I opened the door without thinking.

And wouldn't you know it, I saw Marshall Brown walking in the hallway. His eyes widened in surprise when he saw me, and he shot a glance at the door's number. Fuck! He would know I hadn't just waltzed out of Henry's room.

I gave Marshall a sheepish look before heading down the hallway in the opposite direction, toward Henry's room. Like Morgan, Henry was also a senior and therefore had a private room. It was a nice perk, since it allowed us time to be alone whenever we wanted.

Sucking in a nervous breath, I quietly opened Henry's door. I suppose I expected to see Shandra in the room with him, so when I saw Henry's tall, muscular body stretched out on his double bed—alone—I felt a profound sense of relief. And guilt.

I slipped into the room, closing the door behind me.

Henry shot up instantly. "Where've you been?" he asked groggily.

"I was . . ." Damn, what could I say? There was no way I could tell him the truth. Even if he and Morgan were tight, he certainly wouldn't appreciate my spending the night in Morgan's room.

So I said, "I needed some space."

"Where'd you go?"

"Where you couldn't call me. I was in a friend's room. Someone you don't know."

He eyed me as if he was trying to figure out if I was telling him the truth. "Where do you think I was?" I asked.

Ignoring my question, he said, "Come here."

My stomach fluttered as I made my way across the room. When I reached Henry's bed, I eased onto its edge. I wasn't sure if he was going to hug me or slap me.

"You still pissed?" he asked.

I shook my head.

He lifted one corner of the sheets, a silent invitation for me to join him. I pulled my dress over my head, tossed it onto the floor, and slipped under the covers beside him. I lay with him spoon-style.

He put his arm around my waist and, content, I closed my eyes.

My mind wandered to when I first met Henry. I was in the cafeteria at my high school in Charlotte, gathering my knapsack as I prepared to leave. My two friends had hurried out of the room without me, as they had to meet with a study group about some exam before the next class. That left me alone at my table.

I suppose I'd been deliberately lingering because I was hoping that Henry Reid, who was a year head of me, in tenth grade, would notice me. He didn't know who I was, but everyone at our high school knew him. He was touted as one of the most promising football players in our school, despite his young age. And ever since I'd laid eyes on him, I'd felt instinctively that he was my soul mate.

Even though he had yet to utter a word to me.

He was two tables behind me with a group of his friends, hanging out and laughing. I stole a glance over my shoulder at him, sighing dreamily. When I turned back around, I gasped. Hunter Mathis, a senior who'd made it clear that he was interested in me only a few weeks earlier, was standing at my table. My stomach sank.

"Hunter, hi." I tried to be cordial, though I didn't like him. He creeped me out. "I was just leaving."

I tried to sidestep him, but he gripped my arm. "Leaving so soon?" he asked casually in a way that made my skin crawl. "Where are you going?"

I swallowed. "I'm, uh, meeting someone."

"I'm right here, baby."

I didn't meet Hunter's eyes. They unnerved me. "Seriously, Hunter. I—I've got to go."

Then he did something that really shocked me—he yanked me against his chest and locked an arm around me. I let out a squeal, then began to squirm.

"What's your problem?" Hunter demanded. "Any girl in this school would kill to go out with me, yet you're too good for me? I don't think so."

The next thing I knew, Hunter was being jerked away from me. Someone's fist connected with his jaw, but I was too stunned at the time to realize the fist belonged to Henry. A bunch of guys quickly surrounded Hunter, and in the commotion Henry approached me and put two hands on my shoulders. He looked into my eyes and asked, "Are you okay?"

I could only nod. And despite the fear I'd felt where Hunter was concerned, I also felt a spark of hope.

Henry Reid had saved me.

Oh, I'm sure any number of other guys would have

come to my rescue if he hadn't, but Henry was the one who'd taken the first step. For me, that solidified the crush I had on him. He insisted on walking me to class, and stopped by my table in the cafeteria the next day to say he'd gotten into trouble for being late to his own class but added that it had been worth it. Every day we talked more and more, and within a couple of months we'd become an item. We dated all through high school, and when Henry decided to go to UB—his father's alma mater—I knew I had to go there as well.

Now Henry's hands skimmed my stomach as they inched toward my crotch. My eyes flew open. Through my panties, he stroked my vagina. I moaned softly against his touch.

Slowly I turned and faced him, this man who had been my hero that long-ago day in high school. With everything that was happening between us, would he still be my hero? Were we still meant to be?

His lips immediately came down on mine, and in that moment I completely forgot about our problems and Shandra. I thought only of Henry and my love for him.

4

I WAS HIGH off my lovemaking session with Henry, so much so that when I walked into the sorority house and saw all my sorors crowded in the common room, I couldn't help gasping in surprise. Damn! How could I have forgotten that we had a meeting that morning?

I crept forward and tried to slip quietly into the seating area near the back. No such luck. Katrina, our chapter president, saw me and flashed me a look of reproof. Tall, thin, and light-skinned, she had been some sort of beauty queen in Atlanta and was classically gorgeous, but when she frowned, her beauty disappeared. Katrina took sorority matters very seriously. She didn't care how or where we spent our free time, but sorority meetings were priority number one.

"I'm glad you could join us, Phoebe," Katrina said. There was no mistaking the sarcasm in her tone.

"Sorry I'm late," I mumbled. I spotted Miranda and headed toward her, then realized that the woman sitting beside her was Camille. Holy! What had she done to her hair? Sometime overnight she'd chopped almost all of it off, and it was no longer black but auburn. I wasn't sure it suited her chubby face. Camille was also gnawing on her thumbnail, something she did when she was stressed. Had she and Kevin broken up? She'd gone blond for a while after one of her relationships ended the previous term.

Unlike Miranda, who fell in love at hello, Camille feared commitment. She didn't admit that, of course, but it was obvious to me. I'm sure her problems stemmed from the fact that her father had abandoned her and her mother when she was just three years old.

Her new look was so drastic, I couldn't take my eyes off her as I dropped down on the sofa between her and Miranda.

"Where have you been?" Camille whispered. "Henry was calling all night."

"I ended up—" Katrina glared at me, so I promptly shut up. When she looked away, I whispered, "Tell ya later." Silently I added, *And you'll tell me about your hair!*

Katrina's eyes did another sweep of the room. "All are present now," she announced in her oh-so-official "I'm in charge" voice. "The meeting can begin."

Katrina wore an oversized pink T-shirt with our sorority letters on it, as well as white shorts. In fact, everyone in the room was wearing pink, as we always did for our meetings. Thankfully, I'd been wearing a pink dress to the party, so at least I didn't look out of place.

Pink and white are our sorority's colors. We're known on campus as the sisters in pink.

As Katrina stepped forward, we all got to our feet, held hands, and formed a circle. Katrina said a short prayer, as was the sorority's custom before any meeting. Then we all chanted in unison: "Our founders, we honor you. Our sorors who have paved the way before us, we strive to continue your legacy. Each day we work hard to achieve that goal. With self-sacrifice and caring, what we do makes us whole. Our women are the smartest, the strongest, and have the most zest. Alpha Sigma Pi, we are the best!"

At the end of the cheer, we threw our linked hands into the air. Then we separated and settled back into our seats.

"There's a lot we have to discuss before we head off for classes," Katrina began. "The first thing being fund-raisers. Charlotte."

Charlotte, the fund-raiser chair, stood from her seat near the window. "Morning, sorors."

"Morning."

"I really hate to say this, but our first fund-raiser, the Welcome Back Bake-Off, was a horrible disappointment. People just didn't support this event the way they have in the past. Obviously we need to do a better job of getting the word out. And we have to do more work. So, in the meantime, I'd like us all to think about other fund-raising ideas, because we need to make more money this year."

Monica, the treasurer, echoed that point. "Running a sorority house is very expensive. A few of you haven't paid your dues yet. You need to do so yesterday."

Beside me, Miranda's lips turned down in the slightest of frowns. She was one of the few who hadn't yet paid. Unlike most of us, she didn't come from a middle- or upper-class family. In fact, her mother lived off of social assistance. Miranda had gotten a scholarship because of her grades, but that didn't cover all her college expenses. For extra cash, she worked part-time as a waitress at a pancake house off campus. We became friends during our freshman year, and because of me, she ended up pledging this sorority.

"In the past, the black sororities and fraternities on this

campus never had dorm houses," Monica told the group. "But as we know, in the past five years, that's changed. However, we have to do our best to make sure the bills are paid, or we won't have this luxury anymore."

"Yeah, yeah," Camille whispered to me. "Like she doesn't tell us that every chance she gets."

"Phoebe." Katrina's gaze landed on me. At first I thought she was going to reprimand me because Camille had been talking. But she said, "Can you give us an update on how the pledges are doing?"

At the beginning of the year, I had been assigned as the chair of the pledge process. That meant I oversaw them in all aspects of sorority life until they crossed over. I came up with various tasks they had to complete—mostly the kinds of things our sorority had always done with its pledges. Like the ritual where the pledges brush our hair at night and sing various Alpha Sigma Pi songs. Or scrub the toilets with a toothbrush. Some tasks were fun, others a test of patience.

I smiled as I stood to face my sorors. "As you know, we're into our third week of the pledging process, and so far, so good. Except for . . ." I couldn't help thinking of Shandra at that moment, how my dislike for her had turned to hate. Katrina had always said that our meetings were the place to air issues we might have with any of our sisters, and I was tempted to mention Shandra's obsession with Henry. Tempted, but not stupid. If I brought up Shandra at that moment, my sorors just might think I was jealous and possessive—exactly what Henry had said the night before. Besides, I didn't want to make it look as though I didn't have the pledges under control. "Except for some complaints from the pledges that they're not able to keep up with their schoolwork," I finished. "I've assured them that we all did it and that we maintained decent grade-point averages as well. So, in other words, everything's going just fine." I added, "I think we have a really good group of girls this year."

The meeting went on for a while longer with more sorority business, including our current philanthropic efforts and the upcoming party we were throwing. When I thought that Evelyn, our secretary, was going to officially adjourn the meeting, Katrina stood instead.

"Ladies, you know how I feel about our sisterhood. I believe that no matter what we go through, we have to do what we can to be tight. Sure, we're gonna bicker and have issues, but we need to try to work them out. If there's a problem, this is the forum to deal with it. That said, are there any issues anyone would like to discuss and resolve here?"

I glanced around the room. So did everyone else. No one spoke up.

"All right, then," Katrina said, sounding unconvinced. Her eyes landed on me, and I couldn't help wondering why.

Evelyn then adjourned the meeting, and I headed out of the common room with Camille and Miranda. I was more than ready for a shower.

"I do believe those are the same clothes you were in last night," Miranda said in a singsong voice. "But if you weren't with Henry—"

"Phoebe."

Hearing my name behind me, I halted, then turned. Katrina was looking at me. "Yes?"

"I need to speak with you for a moment."

Camille shot me a curious look. "What's this about?"

"Not sure," I replied. I really wanted to ask why she'd drastically changed her look, but I didn't have the time. "Look, I'll catch up with you guys later."

"Saved by the bell," Miranda said, giggling. "But you still have to tell us the dirty details!"

I smiled meekly and gave a wave good-bye. Katrina was

at the window with Donna, the chapter's vice president, and Evelyn. I approached them, asking with a smile, "What'd I do?"

Evelyn wouldn't meet my eye. Donna looked at me with a poker face, the one she was famous for. I swear, she never smiled. She was attractive with her smooth dark skin, but there was nothing warm about her.

I turned to Katrina. Her chest rose and fell with a deep breath. "Shandra spoke to me last night after the party," she began. "She had a lot to say about how you've been treating her."

"How *I've* been treating *her? Are you kidding me?"

"I'm afraid not," Katrina replied.

"She's the one who's been completely disrespectful, going after my man like she's the biggest whore on campus."

"I know she's been a little . . . difficult," Donna said. "Clearly Shandra still needs to learn a thing or two about sisterhood, and we understand your frustration, Phoebe. But you can't attack a pledge."

"Attack a pledge?" I repeated in disbelief. I looked from Donna to Evelyn. "You saw how she was acting. You came to talk to me about it."

"I know. I told them."

"According to Shandra," Donna said, "you've been harassing her because she's a legacy. She says you're jealous of her because of that."

My mouth nearly hit the floor. "Like I have a reason to be jealous of that bitch."

"Phoebe, you don't seem like yourself," Katrina said. "You're sounding really hostile."

"That's because I don't like being accused of bullshit! I'm not jealous of the fact that she's a legacy. Her ancestors could be founders of this sorority, for all I care. What matters to me is that she's been going after my man with no regard for me. Wouldn't that piss you off?" I looked at Katrina, then Donna, and finally Evelyn.

"Like Donna said," Katrina began, "we understand your frustration. But the problem is, Shandra wanted to lodge an official complaint and—"

"An official complaint?" I interjected, aghast. "She's lucky I didn't make mincemeat of her face. The bitch deserved that and more."

Katrina held up a hand. "Phoebe, cool it for a second."

"What are you planning to do—report me to the dean or something? And you expect *me* to cool it?"

"I'm only telling you what Shandra said," Katrina pointed out. "She was pretty adamant, wanting to take immediate action, but I told her we would talk to you, try to smooth things out. I think it'd be a good idea if we all got together, sat down and had a meeting—"

"Screw that. I do *not* want to see that conniving bitch."

Donna gave me a look of concern. "I can't help wondering if you're still the best candidate to be in charge of the pledge process."

"Because of Shandra? You're kidding me, right?"

Donna looked to Katrina, as if she was deferring to her.

"Listen," I went on. "This is the deal. Shandra was all over my fiancé last night and I mean *all* over. She knows Henry's off-limits. I'd already talked to her about her hitting on him a couple of weeks ago. What was I supposed to do—sit around and let her steal my man from me, like she did to Evelyn?"

Evelyn's jaw flinched. Then she crossed her arms, saying, "I'm with Phoebe on this one. She has a point. Shandra has to learn—"

"*Your men* have to learn to keep their dicks in their pants," Katrina spat out. Then, "Sorry. I'm not trying to be insensitive. But Shandra's a legacy—"

"Ah, so that's what this is really about," I said. "You

don't want to reprimand Shandra because of her mother." And her aunts. They were influential in our sorority, always on some board or other. In fact, Shandra's mother was the vice president at the sorority's national headquarters.

Katrina sighed, exasperated. "Try to ignore Shandra," she told me. "As hard as that might be, try. And, please, don't pick any fights with her. Maybe it's not fair, but we can't ignore who her mother is—or the stress she could give us if Shandra complained to her."

I frowned. A beat passed. "As long as you're not going to tell me to *apologize* to her."

Katrina only stared at me. Donna, too. Evelyn looked away.

"Hell, no. I am not apologizing to Shandra. She can kiss my ass first."

Katrina's jaw tightened. Clearly she didn't like my answer, but after a moment she said, "Fine. But, please, if you care about this sorority, stay out of Shandra's face. Okay?"

As long as she stays away from my fiancé's penis! I thought but didn't say.

"Yeah, sure," I mumbled. "Is that it?"

"We're not the enemy," Katrina told me.

"Uh-huh," I said. Then I turned and walked out of the common room.

5

I WAS PISSED.

Either I was going to head out of the building and go for a run or I was going to take a hot shower. Considering that I was still wearing my clothes from the night before, I opted for the shower.

And I'm glad I did. The shower refreshed me and helped assuage my foul mood. I still wasn't happy, but at least I felt better.

In my room a short while later, I threw off my towel and headed to my dresser. The knock on my door had me quickly scooping up my towel and rewrapping it around my body. I hurried to the door.

I opened it a crack. Saw Evelyn's face. Inwardly, I groaned. "Yeah?"

"Can I come in for a minute?"

I hesitated. "Why?" As far as I was concerned, she could have stood up more for me earlier, but she hadn't. Why should I be friendly with her now?

"Just give me a few minutes, okay? You'll understand."

I pulled the door open wide, saying, "I'm not dressed."

"I won't be long."

She stepped into the room and stood a few feet away from me. She was a couple of inches taller than I was, which put her at about five-foot-ten. She was dark-skinned and pretty, despite the faint acne scars on her forehead. Her short black hair fell in soft wisps about her round face, a face that had gotten fuller in the months since the breakup with her boyfriend, as she'd put on at least ten pounds.

Evelyn breathed in and out slowly. "About earlier, I want you to know you have my support—"

"It didn't seem like it. You needed to tell Katrina and Donna what Shandra's really about."

"Believe me, I tried. They don't want to hear it."

I frowned, not saying a word.

"I went through all this with them in January, when Shandra went after my boyfriend."

At the time, Shandra had been a freshman. Knowing she planned to pledge the Alpha sorority, she became a fraternity sweetheart—a girl who hung around the fraternity house. At that point, Shandra would have been spending a lot of time with our fraternity brothers, so I'm sure that's when she got to know and went about sinking her claws into Jonah, Evelyn's man.

"We knew she'd be pledging this sorority because she's a legacy," Evelyn went on, "but I tried to tell the board they needed to rethink that. Shandra doesn't know what sisterhood is about. I don't care if her mother is vice president."

"I couldn't agree more," I said.

"The problem with Katrina is that she acts like this sorority is her friggin' life. Like we have to give Shandra carte blanche to be a fucking whore, just because she's a legacy."

"I figured that out already." The top edge of my towel started to slip, so I grabbed onto it, secured it in place.

Evelyn's eyes softened. "All I wanted to say is that I've got your back. Maybe you can't do anything to get rid of Shandra, but if you want to talk to me about this anytime, know that I'm there for you."

My lips pulled in a slight smile. "Thanks."

"Well, I won't keep you. I'll let you get dressed."

I took the towel off my head and shook my hair as Evelyn headed for the door. But as she was about to head out, an idea struck me.

"Evelyn?"

She turned. "Yeah?"

I walked toward her, saying, "I think I'd like that. Getting together to talk. Maybe even today. At lunch?"

Evelyn grinned brightly. "Sure. What time do you want to meet?"

At twelve-fifteen I met Evelyn on the main floor of the Student Union. Together, we made our way into Putnam's, the cafeteria. I opted for the chicken fingers instead of egg-plant parmigiana—it's pretty hard to screw up chicken fingers. To make it a healthier option, I got a large green salad as well. Evelyn got the exact same order, but she chose a diet cola while I chose my favorite cafeteria drink, grape juice.

We entered the large cafeteria and chose a table to the right where no one else was sitting. I didn't want anyone within earshot, given what we were going to discuss.

"Evelyn, I appreciate your being here for me. I really need an outlet to vent." We weren't exactly close. She was a year older than I was, and we'd pledged a year apart. So she wasn't one of the friends in my inner circle.

But clearly we had a lot in common. Shandra had sto-len her man, and now she was after mine.

"Believe me," she said. "I know what you're going through. Last semester, though, because Shandra wasn't a pledge, just a fraternity sweetheart, there was nothing the board could do. And they outright refused to decline her sorority application."

"How did you deal with her?" I asked.

"Same as you. Tried to talk to her, asked her to respect my relationship."

"And that didn't work?" I asked, but it was a rhetorical question, since I knew the answer. I shook my head. "So what would you do differently?"

"Besides kick her ass?" She chuckled mirthlessly. "Talk to her again, I guess. Maybe be a little more forceful. Or maybe I would talk to Henry, really get him to understand what Shandra's like and what she's up to."

I nodded absently. Of course, I'd already done that. I ate a cucumber slice, then asked, "What was it like for you? Did you feel your boyfriend slipping away? Or did he just leave? Because I feel . . . I feel like Henry isn't as attentive anymore. He's more impatient. Less available."

"Shit."

"What?"

"That's exactly what Jonah started to get like with me. I came out and asked him if he was having an affair. I'm not stupid. I saw her hanging all over him, the way she looked at him. I know how these things happen. But I figured that even if he'd slept with her, he wasn't going to jeopardize our two-year relationship over her."

"But he did," I said, stating the obvious.

Evelyn's eyes got misty, surprising me. "Told me Shandra was the love of his life. Of course, I freaked. Just lost it. I wanted to know how he could say that, when we'd been together for two years. And you know what—Jonah point-blank told me that Shandra could please him sexually in ways I could not."

"No!"

Evelyn nodded. She wiped at a stray tear. Even after

several months she was still hurt by what had happened. I couldn't help feeling bad for her. When Jonah had dumped her, we'd seen her unravel, and some people had judged her harshly for loving so much. I admit I was one of those people. Now I had to wonder if I would be any different if Henry dumped me.

"Henry tells me I'm acting like a jealous girlfriend," I told Evelyn.

"Isn't it funny how guys will accuse us of being jealous when they're doing *nothing* to make us feel secure?"

"Tell me about it!"

"If you want to keep your man, you need to hang on to him now more than ev—" Evelyn stopped abruptly, her eyes wandering over my shoulder.

"What?" I asked.

When her eyes narrowed into a glare, I quickly turned around.

And then, Lord help me, my heart stopped. Shandra had just entered the cafeteria.

With Henry!

"Oh my God."

"I swear, that bitch never gives up," Evelyn said, shaking her head.

"I can't believe what I'm seeing. Just this morning I talked to Henry about her. He *knows* how I feel. What the hell is he doing with her?"

Henry didn't see me. Shandra clung to his side as they searched for a table, as though she was his girl.

I sat there in stupefied horror, watching them. I felt sick enough to throw up.

Finally Henry's gaze caught mine. He faltered, surprised. I scowled and looked away.

My feeling of nausea was slowly and surely replaced by rage. I thought I was pissed the night before, but that didn't compare with what I felt now.

I wanted to charge over to them. I wanted to dump my salad on Shandra's stubborn head.

Enough was enough. I was more than ready to inflict some pain on this bitch.

"I'll bet she hangs around the fraternity house, stalking him," Evelyn said. "So when he's ready to go out for lunch, she's like, 'Hey, I'll go with you.' When she decides she wants to go after someone, that's it. Nothing stands in her way."

"But I talked to Henry," I said, glancing his way. "Only hours ago."

Evelyn placed a firm hand on my arm, and I met her gaze. "Even the strongest man can fall victim to temptation. It happened to Jonah. And you know what—she dumped his ass after two months. Broke *his* heart." She grinned. "I have to say, that was the best revenge."

I was only partially paying attention to Evelyn. Emotions were making my head hurt. Anger and pain.

Jealousy.

I couldn't stop myself from looking Henry's way again. Even with their backs to me, they looked so damn cozy, sitting side by side.

"You know she's doing that for your benefit. Getting close to him like that."

The awful truth hit me then, and I blurted out, "It's obvious I won't get through to her with any more chats. It's like she needs to be taught a lesson."

Evelyn's eyes slowly narrowed.

My words shocked me, but as I thought about them, I knew I didn't want to take them back. "Not that I'd hurt her, of course," I quickly said. "But . . ." My voice trailed off.

"But what?" Evelyn prompted.

A really nasty thought filled my brain, the kind I didn't want to voice. It involved pain—a lot of it.

"Phoebe?"

"Nothing."

"The expression on your face doesn't look like nothing. Tell me what you're thinking."

I sighed deeply. "You really want to know?"

She nodded.

"Maybe it's crazy," I began in a lowered voice, "but I was thinking of . . ." I paused. "Of some kind of initiation. Tailored just for her. The kind that will teach her a lesson not to mess with me."

"Oooh." Evelyn grinned evilly. "Now, that's an idea."

"You think so?"

"Absolutely. I wish I'd thought of it in January."

I pondered the idea for a moment. Realistically, I *could* do it. I was in charge of the pledge process. It'd be easy for me to set something up, lure Shandra there. . . .

My eyes met Evelyn's excited gaze. Suddenly I became wary. Evelyn may have said that she was there for me, but she was still on the sorority's board. What would stop her from telling Katrina and Donna what I'd just suggested? Hell, what if this was a trap to see how far I'd go?

I decided I couldn't trust her. Well, not so much that I couldn't as that I shouldn't.

"I admit, the idea's appealing," I conceded. "But I can't really plan something like that. The sorority's stand against hazing is clear."

"So don't make it a sorority activity."

"The university also has a strict no-hazing policy."

"Then you just have to be a little creative." She raised an eyebrow. "Maybe I can help."

"No." I pushed my chair back and stood, even though I'd hardly eaten any of my lunch. Seeing Shandra with Henry had instantly killed my appetite. "It was a crazy idea. The kind you think of when you're frustrated. But I would never hurt Shandra. Besides, I don't have a reason to. Henry and I are engaged. He'd never do anything to jeopardize that."

"You willing to bet your two-carat rock on that?" Evelyn glanced Henry and Shandra's way. "Because they look pretty comfortable to me."

My stomach tightened painfully.

"Remember what I told you. How she got to my boyfriend. You think about that, Phoebe. Think hard."

6

I COULD DO nothing but think about Evelyn's words for the rest of the day. Just how close were Henry and Shandra getting? Had they crossed the line to fucking, or were they simply flirting?

I trusted that Henry loved me. He loved me in a forever kind of way because he wanted me to be his wife. Shandra could try all she wanted, but she couldn't come between us.

Could she?

I have to admit I wasn't feeling so sure anymore. Henry had practically become a stranger to me. Where was the man who used to call me at various times of the day, just to say how beautiful he thought I was? To tell me he missed me, even if I'd just left his room five minutes before? In high school Henry had been a total romantic, bringing me flowers at school, or stuffed animals. Chocolate for no reason. He would run to me after a football game and openly kiss me. I knew he'd often suffered ribbing for being such a romantic fool, but he'd never worried about what his friends thought. He'd always told me that he thought I was a queen and he was going to treat me as such.

That kind of attention was intoxicating. Our relationship had been storybook romance, right to the point where he'd proposed to me at the Skylon Tower in Niagara Falls. And beyond, of course.

But it wasn't just the romance that swept me off my feet. It was Henry's sensitive nature. In eleventh grade, when my favorite uncle was killed in a head-on collision with a semi, I don't think I would have gotten through that awful time if it wasn't for Henry. He'd rushed to my side the night I got the news, and he'd been my rock for months on end when I'd tried to cope with the senseless loss of Uncle Manny. He was with me through every step of my grief, as if my uncle were one of his own family members.

What had gone wrong? Here I was, tempted to sleep with someone else, and I doubted my fiancé's fidelity.

After I saw him in the cafeteria with Shandra, Henry called my cell a few times, but I didn't answer, and in the past few hours he hadn't tried me again. Let him think I was mad at him, because I was. Hopefully my giving him the cold shoulder would make him see how much he had hurt me, and if he loved me, he'd make sure to smarten up.

God, I hoped so. Because I couldn't lose Henry. He meant everything to me. Our relationship so far had been a fairy tale, and I wanted our happy ending.

As I looked up from my philosophy textbook, my eyes wandered to the digital clock on my night table. It was 8:32. I hadn't seen Camille since that morning. Where the heck was she? If ever I needed her, it was then.

It was almost an hour later when the door opened and, relieved, I swiveled my chair around to face it. I needed someone to help me forget about my misery. Talking to

Camille about the reason she'd cut and dyed her hair would certainly do the trick.

"Hey, Cammy. It's about time you showed up."

Camille strolled into the room and dumped her backpack on her bed. I expected her to playfully scowl at me and crack some silly joke about how I was moping around in the room when I should be chasing Morgan—like Miranda, she seemed to think we'd be great together—but instead, she looked serious. In fact, she looked so serious that it scared me.

"What?" I asked, my stomach lurching. "Is it your mother?" Her mother was undergoing treatment to battle breast cancer, and as far as I knew, she was okay. Doing well. But a setback could come at any time.

"My mother's fine."

"Thank God." A breath seeped out of me. "Then why do you look like someone's died?"

She slowly crossed the room, walking toward me. "Phoebe, I just saw something." She stuck her thumbnail in her mouth and began to chew on it. "All the way over here, I debated what I should do. Part of me thought I can't tell you. That maybe I'm assuming the worst. But you're my best friend. And you have a right to know. Even if it's gonna hurt."

I was starting to panic. "Know what?"

Camille took a seat on my bed, across from my desk. She exhaled heavily. "I was in Cole's room. And before you ask, yes, I dumped Kevin. He was too . . . clingy."

"And now you're seeing Cole?" I couldn't help interjecting. This was classic Camille. As soon as things started to get serious with a guy, she dumped him and moved on to someone else. This time, though, I knew that she really liked Kevin. She had to be hurting over the breakup, and she'd no doubt taken her frustration and inability to commit out on her hair.

Maybe her feelings for him had scared her?

"Cole is cool," Camille said hurriedly. "I think we're . . ." Her jaw flinched, an indication of how conflicted she was. "We're a better match."

"Camille . . ."

"Please, Phoebe. Let me finish what I'm trying to say. This is important. When I was leaving Cole's room, I saw Shandra. Phoebe, she was coming out of Henry's room."

Instantly I went cold.

"I don't know what that means, but to be *in his room*—"

"No . . ."

"Like I said, maybe I'm assuming the worst. Maybe—"

"Please!" I shot to my feet and covered my ears. "I can't deal with this anymore. Shandra can't keep doing this to me. I can't keep letting her. I have to make her stop. Teach her a lesson."

The words poured out of me, as if they had a control all their own.

"Whoa, Phoebe. Slow down."

"No, I'm not going to slow down. I can't sleep anymore. I'm stressed to the max. I've talked to Henry about her, I've talked to her about Henry, and what good has it done? She's going to steal my fiancé away from me, just the way she did to Evelyn."

"Talk to her again—"

"How many times do I have to talk to her? Three? Five? Twenty-five?" I shook my head. "That's not working. I have to do something else—something drastic."

"Drastic? Like kicking her ass?"

I finally took a calming breath. *Was* that what I was saying? The reality shocked me, because it was. I wanted to use her face as a dartboard. I wanted to put on steel-toed boots and kick her until she puked blood.

"Phoebe, you're letting Shandra do exactly what she

wants—get to you. You know, I'll bet anything she was in his room because she was trying to work her charm, but Henry knows better than that. If I were you, I'd talk to her again. Better yet, I'd ignore her."

I didn't respond. My mind was elsewhere. It was consumed with wicked thoughts of how I could hurt Shandra. The way she was hurting me.

"Phoebe?"

"Yeah," I said quickly. I sat back down. "I guess you're right. I should ignore her."

"Exactly."

Camille's stomach rumbled loudly, and she made a face. "Okay, I can't put it off any longer. I've got to get some food." She squeezed the layer of fat on her stomach. "No matter how much I starve myself, I can't seem to lose these extra pounds."

"You shouldn't starve yourself," I told her. "It's all about eating healthy." Camille was what I'd describe as "thick," and no matter how much she exercised, she couldn't get below 160 pounds. I thought she looked pretty good at that weight, but she was currently about 180, which was heavy for her five-foot-six-inch frame. Lately, her weight had been yo-yoing because she alternated between starving herself and pigging out on junk food. Something else she did when she was stressed. And with her mother's illness, she had plenty to be stressed about.

"I'll look for a yogurt," Camille said, but she frowned, which told me she really wanted a bag of Doritos. "Or maybe make some low-fat popcorn. Want me to pick you up something?"

"No. I'm fine."

She started across the room. "And when I get back, I want to hear all about where you were last night. Maybe you have some juicy news about Morgan. . . ."

"And you can tell me about Kevin." But I was no longer interested in hearing about him. I could think only of Henry.

"I already told you everything."

"Yeah, right," I countered in a jovial tone, as if her bombshell hadn't rattled me to the core. Then I tried to force a smile, but I'm not sure I succeeded.

How could I smile when inside I was dying?

7

HENRY LOOKED DEEPLY into my eyes and said, "I don't love you anymore, Phoebe."

My hands went cold in his. "W-what?"

"It's over. I'm sorry, baby."

"O-over?"

He nodded but wouldn't meet my eye.

I sucked in a breath, but it was hard to force it down. "I—I don't understand."

Now he looked me square in the eye and said, "I'm in love with Shandra."

Henry's words were like a knife piercing my heart.

"I'm sorry," he said. "I didn't mean to hurt you."

"No, Henry. You can't mean this." He moved backward, walking away from me. "No, please. *Noooooo!*"

I bolted upright, screaming. My hands reached for Henry, but all I felt was air. It was then that I realized I was in my darkened room, in my bed.

I'd been dreaming. But, God, what a dream.

"Hey," Camille said, her voice groggy. "You okay?"

"Sorry," I mumbled. "I had a . . . a nightmare."

I lay back on the bed, getting comfortable against the pillows. To my surprise, my cheeks were wet. I brushed away the tears.

I'd only been dreaming, yet I was devastated. And I do mean that literally. What would happen if Henry dumped me for real?

As I made an effort to calm my breathing, things became crystal clear to me. I couldn't let what had happened to Evelyn happen to me. I couldn't let Shandra steal my man. Henry was my everything. My reason for living. My entire identity, my life, was wrapped up in him. As sad as it may sound, it was true.

And that's why I couldn't sit by and take a wait-and-see approach. I had to do whatever was necessary to get Shandra to back off of Henry.

Immediately.

For the next few hours I tossed and turned, sleep eluding me. How could I sleep when all my thoughts were on how to get rid of my problem?

At some point, though, I must have drifted off, because I woke with a start and saw sunlight spilling into the room. A glance at the clock told me it was after eleven. Eleven! Well, I'd been tired and still was, truthfully. Thank God it was a Saturday morning and I wasn't missing a class.

I looked across the room. Camille was gone.

I snuggled beneath my warm comforter, thinking that it was just as well. I wanted to talk to both her and Miranda at the same time, tell them of a loose plan I was formulating. A way to get Shandra to back off once and for all.

I hadn't seen Miranda since the previous morning. Before the party, she and Damon, the guy she was seeing, had been having some problems. Actually, he'd told her it was over a few days before and she'd been trying to win him back. Since I hadn't heard from her, I suspected she and Damon had worked out their issues and were probably having a marathon sex session. I didn't like Damon, but Miranda was madly in love with him—even if they'd been seeing each other for only a couple of weeks. I'm sure Damon liked the sex Miranda so freely offered, but I didn't know what she saw in him other than his good looks.

Every time a guy broke up with her, Miranda was crushed. But she didn't get it. By her own admission, she spread her legs for a guy right away, and she was naive enough to mistake sex for love. Don't get me wrong, I loved her to death—but I really wished she would see the error of her ways. She deserved a guy who was into more than what she gave him sexually.

The first time I met Miranda, I was at the restaurant where she worked. It was a Sunday morning, and I was with Henry for breakfast. Miranda was our waitress, and my first thought of her was that she was as cute as a button. She's one of those people who has maintained her childlike face despite the years that have passed. Coupled with the fact that she was only five feet tall, people often thought she was much younger than her actual age.

That morning she greeted me and Henry with a wide grin that was warm and inviting, and I liked her immediately.

But when we'd finished and she came out to give us our bill, I was instantly alarmed. I could tell she'd been crying.

"Ready to go, babe?" Henry asked me after dropping money onto the table.

I watched as Miranda walked away. "Do you think she was crying?"

"Who?" Henry asked. "Oh, you mean the waitress?" He shrugged. "I don't know."

"I think she was," I said.

"And?"

"And . . . I think that maybe I should go talk to her."

"You're serious?" Henry asked.

"Yeah," I answered. "I like her. She seems real nice, don't you think?"

"I guess."

I waited until I saw Miranda come out of the kitchen, then I took the cash and our bill and headed toward her. She was dabbing at her eyes but forced a smile nonetheless.

"Here you go," I told her, putting the money into her palm. "No change necessary."

"Thank you."

"Hey. Is everything okay with you?"

She nodded.

"Excuse me for saying this, but you don't look okay." When she looked at me in alarm, I continued. "If you want to talk to someone, I'd be happy to listen."

And then Miranda started talking. Nonstop. About some guy she had dated in high school, and how she'd just checked her cell messages to hear that he'd broken up with her. She'd loved him for years, something I could understand, given my relationship with Henry. But while she loved Jerome, she knew he wasn't good for her. He'd already spent some time behind bars for drug possession, and he was hanging with the wrong crowd.

We talked until Miranda's manager yelled at her to get back to work. Hurriedly, we exchanged numbers. During our first phone call, I learned that she was also a student at UB, though she lived with her mother instead of on campus. The more we chatted, the more I empathized with her situation. Miranda had had a bit of a hard life, growing up in poverty in a one-parent household. She'd never known her father. She had excelled in school and got a scholarship to UB, but that didn't cover housing. So, she was largely out of the loop when it came to campus events.

Miranda and I just clicked, as if we'd been friends since grade school. She started hanging out with me, started meeting new guys. Started dating—if you could call it that. I'm no shrink, but my thought is that because she never knew her father, she was looking for a father figure around every corner. At a party, if she met a guy she found attractive, she was likely to be in his bed before the night was out. Guys got to know her as easy. I tried to steer her along a better path, but I wasn't her mother.

I did think she could benefit from the friendship of other women, however, the sisterhood of a sorority. Which is why I encouraged her to apply to the Alpha Sigma Pi sorority with me. My mother was an Alpha, so I always knew I'd pledge.

It was when we were both pledging that we met Camille. One of our first tests of sisterhood was to jump into a pool of frigid water in T-shirts while wearing no bra, then do some sorority chants on the lawn of the Zeta house with our fraternity brothers watching. Miranda and I had been standing beside each other, and Camille was in front of us.

During our second chant—which boasted our sex appeal and how we had eyes only for the Zetas—a couple of the guys standing to my right began to jeer.

"Who wants a fat bitch like that?" I heard one of the guys say. Then a few of them started to laugh.

In front of me, Camille shot a glance in their direction, at which point one said, "Yeah, tubby. We're talking about you."

Maybe it was remembering what it was like to be harassed by Hunter Mathis in high school, but I got so pissed, I stopped singing and charged right over to the three losers. I addressed the middle one who'd insulted Camille. "You actually have the nerve to call someone a fat bitch when you're as ugly as sin?"

The few guys surrounding him started to chuckle.

"Phoebe," I heard someone say. I was certain it was Big Sister Katrina, but I ignored her.

"You ought to be ashamed of yourselves," I went on. "Picking on someone because of her weight. At least a person can lose weight. You can't change your face."

There were snickers all around then. Someone gripped my arm. I whipped around, expecting to see Katrina, but instead Camille faced me.

"It's okay," she said. "Ignore them," she went on, but a small smile played on her lips.

Big Sister Katrina appeared in front of me then. "Pledge," she said sharply.

"Tell these guys not to be assholes," I told her, not caring if she reprimanded me by giving me some tedious task to complete, like cleaning the shower stalls.

"They were really rude," Miranda concurred.

Camille looked at us both with appreciation.

"Fine," Katrina said. She looked at the guys, then back at us. "We're finished here, anyway."

Before we started off, Camille squeezed my hand. "Thanks again."

"No problem."

I started when two hands slipped around my waist. And then I grinned. I knew those hands. I turned to see Henry.

"I'm proud of you, babe." He lowered his head to kiss me on the lips. "Kyle's a real shithead."

"I didn't even see you," I said. "I thought you weren't out here."

"I only came out now. Saw you giving it to Kyle."

"Pledge, let's go!" Katrina called.

Henry and I held hands for a moment, not wanting to let each other go. "I'll see you later," I told him.

I hurried to take my official place with the other pledges.

We marched back to the Alpha house in our "line"—the formation we always took from shortest to tallest.

Once we were inside the sorority house, our task was complete and we were on our own time. Camille, Miranda, and I hung around in the common room, talking about the experience, and wondered why some guys were worthless assholes. Camille had acted nonchalant about the whole thing, though I could tell what Kyle had said fazed her. As well it should.

Camille confessed that no one had ever stood up for her like that before, and we kept talking well into the evening about all kinds of things. As when I met Miranda, Camille and I had an easy connection and I knew that night that we'd be friends for life.

As I accepted that I wasn't about to fall back asleep, it dawned on me that I wasn't about to see Miranda anytime soon. This was Saturday morning, and she would definitely be at the pancake house where she worked. Saturday morning was one of the restaurant's busiest shifts.

I was still tired, but my mind was churning with thoughts of Henry. Not only that, but my bladder was full. I threw off the covers and hurried out of the room. A short while later, determined to start my day, I returned to the bathroom to shower and brush my teeth.

When I stepped out of the shower I saw Angelina, one of my sorority sisters who had been on line with me when I pledged—meaning we had been in the same pledge class. She was making her way to one of the three shower stalls.

She gave me a bright smile. "Looks like I'm not the only one getting a late start today."

"Nope," I replied, returning her smile.

"Have you eaten yet?" she asked me.

"No, not yet."

"You want to head out and get something? I hear the eggs at Putnam's are putrid today, so I'm staying away. I feel like going to the Commons and getting a Whopper at Burger King."

"I have to admit, that sounds delicious," I told her. And it did. Any other time I'd take her up on the offer. "But I'm actually meeting Henry. We're going downtown to get a bite."

Angelina looked at me oddly. "Isn't Henry playing to-day?"

Shit. The football game. "Oh, right. Yeah, of course. *Of course!* I guess we both forgot about that when we made these plans." I laughed airily. "But you know, he's proba-bly gonna send me out to get him a sandwich or something if he doesn't have time for a meal. He always does." I rolled my eyes, as if it were a chore.

"Oh." Angelina sounded disappointed.

"And I have to get ready for the game, of course."

"Of course," Angelina repeated, her voice deadpan.

"Rain check, okay?" I asked.

"Sure," she said.

We parted ways. She went into the shower stall and turned on the faucets. I made my way out the bathroom door.

I felt bad for lying to Angelina, since I really did like her, but I had plans of my own. The kind for which I needed to be alone.

I wanted to go for a drive, see if something I was think-ing about as I'd tossed and turned in the wee hours of the morning would even be feasible.

The University of Buffalo is officially in Amherst, which is about fifteen minutes outside of downtown. It's scenic there, with lots of trees. The fall is especially pretty, with the leaves turning to vibrant reds and oranges.

I concentrated on that view as I drove away from Greek

Row and onto John James Audubon Parkway. I drove alongside the woods, which were spectacular in their beauty. But my thoughts soon turned from nature's beauty to the ugliness hidden in the woods. The killer who still stalked.

God, I'd been crazy to head out there alone the night of the party. But I'd been so distraught. I still couldn't believe that I hadn't cared if I lived or died that night, because deep in my soul I knew that wasn't true. I wanted to live. And I wanted the great future I'd always dreamed about having with Henry.

It was an unusually warm day for late September, so as I drove off the campus I put the top down on my convertible baby blue BMW. The car was a gift from my parents for graduating high school. Some people called me spoiled. I didn't think I was. I knew how hard my father had worked as a defense attorney. And my mother had single-handedly started and made a success out of a bakery business. I didn't take anything for granted, even if I enjoyed the treats that money could buy—especially as an only child. My mother's business, Something Tasty, had expanded over fifteen years to include four stores in our hometown of Charlotte, North Carolina. She was often featured in articles as a local success. My father as well.

I took the 33 Expressway toward downtown. The feel of the wind blowing through my hair was invigorating. If only it would blow my problems away as well.

Of course, it wouldn't. That was something I had to take care of myself.

I'd had a few intriguing thoughts the night before on just how to deal with Shandra. One was to spread some kind of rumor about her, like that she'd screwed so many guys, she had the HIV virus. That should definitely make Henry stay away. I also contemplated bitch-slapping her in Putnam's. I decided against keying the word *bitch* into her car's paint, since that probably wouldn't do dick to stop her from going after Henry.

The idea that was most appealing involved humiliation and some pain. Lots of humiliation. The thought alone had me chuckling as my mind schemed some delicious revenge.

It was perfect—in my fantasy. And I wanted nothing more than to put it into action.

I exited the expressway onto Oak Street. Driving slowly past the buildings, I looked for one that would be the perfect place to implement my plan.

"This could work," I said aloud, eyeing a spot that looked to be an abandoned building. Even if the building and others did house a business, at night at least one of them would afford me the kind of privacy I needed for the special initiation I had in mind for Shandra.

Turning the car around, I turned left onto Broadway, then left again on Elm, heading back toward the expressway. I was determined to locate Miranda and Camille, even if I had to find Camille and bring her to where Miranda worked. I was actually feeling a bit antsy and needed to share my idea with them as soon as possible.

But as I drove, as the reality of my plan seemed more and more real, my conscience started to weigh on me. Could I really do to Shandra what I'd imagined last night? My fantasy involved violence, and I wasn't a violent person. Besides, as much as I wanted to, if I hurt Shandra, she could go to the cops. And then I could kiss my future good-bye.

My future with Henry.

Maybe Camille was right. I was doing exactly what Shandra wanted—letting her get to me.

To exact revenge would prove that she had power over me—and that I thought she had power over Henry. Not to mention that I'd be putting one foot in my grave at the same time by risking the chance of getting arrested.

"It's a stupid idea," I whispered. "Completely stupid."

Instead of thinking of revenge, I turned on the radio to WBLK and started singing along with Kanye West. I was determined to enjoy the rest of my drive back to UB.

I wasn't going to let Shandra take any more away from me than she already had.

8

I DIDN'T HEAD back to campus. Instead, I went to the Galleria Mall to shop. Shopping never failed to lift my spirits.

At 5:05, with a trunk full of new fashions I did not need, I was en route to Greek Row. That's when my cell phone started singing 50 Cent's "In Da Club," the song I'd selected instead of an actual ring tone. I dug it out of my purse and glanced at the call display.

Henry.

Given the time, his football game would have ended only a short while before. I debated answering his call, and it wasn't just about being angry with him. It was about my dream—how he'd told me he didn't want me anymore. Had my dream been a premonition? I couldn't talk to him if he was going to tell me our relationship was over.

"Oh, stop being silly," I told myself. "Answer the phone."

But it stopped ringing.

"Damn," I muttered, and bit down on my bottom lip.

Seconds later 50 Cent started singing again, and I quickly pressed the talk button. "Yeah?"

"Why aren't you answering your phone?"

"I couldn't get to it," I told Henry.

"Where are you?" he demanded.

Ah, so he was pissed that I wasn't at his game. I had deliberately not gone, hoping he would miss my presence. Maybe this was the wrong tactic, but I wanted him to know what life would be like without me if he kept being a jerk.

"What was Shandra doing in your room last night?" I asked him.

"Huh?"

"What was Shandra doing in your room last night?" I repeated the question slowly, but my voice was louder. I didn't want to lose Henry, but I'd be damned if I sat by as he made a fool of me.

"What the hell were you doing in Morgan's room yesterday morning?" he countered.

Alarm made my body freeze.

"Yeah, that's right. You didn't think Marshall would tell me? He saw you coming out of Morgan's room real early. Early enough that it meant you spent the night."

My stomach lurched. *Shit, shit, shit!* "I wasn't fucking him," I blurted out. "Can you say the same thing about Shandra?"

"What is your problem? You are always going on and on about Shandra. You know what—I don't have time for your jealousy."

"You don't have ti—"

Click.

The motherfucker! I pulled the phone from my ear and tossed it onto the passenger seat.

My hands started to shake, that's how enraged I was. Instead of heading back to my sorority house, I found myself heading farther on Frontier, closer to Skinnersville

Road. That area behind Greek Row had a large stretch of field on which sat both tennis and basketball courts.

Every Saturday afternoon once the football game was over, a handful of Zetas got together to play basketball. Many of my Alpha sorors liked to gather to watch the guys play.

Morgan, without fail, would be shooting some hoops.

I turned onto the driveway that led to the courts. Guys without shirts were running around on the court farthest away. My eyes searched the various sweat-slicked brown bodies. And then I saw Morgan.

Keeping my eyes on him, I veered the car slightly onto the grass. He captured the ball and did an impressive layup into the net. The girls sitting on the grass cheered.

I put my car in park but didn't cut the engine. Instead, I turned up my stereo, blaring Usher, and all eyes flew my way. Okay, that wasn't so subtle, but I wanted to get Morgan's attention.

I did. He looked my way, his eyes growing wide in surprise. Normally I didn't watch the Zetas shoot hoops after Henry's games. I waved at Morgan and smiled.

A moment later he excused himself from the guys and trotted toward me. "Hey," he said, grinning from ear to ear as he reached my car.

"Hey, you."

He braced his hands on the edge of my door. "You're all dolled up."

"It's the sunglasses." I pushed them up to rest in my hair. "And the car," I added with a sweet smile as my eyes roamed over his bare chest. There I was, flirting with him again.

"Daddy's little girl."

I giggled. Morgan was right. I was definitely a daddy's little girl.

"*Spoiled* little girl," Morgan added.

"Not spoiled. Just special."

"Special is right."

"What are you doing now?" I asked him.

He glanced over his shoulder. "We were just about wrapping up. Why?"

"Want to get something to eat? And I mean real food. Somewhere away from campus."

Morgan nodded. "Sounds like a plan. I need to shower, though."

"Can you make it quick?"

"How quick?"

"Like five minutes? Ten minutes max? I'll wait for you in front of the Zeta house."

"You could always join me," he said, his eyes dancing playfully. "Wash my back."

I threw my head back and chuckled. "But then the shower definitely wouldn't be a short one."

Morgan held my gaze for a moment and I thought, *Oh, shit.* Had I gone too far with the flirting?

At least I wasn't thinking about Henry.

"You're right," he said. "A shower with you would definitely be a long one." Then he gave me another charming smile before running off toward the basketball court. My eyes roamed his body from head to toe. Long, lean, and sexy, he was definitely a hottie.

He slipped his T-shirt over his head, and I sighed. Then I did a U-turn and headed back to Frontier Road. There was still a smile on my face, courtesy of Morgan. No doubt, he was a great catch, but as far as I knew, he didn't date. At least not seriously. Not since his girlfriend from high school had broken his heart a year and a half ago.

Maybe if I hadn't already been involved with Henry, we could have had a relationship. I did have a soft spot in my heart for him and probably always would.

A few minutes later, as I pulled my car in front of the

Zeta house, an idea came to me. All night I'd been thinking of ways to hurt Shandra, but I suddenly thought of a better plan.

To make *Henry* jealous.

Give him a dose of his own bitter medicine.

I mean, what better way was there for Henry to see how hurtful it was to flirt like a fool than for *me* to flirt in front of his face? I could whine and snivel and beg him to smarten up, but he'd keep saying I was just being irrationally jealous.

But my idea—it was guaranteed to make Henry take notice.

I chuckled as I slipped my sunglasses back over my eyes. Oh, yeah. This would be priceless.

9

MORGAN WAS FAST. Lightning fast. No more than seven minutes passed from the time I parked in front of the Zeta house to his meeting me at my car.

And, damn, he looked *fiiii*ne. Dressed in a black leather jacket and black jeans, his body looked honed to perfection. I was dressed in Baby Phat jeans with brown suede boots, a white T-shirt, and a suede jacket that matched the boots. If I'd gone to the game, Henry would have seen how cute I looked.

"Get in," I told him.

He didn't open the passenger-side door. Instead, he hopped over it and onto the leather seat.

"You're so smooth," I joked.

"Where are we going?"

"Applebee's." My stomach tickled a bit with the mention of the place. "That all right?"

"That's cool."

Morgan buckled up and I hit the gas with a little too much force. "Sorry," I said sheepishly.

"No problem."

Feeling a little guilty for what I was planning, I glanced at Morgan, having second thoughts. Maybe this wasn't such a good idea after all—getting Morgan into my problems with Henry. Maybe I should tell him I had a headache and leave well enough alone.

"Listen, Morgan—"

I stopped short when I saw his eyes bulge.

"Phoebe, stop—"

I whipped my gaze ahead of me. Then slammed on the brakes. The tires squealed in protest, but the car stopped just before I ran down Shandra.

Shandra jumped backward in shock, then glowered at me.

"God," I muttered. "Why is she always here? Does she live at your fraternity house now?"

"You know she's one of our sweethearts."

"She's a bitch, that's what she is." And then I almost blurted out my plan. But something made me hold back.

Maybe the hope that Henry and I would be screwing our brains out before the night was over, both laughing over the pathetic Shandra James.

But I couldn't help wishing that I hadn't stopped.

That I'd run her over.

I was nervous when I parked the car outside of Applebee's. I could only hope my plan didn't backfire.

"I don't really think I'll get drafted by the NBA," Morgan was saying as we walked into the restaurant. "So, I really have to think about what I'm gonna do with the rest of my life."

"Uh-huh," I agreed absently.

"Ultimately, I'd like to be a coach."

He stopped talking when the hostess, a short freckle-faced redhead, smiled broadly at us. "Table for two?"

"Yes," Morgan and I said in unison. There were a few families in the waiting area, so I asked, "Will it be a long wait?"

"Nope," the hostess replied. "There's one table for two open right now."

I held my breath as we followed the redhead into the restaurant. I saw Henry's table immediately. It was the long one in the middle of the room, where he and his teammates were dining.

"Right here." The hostess placed the menus on a two-seater near a window. It was in Henry's line of sight.

"Thanks," I mumbled. I took the seat that would face Henry, hoping Morgan hadn't seen him. My plan was for Henry to see us together, get insanely jealous, and realize that he didn't want to lose me. If he was smart, he'd know this was about Shandra and also know that it was time for him to smarten up.

"I feel like having wine," I said. My voice faltered slightly. I hoped he didn't notice.

"Are we celebrating something?"

I shook my head. "I'm just tired of beer, aren't you? Especially after the frat party."

"True dat."

Lifting the plastic-encased drink menu on the edge of the table, I said, "Or maybe one of these nice fruity drinks. Like this margarita. And by the way, I'm paying."

Morgan shook his head. "No, you're not."

"I invited you, so yeah, I—"

"What the fuck?"

Scared shitless, I jerked backward as my eyes flew to the right. There stood Henry, and he looked madder than I'd ever seen him.

"What the hell are you doing here with Morgan?"

"I—"

"Yo, Henry." Morgan chuckled nervously.

"Fuck you, Morgan."

"Baby." I reached for Henry's arm, but he swatted my hand away.

He glared down at me. "You fucking him?" he demanded, loud and aggressive.

"Henry, there are kids in here!" I said in an urgent whisper.

"Does it look like I give a shit about that?"

I lowered my face and groaned.

Morgan got to his feet, holding his hands out in a sign of surrender. "Relax, man. You know I wouldn't disrespect you like—"

And then Henry punched Morgan in the gut, catching Morgan off guard. Morgan doubled over, winded, and I jumped to my feet and screamed.

Henry dug his fingers into my upper arm. "How dare you come here to flaunt this in my face, knowing I'd be here with my team?" His fingers tightened.

I saw unadulterated rage on his face. Felt it in his touch. "Ouch . . . baby."

Recovered from his blow, Morgan punched Henry in the face. The force of it caused him to loosen his grip on me. The next instant, Henry flew backward. People around us screamed as he crashed into a table, landing on the couple's dinners.

Paralyzed with fear, I stood there, watching Henry, wondering what would happen next.

Then he started to rise.

Whimpering, I stepped backward until my body hit Morgan's. Henry was out of control, and I had to do what I could to protect Morgan from him. I'd never seen Henry look so terrifying in my life.

But Morgan moved me to the side, clearly ready to face down Henry again. I grabbed Morgan's hand, pleading, "No, Morgan. Let's go." Surely some petrified staff member had already called the police—something we didn't need.

"Henry, what are you doing, man?" one of his teammates asked. "You want to get arrested?"

The warning didn't stop Henry. Giving Morgan a fierce look, he advanced.

"You don't even love Phoebe," Morgan spat out. "If you did, you wouldn't be screwing Shandra."

My eyes flew to Morgan's. And then Henry lunged at him, slamming into his body and knocking him against the window.

"Henry, no!" I cried out.

"Go on." Morgan looked at Henry with defiance as Henry gripped him by his shirt. "Tell your *fiancée* what you do when she's not around."

My knees buckled, and for a moment I thought I would collapse. Somehow I found the strength to force myself between the two of them. I was stuck in the middle as they tussled around me. Thank God several of Henry's teammates appeared and began tearing him and Morgan apart.

"All right, all right." Henry stepped backward and glanced around, seeming to realize for the first time that everyone in the restaurant was staring at us. Then he shot me a lethal glare before stomping off.

It did not escape me that he never denied Morgan's allegation.

10

THE NEXT MORNING I stayed in bed as though I were dying or something. I was completely listless, unmotivated to move even a muscle. Something was going on inside me, a kind of despair that sucked the life out of me.

Camille urged me to get up and go downstairs with her to enjoy one of the perks of being a big sister in our sorority. During the pledge process, every Sunday morning the pledges gathered in the common room and brushed our hair. They also painted our toes and fingernails if we wanted, and they even gave massages. It was basically a "pamper me" morning and a highlight of the week.

But that morning I wasn't in the mood. My head was pounding as if a little hammer were inside it, chipping away at my peace of mind. All I could do was clutch Miffy, my favorite teddy bear, which I'd owned since I was four, for comfort.

I'd blown things royally the night before. My plan didn't just veer off course, it completely failed. Morgan and

Henry could have killed each other, and it was no one's fault but mine.

After we'd left the restaurant, Morgan was fuming. Once in my car, he let me have it. Told me that he felt used by me, that I'd set him up. I apologized over and over. It was the only thing I could do. The last thing I wanted was for him to feel used. But could I blame him? No. I wasn't even sure he still wanted to be my friend, which was why, as I drove back to campus, I didn't ask him to elaborate on what he'd accused Henry of.

And if I'm entirely honest with myself, I guess I didn't want to hear more. I didn't want to face the truth that Henry might have been unfaithful.

Henry . . . Pain stabbed my heart as I thought of him. I knew I would never forget the look he gave me at the restaurant for as long as I lived. I dreamed about the look all night, in my now-recurring nightmare where Henry tells me he no longer loves me.

"Henry, I hope you don't hate me," I said softly. My stomach knotted with the very thought.

Exhaling a slow breath, I sat up in my bed. Henry had had the night to cool off, and I hoped he was in better spirits. It was time for me to talk to him and smooth things over.

I reached for the phone on my night table and dialed his room number.

"Hello?" It took him four rings to answer, and he sounded as good as I felt.

"Baby," I began tentatively. "It's me."

"I can't talk to you."

Henry hung up the phone, and I burst into tears. I shook uncontrollably as I cried. I cried until my eyes were swollen and my throat was raw.

My entire life was falling apart. I felt out of control.

Powerless. Distraught in a way I had never before experienced.

Henry and I were in love. Had been for five and a half years. We were supposed to get married. Married! Did that mean nothing to him?

Was he really screwing Shandra behind my back? Why wouldn't he even talk to me?

I called him again. He didn't answer the phone.

I called again. He answered, barking, "What?"

"I just want you to know, I'm not sleeping with Morgan."

No answer.

"We can get through this, Henry. As long as . . ." I had to stop, or else I was going to start crying hysterically. I realized then that I loved Henry more than life. It was a scary thought, but true. "As long as you're not sleeping with Shandra. You're not, right? Please tell me what Morgan said was a lie."

"You're unbelievable," Henry muttered. And once again, he hung up on me.

I replaced the receiver and curled into a ball on my bed. As I bawled like a baby, I seriously thought the pain of Henry's rejection would kill me. Everything about our relationship up to that point had been the stuff of every girl's fantasy—a fantasy he'd promoted with his sensitivity and frequent romantic gestures. How had he changed so drastically?

I'm not sure how much longer I cried, but at one point I realized that crying was going to get me nowhere.

I had to see Henry.

Go to his room and talk to him. That way, he couldn't hang up on me. He'd *have* to talk to me. And I could make him see how much he meant to me and how much we still belonged together. Before Shandra had disrupted our lives, we'd always been able to talk out whatever problem we were going through.

Of course, before Shandra, our problems were nothing the average couple didn't experience. Misunderstandings over small things, like a forgotten date. Or the occasional drama if he thought I made eye contact with a guy who had checked me out a little too long. Nothing major.

A few minutes later I was dressed and almost at my door when it suddenly opened. Camille appeared, looking as startled as I felt.

She smiled and flashed her fingers at me. "What do you think? Does royal blue suit me?"

"I'm sorry. I've got to go."

"Phoebe—"

I didn't stop. I flew past people in the hallway and downstairs without so much as a glance or a hello. I didn't break stride until I was in the Zeta house at Henry's door.

For a moment I hesitated. Then I turned the knob. It opened.

Henry was in bed, a pillow over his face. He was a vision of what I must have looked like a short while ago. And just like that, my heart melted. I felt his pain, because I was feeling the same thing. How did we get to this point, where our relationship was falling apart?

He heard me when I started to walk across the floor and dragged the pillow off his face. His eyes widened in surprise as he looked at me.

I climbed on top of him, straddling him. It wasn't a sexual move but one designed to keep him in place. My hair flowed down the sides of my face as I stared into his eyes.

"I'm sorry," I found myself saying. And I knew then that it didn't matter if Henry had slept with Shandra, because I wasn't going to lose him to her. I was going to fight with everything I had to make sure Henry remained my man.

"I'm so sorry," I went on. "I wasn't thinking. I was just—I don't know. Can you forgive me?"

"I hate when we fight."

"So do I."

Henry looked thoughtful for a moment, as if he was going to say something but didn't.

"What?" I asked.

He shook his head. "Nothing."

"You don't forgive me?" I asked, my heart sinking.

Henry replied, "Let's forget it. In fact, why don't we do something nice tonight? Maybe have a romantic dinner in Niagara Falls or something."

"I'd love that," I told him. Somehow I kept my voice from being overexcited, when in fact I wanted to scream with joy. We'd gone off track in our relationship, and we needed time together as a couple. And romantic dinners were completely Henry's style—and something I loved doing with him.

"Great." Henry had an easy smile that warmed his entire face. It didn't take a rocket scientist to figure out why women were attracted to him. It was that smile that had won me over in high school, before he'd ever uttered a word to me.

"Meet me here at six," he said. "We can take my car."

"Casual or formal?" I asked. My vagina was thrumming against him, and I felt him growing erect. Our bodies were speaking to each other in a language all their own.

"Wear something nice. We'll go somewhere nice."

"And in the meantime . . . what do we do before then?" My voice lifted on a suggestive note.

Ever so slightly, Henry moved his groin against me. "What did you have in mind?"

As I lowered my head toward his face, I linked my fingers with his. "I can think of something." I kissed his cheek, then met his gaze again. "You know I love you, right?"

"I know."

Then I kissed him on the mouth, and he kissed me back. God help me, it was like heaven.

We undressed hastily. And when his penis entered me, we found our paradise lost.

11

I WAS STARING at Henry with what I knew had to be a completely lovestruck expression. If he hadn't already proposed to me, I would have sworn that's what this dinner was about.

We were seated in the revolving restaurant on the top of the Skylon Tower on the Canadian side of Niagara Falls—the very place he had proposed. The restaurant's main feature—other than being hundreds of feet in the air—was that it slowly rotated as people dined, affording one an incredible view of the city and the beautifully lit falls below.

A bottle of chardonnay sat on the table between us. I'd had two glasses and was already tipsy.

I took another sip of my wine, then said, "I'm so glad we're out like this. Away from campus for a while. This is really nice."

Henry nodded his agreement. He reached for his wineglass. Fiddled with the stem. "Yeah, this is a great place."

"Not just a great place." I reached across the table and

covered his hands with mine. "This place will always be very special for us. Thank you so much for bringing me here, back to where you proposed to me. It's made me remember all the good in our relationship, and that we're soul mates, just like you told me when we first started dating."

Henry sipped his wine.

"I didn't want to mention this yet, in case it doesn't happen," I went on, "but last week, just before the Zeta party and everything got crazy between us, I spoke to my mother and she said that *Charlotte Bride* is interested in possibly covering our wedding! They'll follow us in the days before the wedding, be there at the big event. Isn't that great?" My problems with Shandra had unfortunately kept me from enjoying this fabulous news, but I was determined to put Shandra and all the unpleasantness regarding her behind me.

"*Charlotte Bride*?" Henry finished his wine, then reached for the garlic bread.

I continued. "With the interest from *Charlotte Bride*, I was thinking we should set a date. Maybe the third week in June. I've always wanted to be a June bride."

Henry cleared his throat and tapped lightly on his chest. I looked at him in concern. "Sweetheart? What is it? Did the bread go down the wrong way?"

"No, I'm fine."

"Then why are you frowning?"

He took a deep breath, not meeting my eye. "Phoebe, there are things . . . things we need to talk about."

"Of course. If we're going to get married in June, we have to get cracking right away. There's so much to plan! But my mother said she can take care of hiring a wedding planner, getting the invitations printed, and—"

"Phoebe."

Henry's firm voice made my smile disappear. I suddenly

realized that he wasn't sharing the excitement I felt. In fact, he didn't look happy at all.

"What is it?" I asked him. "What's wrong?"

A few seconds passed before he said, "It's us."

I stared at him for a moment, my eyes narrowing. Then I chuckled nervously. "What about us, baby?"

"Things have been . . . real messed-up recently," Henry went on. "We haven't been getting along like we used to."

"I know. And I know that's why you brought me here, Henry—so we could refocus on our commitment to each other. And it worked. I'm ready to work past all our problems the way any engaged couple does."

"That's the point." Henry paused. "Maybe we shouldn't be."

For a few seconds I didn't even breathe. I wasn't even sure I had heard him correctly.

I finally asked, "What did you say?"

"I hoped that tonight would give me clarity on our relationship. Make me realize that we didn't make a mistake getting engaged. But maybe we've been going through problems because we're too young to be taking such a big step. Hell, Phoebe, we're at the stage where we're figuring things out."

Oh my God. Oh my God.

"Don't you think marriage is too big a step right now?"

I forced in a few deep breaths. "Henry, why are you talking like this? Just this morning we had such an incredible time making love, and then you said you wanted to go somewhere nice. . . ."

"I'm just telling you how I feel."

"Telling me how you feel!" I shrieked, and everyone on our side of the restaurant looked my way. "What you're saying makes no sense. We've been together for five and a half years, Henry. Right from the beginning, you told me you knew we were soul mates. How could marriage be too big a step when you know it's right?"

Henry groaned uncomfortably as he looked around. "Phoebe, please keep your voice down."

"You break up with me and you don't expect me to be upset?"

"I didn't say I was breaking up with you. I said we should slow down."

"And let me guess—see other people?"

Henry shrugged. "Can you deny that you're attracted to Morgan?"

I gasped loudly, shock overwhelming me. Then I recovered. "So this is about Morgan? Or is it really about Shandra? Is this because you're attracted to *her?*"

In the several seconds it took Henry to respond, the restaurant started spinning out of control. Or was that my head?

"Maybe I am," Henry finally said.

All my air left my lungs in a rush. My head was spinning so fast, I thought it would break off my neck and fly into orbit.

"I love you enough not to lie to you, okay?" he said after a moment.

"You love me, but you're attracted to Shandra. Right?" And then I started to cry.

"It's not like I love her or anything."

"*Love?*" I croaked. "Oh my God."

"Phoebe—"

"Why are you doing this? What's happened to you?"

"Phoebe, listen to me. I didn't say I loved her. It's just—"

"What—your penis?" I spat out. "You pathetic jerk!" I threw my wine in his face and jumped to my feet.

"Fuck," Henry muttered. He glanced around at the people who were staring, then got to his feet as well.

My hands were shaking so much, I could hardly grab the strap of my purse off my chair, which delayed my getting out of there.

Henry reached for my hand. "Baby, you have to calm down."

I was angry. "Go to hell."

Looking around the dimly lit restaurant, with candles burning on tables between couples gazing into each other's eyes, I felt incredibly stupid. There I was, thinking that Henry had taken me to this romantic place where he had proposed because he wanted to make our relationship stronger, and instead he only wanted to dump me. I turned and marched one way around the circular restaurant, then realized I was heading the long way toward the elevators, so I spun around to go in the other direction. I saw Henry throw a wad of money down on the table before starting after me.

Fucking rotating restaurant. I couldn't make a clean break, even though I wanted to. I had to wait for the elevator. Which gave Henry plenty of time to get to me.

I ignored him when he got to me at the bank of elevators. He sighed and said, "I took you here hoping we could talk—calmly."

"You mean you thought you could dump me without my making a scene. But you were wrong."

The elevator opened, and after half a dozen people spilled out, I hurried on. Henry followed me. Tears were streaming down my face, so I stood facing the wall.

When Henry put his hands on my shoulders, I shrugged them off. "Don't touch me!"

"All right," Henry said. A beat passed. "I care about you, you know I do."

"You used to love me." I gripped my belly as a sharp pain, like a knife blade, sliced through me.

"If we're meant to be, we will be. But right now I need

a break. You know we do. You don't even trust me. You keep harassing Shandra."

I whirled around. "What did you say?"

"Shandra's told me—"

"So *that's* what this is about? That fuckin' bitch has been bad-mouthing me? And you believe *her?*"

"Honestly, Phoebe. You've got to calm down. How am I supposed to drive back with you like this?"

"Oh my God." Hysteria took hold of my emotions, and I began sobbing. "Now you're gonna abandon me here!"

"That's not what I said."

"No? Then why did it sound like that?"

Henry groaned. "Just take a deep—"

Henry stopped abruptly as the elevator door opened. A handful of people about to get on eyed us both with interest. Henry put a hand around my shoulder as though he were a concerned lover and ushered me out of the elevator.

The drive back to campus was an entire blur. I had seriously considered taking off and finding my own way home, that's how much I couldn't stand the idea of being near Henry right then. But being across the border with my passport in Henry's car would have caused a mess of problems. And if I were completely honest with myself, I wasn't ready to be out of Henry's company. His bombshell had devastated me, and I kept expecting him to tell me that he hadn't meant what he said, that he still loved me and wanted to marry me.

But he didn't. He played an old-school hip-hop CD all the way back to campus. Every so often he'd sing some of the lyrics. It was like salt in an open wound. How could he be so friggin' carefree at a time like this?

I, on the other hand, sat silently, staring out the window and wondering how I could go on.

For over five years, Henry had been nothing but a

wonderful, loving, romantic boyfriend. He had been passionate about me in and out of the bedroom. We had clicked in every way. I'd had the kind of relationship with him that I read about in the romance novels I devoured. And now he was taking that away from me?

How could this be happening? And what was Henry going to do—start dating Shandra?

I couldn't stomach the thought.

When we got to the sorority house, Henry reached for my hand. My heart ached as he touched me, even though my brain told me I should get out of the car and slam the door behind me.

"I do love you, babe," he said softly. "I want this to work."

"Yeah, whatever."

That was all I could manage to say without becoming a weeping mess in his car. I threw open the BMW's door and ran off.

Henry called my name, but I didn't look back.

12

I WAS AWARE of the door to my room opening, but I didn't have the strength to even move.

"What if you're wrong?" Miranda was saying. "What if Kevin didn't sleep with Tricia?"

"Gimme a break," Camille responded. "Look at her. Pencil-thin, really pretty."

"And you're a beautiful full-figured woman. Camille, you saw them talking a few times. Big deal. Kevin is totally into you. Why don't you give him another chance?"

"It's too late. I'm seeing Cole."

"Oh, I don't believe you. Why do you always do this? How long is it gonna last with Cole?"

"At least I'm not lying to myself. Girl, I told you not to go back to Damon and you didn't listen. Sure, he was happy to screw you again, but where is he now?"

"He's probably been busy with his work at the paper," Miranda said.

"Come on."

"It's possible."

"Miranda, you have to move on. Kick him to the curb."

"Maybe you're right. Maybe he is an asshole. Why do all guys turn into jerks after the first week?" Miranda sighed as she sat on my bed. "Hey, where's Phoebe?"

"Speaking of assholes," Camille began, "can you believe how Henry's treating her? You *know* he's screwing Shandra." From my hiding spot in the closet, I couldn't see her.

"Maybe not," Miranda said. "Shandra's obviously after him, but that doesn't mean he's stepped out of line."

"Right." Camille's voice was dripping with sarcasm.

"Something must have happened at dinner, though. When Henry showed up at the Zeta house, he didn't look happy."

"They probably had another fight."

Miranda turned—and screamed. I didn't even flinch.

"What?" Camille asked, alarmed.

Miranda slowly got off the bed and crept toward the closet, as though she thought I might be an axe murderer hiding behind designer clothes. I'd gone to the closet when I returned to my room because it was the only thing that resembled a dark hole, and I wanted desperately to disappear.

"Phoebe?" she asked cautiously.

Camille appeared by Miranda's side, and she too peered into my hiding spot. "Phoebe, what are you doing in the closet?"

I didn't answer. Together, Miranda and Camille pulled me out of the small dark space. They escorted me to my bed as if I were a cripple.

"Phoebe, talk to me," Miranda said. "What's happened to you?"

Camille stared at me with a mixture of fear and concern on her face. "Did someone hurt you?"

I tried to breathe but gasped instead.

Miranda wrapped an arm around my shoulder. "Oh, baby. We're here now."

"H-H-Henry . . ." was all I could manage.

"What'd he do?" Camille asked.

I could only cry harder, reliving the whole dreadful incident.

"I've never seen her like this," Miranda commented. "Do you think he hurt her? Raped her?" she added in a low, horrified tone.

"Tell us what happened," Camille urged me.

I shook my head.

"If he laid a finger on you, I swear to God . . ." Camille made a fist.

"Let us help you, hon."

"Y-you can't," I sobbed. "N-n-no one c-can."

"Take deep breaths, honey," Miranda said softly. "You have to calm down."

I tried, but it was too hard. "H-Henry. H-he . . . he . . ."

"Maybe we have to take her to the hospital," Miranda suggested. "I mean, if he beat her up, she could be bleeding internally. . . ."

And that's when it clicked. My friends' scared gazes, their words—I got a clear picture of what I must have looked like to them. Like a woman traumatized and on the verge of a breakdown.

I'd let myself become an emotional basket case, but I had to take charge of my life again.

I drew in a shuddering breath, willed myself to calm down. "It's that bitch, Shandra," I said. "Everything that's happened, it's all her fault."

Camille's eyes widened in horror. "He told you he's sleeping with her!"

I swallowed—hard. Then recounted what had happened at dinner with Henry. When I finished my tale, both

Miranda and Camille stared at me with their mouths wide open.

"He broke up with me. Right there where he had *proposed*, with God knows how many people watching. Do you believe it?"

"No!" Miranda exclaimed. "Why would he do that? You don't just break up when you're engaged."

"He thought you wouldn't make a scene," Camille said sourly. "That's why he brought you there."

"Exactly," I agreed.

"But Henry loves you," Miranda said, as if she refused to believe my story was true.

"I can't believe I'm saying this, but I'm not so sure anymore," I admitted sadly.

I remembered that day in the cafeteria with Evelyn, how she'd told me that Shandra had stopped at nothing until she'd stolen her boyfriend.

"This is Shandra's fault," I said. "If only that skank whore had never come into our lives, we'd be happy right now. Just like we always were. I hate her, I hate her, *I hate her!*"

"Did he say if he fucked her?" Camille wanted to know.

"I don't even care if he fucked her. I just wish he'd get over it already."

Camille shook her head. The look of disgust on her face was unmistakable. "I don't know if I could forgive that."

"What's she supposed to do?" Miranda asked. "Just give Henry up because Shandra wants him? You know all she wants is the chase, anyway. Look what she did to Evelyn."

"I'll be damned if I'm gonna lose him to her. To anyone." And I meant it. I'd been with Henry too long for Shandra to fuck things up.

"She needs to be out of the equation, pure and simple.

That's the only chance Henry and I have of making things work."

"Like she's gonna leave him alone." Camille scowled. "You've already talked to her. I kind of thought she was going to back off, but clearly I was wrong."

"That's why it's time to teach her a lesson." I stared at Miranda and Camille in turn. "Let her know there are consequences for messing with me."

Miranda gave me a skeptical look. "You don't mean that."

"The hell I don't. I've been sitting around here, moping, when the solution to the problem has always been in front of me. I just didn't want to accept it."

The day before, I'd dismissed my fantasies of hurting Shandra as infeasible. But now . . . now the idea didn't seem all that far-fetched.

In fact, it seemed necessary.

I knew I could set up some sort of initiation scenario to get to her. I didn't have to hurt her seriously, just shake her up so that she'd understand I meant business.

"What are you saying?" Miranda asked.

"I feel like I'm gonna lose my mind," I said. "I'm not kidding. This is driving me crazy. Once and for all, I have to put a stop to Shandra. Talk to her in a language she'll understand."

Miranda stared at me, then asked, "You mean like beat her ass or something?"

I nodded. "Something like that. For all the hell she's put me through, she needs to be taught a lesson." When Miranda and Camille remained silent, I continued. "I'm not gonna go insane and cut her up or anything. I'm not going to push her over Niagara Falls. I've been thinking about this. . . . I guess what I really want to do is shame her."

"I'm game," Camille said right away. "Shandra is a

straight-up ho, and for messing with your man, she ought to be put in her place."

"Thank you." I got off the bed and hugged Camille. Her support meant the world to me.

Then I faced Miranda. Known as Big Sister Hugs and Kisses, she wanted to see the best in everyone. "What about you? Are you with me?"

"Is it really worth it?" she asked me. "The more you react to her—"

"It's not like I'm gonna kill her or anything. But what's so wrong with humiliating the shit out of her? She needs a lesson in humiliation. I've been thinking about it, and I can do this under the guise of an initiation. But one just for her. We can take her out to some remote spot in the middle of the night, scare her real good."

"And you don't think—"

"Last year when you were all upset over Arnold and wanted to plan some payback, I was there for you. That's what I'm asking of you now. To be there for me."

"I didn't hurt Arnold."

"I already told you, I'm not gonna hurt Shandra," I shot back. "And you may not have physically hurt Arnold, but when the word spread that he was addicted to child pornography, that ruined him. He had to transfer schools."

"I know, and I'm not proud of that." Miranda hung her head low in shame. "Arnold didn't deserve that."

"Arnold may not have deserved the humiliation, but Shandra deserves all that and more." Anger hit me like a slap in the face as I thought of all she had put me through. "Hell, she's humiliated me at every turn. Fucking bitch."

"I do agree she needs to be stopped," Miranda said. "But what about talking to our housemother? Or maybe I can talk to Shandra."

"Shandra complained to the board that *I* was picking on her because she's a legacy. Which is bullshit. I'm a legacy, too, even if my mother isn't some important person on the sorority's national board. You think you're going to get through to Shandra by talking to her when I can't?"

Miranda shrugged. "It's a suggestion."

"It's bullshit," I snapped. "I can't believe you don't want to help me."

Miranda sighed. "I didn't say I wouldn't help you. I know you're not gonna do anything stupid. I'm just concerned about you, that you don't let Shandra get to you."

"I'm so past that. My relationship is falling apart because of her. That bitch has to pay. *Now.*"

13

THE NEXT DAY I had a stroke of good luck. I took it as a sign.

I'd been trying to think of ways to call Shandra out of her room alone under the guise of an initiation, but then I got the news that her roommate, Cassie, had to leave suddenly for a family emergency.

"I think we should make our move tonight," I whispered to Miranda and Camille when we were in Putnam's for lunch.

Miranda looked at me in surprise, then swallowed. "Tonight?"

I nodded. "Her roommate's father had a heart attack and she had to go home. I assume Cassie'll be gone for a while, but who knows for sure. I want to do this as soon as possible."

"You know I've got your back," Camille said.

I stared at Miranda. "What about you—are you in?"

"I told you I was."

"But your face says you don't really want to." I needed her to help me make it happen. My plan needed at least three of us.

"I just . . . does it have to be tonight? I don't know why, but I have a bad feeling. . . ."

"Yes, it has to be tonight. Please, Miranda. I need you. I can't wait another day. Henry won't even talk to me. Never in the years I've been with him has he ever been this . . . cold. It's Shandra's fault. I know that now. With her out of the picture, he'll be himself again, and we'll work everything out." I paused as I took a deep breath. "Meet us in our room at two A.M., Miranda. Everyone should be sleeping by then."

"You're really sure—"

"Yes, Miranda. I am." I was more determined than ever to do this. "Can I count on you?"

"All right," Miranda agreed, albeit reluctantly. "I'll be there."

I was nervous and excited at the same time. Excited that I'd get some payback. Nervous because I didn't want to get caught.

But I had to do it now. I was as ready as I'd ever be.

At five minutes to two, I took a quick walk around the sorority house and found it all quiet. No one was in the common room, studying or watching TV. Which only confirmed that now was the time to act.

I took the stairs two at a time back up to my room. "The coast is clear," I told Miranda and Camille.

Miranda nodded, then pulled her toque over her face. Camille and I followed suit. The black toques revealed only our eyes and our mouths. Combined with the rest of our black clothing, I prayed that if anyone saw us in the dark, they'd never be able to identify us.

"Let's do this," I said.

We took the back stairs down to Shandra's floor. Thankfully, her door was close to the stairwell. It would allow us the opportunity to be quick. The house was quiet, but we couldn't take any chances.

Part of the policy during the pledge process is that the pledges keep their doors unlocked—to allow us easy access to wake them up for middle-of-the-night rituals and so forth.

My hands shook slightly as I opened the door. Then we all crept into the room.

A low-wattage lamp was illuminated on the desk, but Shandra lay sleeping in her bed. I knew she was sleeping because I could hear the bitch snoring.

I exchanged glances with Camille and Miranda. Then I nodded.

We tiptoed across the room. I tore off a piece of duct tape, passed it to Camille, then tore off another piece of duct tape. I placed it on Shandra's eyes at the same time Camille placed the other strip on her mouth.

It took Shandra only a beat to become fully awake, and then she started struggling. Camille and Miranda grabbed her hands and I wrapped her wrists in duct tape. She was breathing heavily now, her nostrils flaring with the frantic effort.

I was surprised at how loud her muffled screams were. "Shut up!" I demanded.

Shandra thrashed, still made noise.

"You must be quiet and still," I told her, disguising my voice. "Your passage into the Alpha Sigma Pi sorority depends on your cooperation."

Only then did Shandra start to calm down. It sounded as if she was making an effort to get her breathing under control. She probably wasn't used to breathing through her nose.

"That's right," I told her in a calmer, still disguised voice. "You pass this, and you're one step closer to crossing over. Do you understand?"

She nodded. Then Camille, Miranda, and I pulled her to her feet. We began walking with her toward the door.

Camille moved ahead of us to peer in the hallway. A moment later she nodded, signaling that all was clear.

Miranda and I whisked Shandra out the door. We followed Camille to the left, where she held the door to the stairwell open. We had planned it all in detail beforehand. From the stairway, there was an exit on the ground floor that led to the back of the building. Miranda's car was parked a short walk across the grass from there. My car was there, too, but I felt it would be safer to take Miranda's car. Thankfully, she'd agreed.

Shandra drew up short when her feet hit the cold concrete of the stairwell. She protested in a muffled voice that no one could understand. But then she stuck a foot high in the air, and I understood what she was trying to tell us.

"You'll get over it," I told her, giving her a shove.

We moved as quickly as we could down the two flights of stairs. My heart raced a mile a minute. If caught, I could always explain it to a stranger or other students as a sorority initiation, but the sorority's board would know that was a lie. They were to be informed of any initiation plans.

If it got back to them, they could report me to the Panhellenic Committee and I could lose my sorority pin.

That couldn't happen. I wouldn't let it.

The cool night air hit us in the face when Camille opened the door. Shandra whimpered loudly. Ignoring her, we all broke into a run, forcing Shandra to run as well. It took only about a minute for us to reach the car, though it seemed longer.

"Here." Miranda pulled her car keys from her waistband and tossed them to me.

I hit the button to unlock the Toyota's doors. Miranda and Camille stuffed Shandra into the backseat while I got behind the wheel.

Then I tore out of the parking lot as if the cops were pursuing me.

I did it, I thought. *I really did it.* I was exhilarated and nervous and scared out of my mind.

For the first few minutes no one spoke, but Shandra's labored breathing filled the air. It was a gasping-wheezing type of sound that drove me crazy. I found it hard to concentrate on driving with the awful sounds she was making.

"Maybe she can't breathe," Miranda said after a while.

"She's fine," I said.

"Listen to her," Miranda urged.

I did. How could I not? She sounded like she was dying.

I was certain she was exaggerating her discomfort, but I said, "Fine. Take the tape off." At least she wouldn't be able to see anything.

The sound of ripping duct tape reverberated through the car. Shandra screamed in pain, then started her tirade. "Are you all trying to *kill* me?"

"You're not dead, are you?" Camille retorted.

"Where are you taking me?" she demanded.

None of us answered.

"What kind of initiation is this?" Shandra asked. "Where's everyone else? Why do you have me on my own?"

"Maybe you should put that gag back on," I suggested.

"No! I can't breathe with that thing on!"

"Then shut up! You're not making the rules," I told her.

Shandra stopped talking, but only for a short while. Not more than a minute later she asked, "That's you, Phoebe, isn't it? And why is no one else here?"

I didn't answer. But I knew I'd screwed up. I'd forgotten to disguise my voice.

"So this is personal," she continued. "Not a real initiation."

I angled my head to glance at Miranda and Camille. Miranda had her toque pulled up, and she met my eye with concern. I knew she was worried about the ramifications, especially given her reluctance in the first place. I couldn't blame her.

"Just shut up and it will be over soon," I told Shandra.

My head was starting to pound. Now that Shandra knew who I was, I couldn't help having second thoughts. Maybe this idea had been an incredibly dumb one. What if Shandra went to the sorority's board? Or worse, to her mother? Surely her mother would have my sorority pin revoked without a second thought.

I shivered, the thought scaring me. I didn't want to lose my sorority pin. What had I gotten myself into?

But then the memory of the look on Henry's face when he'd told me we needed to take a break hit me so hard, emotion welled up in my chest.

My second thoughts quickly vanished. To hell with the sorority. If they kicked me out, so be it. I had to do what was necessary to keep my man. He was more important to me than anything else.

Resolved to get it over with sooner rather than later, I hit the gas. I drove to the spot I had scoped out two days earlier. It was the back of a vacant downtown building with easy access to the 33 Expressway. At night, parts of downtown Buffalo became like a ghost town. I knew there was little chance we'd have any problems executing our plan.

"Where are we?" Shandra asked the moment the car stopped.

I was about to kill the car's engine, but then thought better of it. If we needed to make a quick getaway, the car should be running.

"Answer me, damn it," Shandra said.

"We're someplace special," I told her. "Real special."

14

I GOT OUT of the car and opened the back door. Camille jumped out, and once she was on her feet, we both reached inside for Shandra.

"Don't touch me!" Shandra exclaimed. "Take me back to campus right now, you fucking bitch!"

As we hauled her out of the car, I felt as certain as ever that Shandra was about to get what she deserved. And I felt a sense of power, knowing that I had her right where I wanted her.

"You think it's my fault Henry finds me irresistible? That he loves my pussy so much?"

I pushed her to the rocky ground. She fell onto her face and bound hands, moaning as she did.

"Get up, bitch." I wanted to kick the shit out of her, but I held myself back.

"You can't do this to me. You know who my mother is?"

"I'm in charge of the pledge process," I retorted. "I can do what the hell I want. The board has approved this," I lied.

"Bullshit," Shandra replied.

"You don't make the rules, pledge. I do. And I gave you an order to *get up*." I reached for Shandra, hauling her up by the hair.

She screamed bloody murder.

"You keep that up and you get gagged again," I told her. "Got it?"

"Why are you doing this? I can't see a fucking thing."

Camille gave Shandra's shoulder a shove. "Quit your whining."

"That's Camille, right? Let me guess. That brainless lackey Miranda is with you, too."

Miranda's mouth fell open in shock. Then her eyes narrowed with anger.

"You think it helps you to run your mouth?" Camille asked.

"You all are gonna be sorry," Shandra shouted. "You have no clue who you're messing with."

"Us? Sorry?" I laughed. "Are you on crack?"

"What do you think Henry's gonna say about this?" Shandra asked. "If you think he doesn't give a shit about me, you're wrong. We don't just fuck. We've got something special going. Henry and I, we're closer than you know."

I slapped Shandra across the face. "Don't you dare mention Henry's name." I wanted to do worse to her. Punch her until she puked blood. Instead, I remembered my plan. I had a pocketknife in my jeans pocket and I took it out, opened it up, and cut Shandra's hands loose.

Shandra instantly rubbed her wrists, soothing them.

"Now my eyes," Shandra ordered.

"This is the *brainless lackey* speaking," Miranda said. She walked right up to Shandra, standing inches from her face. "Since you're too stupid to figure it out, *we're* the ones giving the orders. And until you do as we say, you can forget about heading back to the dorm."

"What do you want me to do?" Shandra asked, sounding frustrated. "Apologize? Okay, I'm sorry, Phoebe. Sorry that Henry can't stay away from me."

"Oh, you think you're a funny bitch. Well, how's this for funny?" I punched her in the face.

Shandra tumbled backward, landing against the car.

"Get off the damn car," Camille said, pulling her forward.

"Enough games. It's time for your . . . your test." I looked at both Miranda and Camille in turn before continuing. "Take off your pajama top."

"What?"

"You heard her," Miranda said.

"It's freezing out here. I'm not taking off my shirt."

"Do you want to cross over into our sorority or not?" I asked.

"You can't stop me from crossing over. My mother runs this sorority. You hear me? My mother's the friggin' vice president!"

Shandra shouted the last words, and I had no doubt she was hoping to attract someone's attention.

I pulled my belt out of my jeans. "Take off your shirt, or you'll be very sorry." I whipped the belt against the ground.

"What . . . what was that?" Shandra asked.

"A belt," I replied smugly. "Something your mama clearly should have used on you when you were young but didn't. Now, your top!"

When Shandra hesitated, I whipped the belt against the ground again, saying, "Now."

The loud, cracking sound frightened Shandra into motion. She hastily pulled her pajama top over her head, but held the material over her exposed breasts.

Miranda pulled the pajama top from Shandra's hands.

"Now take off your pajama bottoms."

"Fuck you," Shandra uttered in defiance.

I whacked her across the legs with the belt. "Do it!"

She whimpered for a moment, then recovered. "Fine, you bitches want to see me naked, here you go. Drool all you want, you—"

"Shut up!" Miranda yelled.

For a girl who hadn't been entirely convinced of the plan in the beginning, Miranda was certainly getting into it now. And that was no wonder. Experiencing Shandra's venom firsthand had obviously pushed her over the edge.

We all watched as Shandra dropped her pants. But she didn't stop there. She boldly pulled off her thong under-wear as well. All she wore was a thin platinum chain with a white and pink heart-shaped diamond pendant, an early gift from her mother for becoming an Alpha. The neck-lace glittered beneath the moonlight.

"Now do you see why Henry can't resist me?" Shandra asked boldly.

"You're delusional," I told her. But I said the words around a lump in my throat. Because looking at Shandra's large breasts and hourglass figure, I could see why Henry was attracted to her.

"You're the delusional one," Shandra said. "Because, believe me, Henry loves every inch of my body." She ran her hands down the length of her torso. "And he does things to me I bet he's never done with you."

"Shut up!" I screamed. I was on the verge of tears. "Shut up, shut up, shut *up!*"

"He loves me, Phoebe. Said I'll always have his heart."

I held my tears at bay. "Now you've gone too far, bitch." I raised the belt over her head.

"No," Miranda said, quickly stepping between me and Shandra. "Not yet." She turned to Shandra. "And you call me brainless? You don't have the sense to know when to shut up."

"It's obvious you think you're fine," Camille said. "You think the world revolves around you. And guess what— tonight it will. Skinny-ass bitch."

"That's right." I drew in a few deep breaths, trying to stay in control. Shandra was lying. She had to be. She was trying to get to me.

"Tonight," I continued, "you're gonna do some serious penance for your sins, pledge. Get on your knees."

"Whatever." Surprisingly, Shandra obeyed without a fight. She lowered herself to her knees but went a step beyond that and leaned forward onto her hands. "Henry loves me in this position, by the way. I love when he's behind—"

I whipped the belt across Shandra's butt.

She cried out in pain, then quickly quieted, but I could hear that she was sobbing softly. I'd hit her harder than I'd intended but, damn, Shandra had been asking for it with all the lies she was telling about Henry.

I didn't realize my hands were shaking until Camille took the belt from me. "You okay?"

"Yeah." I cleared my throat. "Course I'm okay."

"Let me have a go at her," Camille offered.

I simply nodded as I took a few steps backward. Damn it, I *knew* Shandra was trying to get under my skin. Why was I letting her?

"So, you like that position," Camille said. "Just like a bitch in heat. Well, bark for us, bitch. And make it good."

"Fuck y'all."

"Fuck us?" Miranda asked. "No, fuck you. Which we might just. There's a huge branch not more than three feet from you. It just might be big enough for you."

"All right," Shandra shouted. "I'll do it."

Shandra hesitated for a moment, then started barking.

"Louder," Camille instructed. "And howl, too."

Shandra barked louder, and she howled as well. The

sight of her on all fours, barking like the bitch she was, made me crack a smile.

Within seconds Camille, Miranda, and I were laughing our heads off.

I glanced around to make sure no one was coming, something I'd been doing periodically since we got out of the car. Satisfied we still had privacy, I said, "Now crawl around. Just like a dog. Yeah, that's it."

I could hardly talk for all my laughter. Oh, but I needed this. Needed to laugh, or I was going to cry.

Camille stuck her wrist under my face, pointing to her watch. I nodded. We'd been gone for a while. We'd have to wrap it up and head back to campus.

"Just one more thing," I whispered to Camille. Then, to Shandra I said, "Roll over. And don't stop till I tell you to."

"Y'all are whores. You hear me? Friggin' whores who need to get a life."

"Roll over, bitch," I insisted, "and this will be finished before you know it. Unless you want another ass-whooping."

Awkwardly, Shandra rolled over and over the gravel, cursing under her breath as she did. "Shit!" she cried. "Something just tore open my knee. I hope you're happy."

"Oh, we're happy," Miranda countered. "As long as you get the point that you have to watch who you mess with."

"That's right." I moved to stand over Shandra's body. "You've been warned. Stay the fuck away from Henry. If you don't, you'll be sorrier than you are right now. And if you breathe a word of this to anyone, you will definitely be sorry. That, I guarantee you." I kicked Shandra's pajama pants at her, then said, "Come on, ladies."

Shandra scrambled to her feet as we started off. "Whoa, wait a second," she said. "What're you doing? You're *not* leaving me here!"

None of us responded. I yanked the driver-side door open.

"No!" Shandra cried. "Don't leave me! I did everything you said."

"I'm sure you'll have no problem charming a trucker into driving you back," I told her. "Hmm, I think I see one coming."

Despite my bravado, my hands were still shaking. I couldn't drive, not like that. "Camille."

She looked up from her side of the car. I tossed her the keys, then made my way around to the front passenger side of the car.

"Don't leave me here! *Please*."

There was something about Shandra's pleading that actually got to me. Maybe because she finally sounded vulnerable and scared, instead of like the Wicked Bitch of Buffalo.

"Someone's coming to get you," I told her. "Just stay here and you'll be fine."

"Please," she cried, ignoring what I had said to her.

I slammed my door shut to block out Shandra's screams. Camille hit the gas, throwing all of us backward as the car surged forward.

I didn't want to, but I craned my neck around to see Shandra. She was on her feet, pulling at the duct tape around her eyes while she futilely ran in the direction of our fleeing car.

"I hate being so mean to anyone," Miranda said, "but she deserved that."

"Absolutely," Camille agreed.

"She'll have plenty to think about while we drive around for a few minutes," I said. "Stupid whore."

"She's got to be freaking, thinking we're not coming back." Camille laughed as she pulled the car onto Oak Street. "Where should we go?"

"Um . . ." I wasn't entirely sure. I knew only that we needed to kill about five minutes. It would seem like an eternity to Shandra. "Maybe turn right at the lights. We can drive around the downtown core, then circle back to get Shandra."

Camille did as I suggested, turning right onto Broadway. Just ahead of us was Lafayette Square, and to the left of that was Main Place Mall.

"Keep going straight past Lafayette Square," I told Camille. "When we hit the traffic circle in front of the courthouse, we'll turn back."

But we didn't get far. Just as we passed the library, there was a loud popping sound. The car veered sharply to the right and slammed into the curb.

We all screamed.

15

"HOLY SHIT. OH my God." My breathing came in rapid pants. Though we clearly hadn't suffered a major collision, I was as freaked out as if we had.

"What happened?" Miranda shrieked. She sounded as scared as I felt.

"I don't know." Camille glanced at me as she put the car into park. "I must have blown a tire."

I slapped a hand to my forehead. "No, not a tire. Not now."

Camille opened the door, and I followed suit. Miranda stayed in the car, as if she were too afraid to get out. I took a few steps forward and instantly saw that the right front tire was flat.

"It's blown all right," I told Camille as she came around to my side of the car.

"Great." Camille groaned. "What do we do now?"

"Maybe Miranda has a spare in the back."

Camille looked incredulous. "Do you know how to put on a spare tire? Because I sure as hell don't."

"Right, right. Well, we'll have to call for a tow truck."

"But that's gonna take time."

"I know," I said. "And we have to get Shandra." I dug my fingers into my hair. "Fuck!"

Miranda opened her door and finally stepped out of the car. "What's going on?"

"Your tire is blown," Camille explained. "Now we'll have to call for a tow truck."

"But Shandra—"

"I know, Miranda," I said. "Obviously, we can't leave her there."

Miranda's eyes flitted nervously between me and Camille. "So what are we gonna do?"

"We have to call someone to pick her up," I answered, my mind churning with possibilities. "What about your ex—Jerome? You said you guys still talk from time to time. Maybe you can call him." Considering that he'd been in and out of trouble with the law, I was certain he wouldn't rat us out if we called him to pick up Shandra.

Miranda's jaw dropped. "You're kidding, right?"

"I'm dead serious. We can't call anyone from UB."

"She's right," Camille agreed. "You're the only one of us who's from Buffalo. You've got friends here."

"I told you this was a bad idea," Miranda muttered. "Damn, I knew *something* would go wrong."

I wasn't in the mood for any lectures. "Time's running out. Can you just call him?"

Miranda blew out a frustrated breath, then went back to the car. She reached inside and retrieved her phone. Camille and I watched her as she made the call.

After about thirty seconds Miranda shook her head. "It went to his voice mail. Look, you're not going to like what I have to say, but maybe we need to call the police. Anonymously," she quickly added. "Tell them we saw a girl who looked like she needed help."

"And what do you think Shandra's going to say to the cops if they go get her?" I asked. "She's going to have to explain how she got there. She's in pajamas, for Christ's sake, with no shoes and no purse. That'll be mighty suspicious, even if she doesn't want to rat us out. No, there's got to be someone else." I turned to Camille. "Hey, what about Cole?"

Camille was chewing on a thumbnail. She didn't speak, just shook her head.

"Why not?" I asked.

"We just can't. Cole—he won't understand."

"Kevin, then?" I suggested. "He'd do anything for you." When Camille's wary eyes met mine, I pleaded with her. "Please, Camille. You know I can't call Henry."

"Kevin is not gonna appreciate this."

"At least he still cares about you. You don't think he'll help out?"

Sighing loudly, Camille walked toward Miranda. "Miranda, let me use your phone."

My stomach was in knots. It was nearly three in the morning, and there was no guarantee we'd reach anyone at that hour. It was all a crapshoot, and in the meantime, the minutes were whizzing by. God only knew what Shandra was doing right then.

Please, let her reach Kevin. Please.

A couple of cars had driven by us, but no one had stopped. Now another car was approaching, and it slowed to a crawl. The window went down, and a middle-aged black man stretched across the front seat. "You ladies okay?"

"We're fine," I quickly told the man. "We blew a tire, but a tow truck is coming."

Satisfied, the man nodded, then continued on. I went to the car to retrieve my phone, realizing that one of us needed to call for help.

"Kevin's not answering," Camille told me as I reached into the car.

"No?" My heart rammed against my chest.

"We can't just stand around here like this," Miranda whined. "Anyone could be driving around here, and Shandra's not going to stay behind that building for long."

"I know, I know." My head was pounding.

"What about Morgan?" Camille suggested. "He adores you."

"Morgan?" I croaked. "I—"

"You can't?" Camille asked. "We don't have a choice."

I wanted to protest, but Camille was right. Calling Henry was out of the question. But I also didn't want to call Morgan, let him know what I'd done. He was already angry with me for the stunt at Applebee's. I didn't want him to hate me.

"Phoebe," Miranda said impatiently.

"Okay, I'll call him." I blew out a heavy breath, accepting that I had no choice. "But one of you has to call for a tow truck."

I felt like shit calling Morgan like that, but I dialed his number nonetheless. As the phone rang I wandered a few steps away from my friends so I'd have some privacy.

Morgan answered after three rings, sounding groggy. "Hello?"

"Morgan, it's Phoebe."

"Phoebe?"

"I know it's late, and I'm sorry. But I need you now. In a really big way."

"What's going on?" Worry filled his voice.

"I . . . It's Shandra. She's downtown—alone—and someone has to pick her up."

"Huh?"

Morgan sounded utterly confused, and of course he would be. I exhaled sharply and started again. "I . . . I did something. To Shandra. An initiation thing," I quickly rambled. "She's okay, and I'll tell you about it later, but I really need you to head downtown and pick her up."

"You're kidding me," Morgan said. "Do you know what time it is?"

"I know. Trust me, I know. I didn't plan on calling you like this, but my tire blew and now we can't go back for her."

"We?"

"I'm with Camille and Miranda," I explained.

"God, Phoebe. At least you're not alone. But let me guess—you've called for Henry to come get you guys, while you want me to pick up Shandra."

"No, I haven't called Henry. A tow truck is coming for us. In the meantime, someone has to get Shandra. We let her think . . . think that we'd abandoned her there."

"Holy shit."

"Morgan, I know you're mad at me, but I really need you right now. Can you do this for me?"

He hesitated. "What if she's gone when I get there?"

"She was naked when we left her. I don't think she'll go far."

"She's naked?"

"We'll talk about it later, okay? Please, can you go?"

"All right," he grudgingly agreed.

I explained to him how to get to the building where we'd left her.

"You're gonna owe me, Phoebe. Big-time."

"I know. Please hurry."

Morgan hung up. I turned to find that Camille and Miranda were standing directly behind me.

"Morgan's on his way," I told them.

Miranda crossed her arms over her chest, then asked, "You think she'll be okay?"

"I'm sure she'll be fine," I answered. "Shandra's behind

an unoccupied building. If I were her, I'd wait there until daylight. Wouldn't you? As long as she stays there—and I'm sure she will—then no one's gonna find her except Morgan. She'll be humiliated but unhurt, which was the point. And scared out of her mind until Morgan gets there, I guess. But that's no less than she deserves."

"I hope you're right," Miranda said. "But I can't shake this feeling that something else is gonna go wrong."

"Nothing else will go wrong," I said, a little annoyed with her doom and gloom. But as I spoke the words, a thought struck me. I hurried past my friends to the car, where I reached inside and retrieved the three toques. Then, looking around to make sure no one was lurking in the bushes, I stuffed the toques into a sewer grate.

"We don't want those lying around the sorority house," I explained. "Just in case."

"Just in case what?" Miranda asked.

Damn, I hated how nervous she sounded. I didn't need that. Not then. I needed reassurance that I'd done the right thing, that other than the flat tire, nothing would go seriously wrong.

"In case Shandra pulls something stupid," I finally answered. "But if she does, it'll be her word against ours. If she's dumb enough to breathe a word of this, we deny, deny, deny. But I doubt she's going to say anything. I'll bet my last dollar that Shandra's not going to be a problem from now on."

16

TWO HOURS AFTER returning to my dorm room, I was too wired to sleep. I couldn't put the night's events out of my mind, no matter how much I tried.

I wish I could say it's because I was overjoyed—which I fully expected to be—but it wasn't. I didn't feel elated after giving Shandra what she deserved. Instead, I felt ambiguous.

Actually, I felt downright empty.

And a little scared.

The fear had started after the tire had blown, and continued with Miranda's worrying all the way back to UB. I hated that I had to get someone else involved in the plan, even if it was Morgan. I felt I could trust him, but I wished he didn't have to know what I'd done.

Still, fear of repercussions wasn't the only thing bothering me, though the reality that Shandra could report me hung over me like a dark cloud. What scared me more—now that I was alone with my thoughts and could be honest with myself—was that never in my wildest dreams would I have thought I could be capable of the uncontrollable rage that had driven me to do what I'd done to her.

Sure, I hadn't beat her to a pulp, but I'd been tempted. Really tempted. I'd been close to snapping and totally losing it.

And I'd been careless. In my haste to get away, I'd left my belt at the scene. The rhinestone-studded belt wasn't one of a kind, but people certainly had seen me wear it. What if Shandra scooped it up as evidence of what I'd done to her?

I told myself not to worry about that. Yes, I wished I hadn't left it behind. I'd have preferred to have it with me, or to toss it as I'd done with the toques—in case it could ever be used as evidence. But that was assuming Shandra would have been smart enough to pick it up. I kind of doubted that. And since she should be back in her room by now—humiliated but otherwise okay—there was really no need to worry over the issue.

Whether I had cause to worry, my body was trembling, as if I had a chill from the inside out. I pulled my comforter up to my neck but after a few minutes I still wasn't warm.

I glanced across the room at Camille, who was lying on her back. Her mouth was open and she was snoring loudly. With her weight gain, her snoring had gotten worse.

At least she wasn't having a problem sleeping.

Rolling onto my side, I looked down at my open sociology textbook and tried to read about the history of the woman's role in society. After five minutes of rereading the same paragraph, I gave up and slammed the book shut. I needed to occupy my mind with something since I couldn't sleep, but the words weren't registering. Why was I even bothering?

Slowly I sat up. There was no point in trying to read when I couldn't concentrate. I was anxious—more than anxious—to hear from Morgan. I figured he would have called me once he'd returned Shandra to campus.

So why hadn't my phone rung?

Miranda's words sounded in my mind. *But I can't shake this feeling that something else is gonna go wrong.*

Had something gone wrong?

No, I told myself. Of course nothing had gone wrong. What could go wrong? No matter how angry with me Morgan was, I knew he wouldn't let me down.

Unlike Henry, who had apparently betrayed me. If I were to believe Shandra's words.

Thinking about all she'd said made my head pound. Oh, I didn't want to believe her, but she'd been entirely too confident, too smug, given the position we had her in, to be lying. And Henry had admitted he was attracted to her, so how far a stretch was it that he'd slept with her?

And not just slept with her, but fallen for her—if I could believe Shandra.

"How could you do this to me, Henry?" I asked quietly. "How could you hurt me like this?"

The more I thought about everything, the more my head hurt. I glanced at the clock radio and groaned. It was five minutes after five. In a couple of hours, I'd have to get up. It was too late to pop a sleeping pill.

I closed my eyes. Tried to turn my brain off.

I couldn't.

Okay, so I had to accept that Henry had most likely slept with Shandra. Or at least made out with her. But no matter what they had done together, I was certain he didn't have strong feelings for her. I would never believe that. She'd been a temporary attraction, if that, and with her staying away from him from now on, we would get our relationship back on track.

We would get married, just as planned. Hopefully next June.

But even as I tried to reassure myself, the thought seemed like an empty one. As though I were lying to myself.

Did Henry really like to ram Shandra from behind? Did he taste her pussy, let her sit on his face—all those things he had done with me?

But worse than the sex, was it possible that Henry was slipping away from me, little by little? After everything we had meant to each other? I could barely stand the thought.

If I didn't have Henry, what did I have?

My thoughts were driving me crazy. I rolled over and glanced at the phone. Contemplated calling Morgan. Then decided against it. He was no doubt in his bed, catching up on his sleep, and I didn't want to wake him up.

In a few hours I would talk to him and find out everything that had happened with Shandra. Hopefully I'd also find out her state of mind and know whether I had to worry about her going to the board. I didn't think I did, but some assurance would be nice.

Lying down, I closed my eyes again. I was desperate to sleep. I thought about Henry, what it would be like when we got back together. How amazing the sex would be, how our intimate bond would be resealed.

Finally I drifted off to sleep, but it was far from peaceful.

17

THERE WAS A hand on my thigh.

My eyes flew open. I whipped my head around on the pillow and nearly had heart failure when I saw Henry's face.

Was I dreaming?

"Henry?" My voice was hoarse.

"Yeah, baby. It's me."

My God, I wasn't dreaming. I turned my body to face him. "What are you doing here?"

"You don't want to see me?"

"Of course I do." Remembering Camille, I quickly looked beyond Henry to my friend's bed. "Where's Camille?"

"She let me in."

"I slept through Camille getting up?"

"She said you were real tired. That you were up late studying."

The memory came back to me in a rush. What I'd actually been up late doing.

"Um, yeah. I was. And I thought sociology would be a bird course." I smiled lamely, even as my heart started to pound with nervous excitement. If Henry was there, it meant he wanted to work things out. Had Shandra already spoken with him that morning and told him she was backing off?

"What time is it?" I asked since Henry's body was blocking my alarm clock.

"Nearly eleven."

"What?" I shot up. I'd missed my morning sociology class.

"Listen," he said softly. "I was hoping we could talk."

Henry's jawline had the shadow of a beard, a look I'd always liked on him. I took a deep breath. "Henry . . ."

"I've missed you," he said softly.

"Have you?" But I knew what he meant. A day and a half apart had seemed like an eternity.

He nodded as he ran a hand along my thigh. "How could I not miss this?"

"But you said—"

"Forget what I said. I was stupid. Guess I got cold feet for a while, with all that talk about *Charlotte Bride* and setting a date. But I realize now that was just jitters."

My heart swelled with so much warmth and love, I nearly started crying. Then caution took root. Was this about me, or about Shandra? It mattered, I suddenly realized. I wanted Henry there because he wanted to be there.

"Jitters?" I asked.

Henry laughed. The sound was warm and wonderful and reminded me of everything I loved about him. "Crazy, huh? We've been together forever. I know you're the one for me."

Emotion overwhelmed me then, but I bit back my tears. "You hurt me so much."

"Oh, baby." He kissed my cheek tenderly.

I wanted to ask him why, but I didn't have the nerve. Maybe I just needed to be happy with the fact that he was back.

He kissed my other cheek. "I'm sorry, baby. I've been a fool. Do you forgive me?"

"Yes." The word slipped out of my mouth on its own.

He lowered his voice to a husky whisper and asked, "When's your next class?"

"Right now." My body was already growing hot for him.

"Want to skip it?"

"Ye—" I began but stopped myself as I remembered Morgan, that I hadn't heard from him yet. And I was desperate to know what had happened with Shandra.

"I don't know, Henry. I think I need to go—"

Henry silenced me with a kiss, and my protests began to melt away. I wanted him more than I wanted anything else.

Still, as Henry and I made love, I couldn't help thinking of Morgan. Wondering when he would call, and what he would say.

18

OKAY, I WAS really starting to shit.

Henry had stayed with me until late afternoon. I hadn't had the heart to tell him to leave. But that meant I wouldn't be able to call Morgan, and neither my room phone nor cell phone rang even once.

Henry and I finally took a break from our lovemaking to get some dinner. It's amazing: when I headed out of my room with him the way I'd done a thousand times, I felt that all eyes were on me. As if people knew what I'd done.

But if they did, wouldn't Katrina have knocked on my door already? No one had.

I held Henry's hand as we made our way to the Student Union. He talked about football, how excited he was about an upcoming game, but I didn't hear more than a few words of what he said. I kept looking all around me, trying to see if Shandra was anywhere to be found. I'm not sure why I was concerned about that, but I was.

Probably because I hadn't heard from Morgan yet.

I saw Shandra nowhere, not even in the cafeteria. Again, it felt that all eyes were on me.

Of course, I was just being paranoid, knowing what I'd done.

Henry and I loaded our plates with shepherd's pie. Henry ate. I picked at my food.

"What's wrong?" Henry asked me.

"Nothing." I forced a forkful of food into my mouth, tried to pretend I was enjoying it. It was like acid going into my stomach.

A short while later I sat up straighter when I saw Morgan walk into the room. He saw me immediately. Panic made my blood freeze. *Please don't come over here now,* I thought. *Please.*

Morgan held my gaze for a moment, then—I couldn't be sure—scowled. Why the hell would he scowl at me?

"Do you swear to me that nothing's going on with you and Morgan?" Henry asked.

My eyes flew to his. "Of course." Damn, I sounded so nervous. "Why would you ask that?"

Henry glanced Morgan's way before meeting my gaze once again. "I'm not stupid, okay?"

"It's just . . ." My mind scrambled for an explanation. "I don't know if he's still mad at me because of Saturday night. But that's his problem," I added sourly.

I reached for Henry's hand, trying to reassure him that everything was okay. But I couldn't help thinking about Morgan.

And then it hit me. Why he'd scowled at me. Shandra must have been a real cow when he went to pick her up.

I actually smiled. Yeah, that had to be it. I could definitely see Shandra giving him a hard time.

I'd get all the dirty details later.

* * *

Camille was in our room when I got back, sitting on her bed with a large bag of Doritos in her lap. She immediately asked me, "Have you seen Shandra?"

"No. But I've been busy all day."

"I'm starting to worry," Camille admitted. "Miranda said she had this dream that Shandra was dead—"

"Dead!" I shrieked. "Oh, come on. I know she fancies herself some kind of psychic sometimes, but if she was, why didn't she know her ex was screwing her sister? She's freaking out, and there's no reason for that. I saw Morgan in the cafeteria not too long ago."

"What'd he say?"

"We didn't get a chance to talk. I was with Henry. But the look he gave me—I think Shandra was a handful when he went to pick her up." I chuckled.

"Oh." Camille popped a chip into her mouth.

"In fact, I'll call him now. That'll put both our minds at ease. Dead!" I chortled. "I can't believe Miranda."

I was still chuckling as I wandered to the room phone and punched in Morgan's cell number. "Hello?" he said, sounding as though his mouth was full of food.

"Morgan, it's Phoebe."

He didn't answer right away, and when he spoke again, he didn't sound as if he was eating anymore. "Yeah?"

"I thought I would have heard from you by now."

He laughed bitterly. "Did you, now?"

I frowned. "Why do you sound like that—like you're pissed off?"

"You don't think I have a right to be pissed off?" he asked incredulously.

He was either talking about the night before or Saturday night. "I know. I haven't been the best friend."

"You might think your little games are funny, but

they're not. I care about you, but that doesn't mean you can take advantage of me."

"Take advantage?"

"Look, I'm with my boys right now—"

"I needed a favor last night. I wasn't trying to take advantage of you."

"A favor," he repeated sourly.

"When we get together, I'll tell you all about it."

"Yeah, and maybe you can tell me what the hell you were thinking, sending me on a wild-goose chase in the middle of the night."

19

MORGAN'S ANSWER THREW me for a loop. So much so that for a few seconds I couldn't speak. But I finally found the voice to ask, "What do you mean, 'wild-goose chase'?"

"Oh, come on, Phoebe. You set me up on Saturday night. Now this. You had me going with that story about the blown tire," he added with a mirthless chuckle. "To think I was worried about you."

"What—"

"Did you think it was funny? Or are you trying to see if I'll be your backup guy if things don't work out with Henry?"

"Morgan, hold up. Are you trying to tell me that *Shandra wasn't there?*"

"No shit."

My stomach bottomed out. "Oh my God."

"She wasn't there?" Camille asked from behind me.

My mind scrambled to make sense of things. How could Shandra have not been there? Morgan had to be lying, I decided. Pulling my leg as payback for what I'd put him through. "You're kidding me, right?"

"Do I sound like I'm kidding?"

God help me, he didn't. The weirdest numbing sensation washed over me. I couldn't think, much less speak.

Camille took the phone from my suddenly cold fingers. "Morgan, this is Camille. Are you really serious? Shandra wasn't there when you went to pick her up?" There was a pause, then Camille said, "No, this wasn't a prank. We really did leave her there. . . . I know. Look, it was an initiation thing. I'll let Phoebe tell you about it. . . . What time did you get there?" I watched as my best friend's face crumbled. "Oh my God."

I motioned for her to give me the phone again, which she did. It smelled of Doritos when I put it to my ear. "How long did you stay there?" I asked Morgan.

"I don't know. Around ten minutes. She's really missing?"

"I . . . I don't know. Maybe she caught a cab or something. I just figured . . . I told her someone was on the way. Why would she take off?" I paused, then asked, "Have you seen her at all today?"

"No, I haven't seen her."

"Can you ask around?"

"Phoebe, what did you do?"

"Just . . . humiliated her. So she'd know to stop messing with Henry."

"Jesus."

"I'm sure she's around here somewhere. I'm sorry you made a wasted trip last night."

"What if she's not okay?" Camille asked me. "Miranda said she had a bad feeling, and then that dream . . ."

"I don't want to hear that shit right now!" Frustrated, I groaned. "Sorry I yelled, Camille. Morgan, let me call you later, okay?"

"Whatever," he replied.

He still sounded pissed with me, but I couldn't worry about that right then. I had to find out where Shandra was.

And I knew the perfect way.

"Up, up, everybody up!" I repeated this mantra as I and my sorors pounded on the second-floor dorm rooms of the sorority house. It was midnight, and time for a surprise initiation for the new pledges.

At least that's what I'd told the board about that night's surprise initiation. But what I really wanted was the proof that Shandra was alive and well and just trying to make me sweat.

One by one doors opened and groggy-eyed young women made their way into the hallway.

"You know the drill," one of the big sisters said. "Get in your line."

The pledges scrambled to get into order. Their "line" went from shortest to tallest. There were fourteen pledges that year, and it wasn't hard to see that Shandra wasn't among those in the hallway.

I rolled my eyes so that everyone could see, then walked to her door. "Shandra," I called. I banged on her door. "Up, pledge."

The door didn't open. I looked around nervously, saw a soror's curious gaze.

"All right, then." I opened Shandra's door. It was empty, the bed unmade. The lamp on her dresser was on.

Just as it had been in the middle of the night.

My heart slammed against my rib cage.

"I haven't seen her," one of the pledges said. "Not all day."

There was a chorus of "neither have I's."

"We were supposed to meet after our African studies class," another pledge said. "She didn't show."

My legs started to tremble. Beside me, Miranda gave me a grave look of concern.

"I . . . We'll deal with Shandra later," I said. I tried my best to sound authoritative. Unfazed. "Now, girls—follow me."

Along with a handful of sorors who were on the pledging committee, I led the pledges outside. This was supposed to be a fun initiation in which we hosed the girls down in front of our sorority house, then marched them through the Zeta house to give our frat brothers a little thrill.

But I could only go through the motions, doing my best to force a smile onto my face.

Inside, I was paralyzed. Paralyzed with fear.

Where the hell was Shandra?

20

THE FEAR DIDN'T leave me all night. In fact, it was like a living, breathing entity. Sleeping with me. Following me everywhere.

I told myself to remain calm, not to assume the worst. But as the day went on and I didn't see Shandra anywhere, the fear damn near turned to panic.

There was no way I could deal with going to the cafeteria for dinner on my own, as I had for lunch. I knew I'd need to talk with Camille and Miranda should Shandra remain missing. So, I left a message for both of them, saying to meet me outside the Ellicott Complex at six o'clock.

"Has either of you seen her?" I asked in a hushed voice as I approached my friends outside the cafeteria.

Both Miranda and Camille looked glum. They shook their heads.

None of us spoke as we made our way into the dining hall, where most of the Greeks ate. Our meal plans allowed us a certain amount of meals per week that could be eaten at either of the major eateries on campus, and we also had a fair amount of campus cash to spend anywhere on campus for whatever we liked. Of the cafeterias and dining halls, Putnam's was the more popular spot, but since I hadn't seen Shandra there yet, I was hoping against hope that I'd see her in the dining hall instead.

Camille, Miranda, and I filed into the dining hall quietly, filling our plates with salad. I scanned the hot-meal choices. Normally I would indulge in the hot and spicy chicken wings, but I didn't think I'd be able to keep them down. So I filled myself a bowl of vegetable soup.

I led the way onto the dining-hall floor. My eyes did a sweep of the room, my stomach sinking with each passing second.

"Okay, this shit ain't funny," Camille said. "Where could Shandra be?"

Miranda's face paled.

"She could be at Putnam's tonight," I explained. "Or at any of the fast-food joints in the Commons."

"And that's why no one has seen her anywhere?" Miranda asked.

We all sat down. "I've been thinking," I continued, "that maybe she's doing this on purpose. To scare us. Hiding out somewhere to make us shit in our pants."

"God, I hope so," Camille said. "But I don't know."

"Where would she have gone?" Miranda asked. "She's got no family in the city, far as I know."

"Maybe she's got a friend nearby," I suggested. "And since this is where her mother went to school, her mother must have friends in the city. Shandra could be staying with any one of them."

"I'd like to believe that, but . . ." Miranda's voice trailed off. She spiked a piece of cucumber with her fork but didn't eat it.

"But what?" I asked. I loved Miranda, but her doom-and-gloom "feelings" were pissing me off.

"But what if there is no friend, Phoebe? What if that's wishful thinking?"

"So, she's at a hotel somewhere," I said. "She's got money."

Miranda snorted with derision. "And you still believe in Santa Claus, too—don't you?"

"Fuck off," I snapped.

"I think what Miranda's trying to say, Phoebe, is that you have to be realistic here. What if something seriously wrong happened to Shandra? What if she somehow found her way back to campus, only to be snatched by that rapist and murderer who's on the loose?"

Miranda whimpered, then pushed her tray away and said, "I'm not hungry."

"Neither am I," Camille said.

"We can't start jumping to conclusions," I said. "That's not gonna help."

"What *is* gonna help?" Miranda challenged. "I told you, Phoebe, don't do this, it's a bad idea."

"But you certainly got into it when you were there!"

Both Miranda's look of hurt and the realization that I was speaking too loudly made me shut my mouth.

"I'm sorry," I said, then buried my face in my hands.

Several seconds passed. Camille finally broke the silence. "If Shandra doesn't show up soon, how long will it be before people start wondering if she's been the victim of foul play? And what if someone saw us? We don't think anyone did, but—"

"Wait," I said, remembering something. I couldn't believe that I'd even forgotten it. How stupid was I? "I'm almost sure now. Shandra has to be okay."

"Why do you say that?" Miranda asked.

"Henry came to see me yesterday morning, and suddenly he was all lovey-dovey again. Told me he wanted to be with me again, that he'd always love me. I didn't want to ask him, but I had the feeling that Shandra went to him after what happened and told him she was through with him."

I looked at Miranda and Camille in turn, waiting to see what effect my words would have on them. Camille's shoulders visibly drooped with relief. "That is a good sign," she said.

"But we need to know for sure," Miranda chimed in. "Why don't you ask him?"

"Are you kidding?" I looked at her in disbelief. "How will I explain that? If she didn't tell him what we did, I don't want to be the one to mention it. We just worked things out."

Miranda frowned. "So, what do we do in the meantime?"

I sipped my soup. It was lukewarm and unappetizing. "We go about business as usual. You might not agree, but I'd bet money that Shandra is doing this on purpose. This is her way of making us pay."

"I hope you're right," Miranda said softly.

"I'm sure I am."

But I wasn't really as confident as I pretended to be. Because through the rest of dinner, I kept glancing around, hoping Shandra would make an appearance.

She didn't.

21

LATER THAT NIGHT I was more certain than ever that Shandra was alive and well. She had to be, given Henry's total about-face. He was being sweeter than ever, hornier than ever, pursuing me the way he had when we first started dating.

I was also pretty sure that Shandra had told him everything we'd done to her. The only reason he hadn't mentioned it was that he knew he had pushed me that far.

At least my plan had worked, and Henry wasn't mad at me. In fact, he loved me more than ever, if our current instant messaging was any indication.

A smile danced on my face as I read Henry's words.

FINEA$$BROTHER: Stop torturing me with what you're NOT wearing, if you're not going to come over.

ALLABOUTHENRY: I know, babe. I wish I could, but I can't.

FINEA$$BROTHER: Why not?

ALLABOUTHENRY: You know why. Besides, don't you think you did enough damage earlier? I'm still sore!

FINEA$$BROTHER: Ha ha ha. That's what I love to hear.

ALLABOUTHENRY: Yeah, I'm sure. Anyway, I should go. I'm supposed to be researching a philosopher for my class.

FINEA$$BROTHER: You want to get rid of me already?

A chiming sound alerted me that I had new mail. I wrote Henry a quick message that I'd be right back, then clicked on my in-box. I saw immediately that the new message was from BUFFALOGIRL.
Miranda.
I opened the e-mail.

Phoebe, I'm really getting scared here. I was out with Damon tonight, and he asked me about Shandra! He made it sound innocent, but he's never asked me about her before. Also, when I got back tonight, people in the common room were asking about Shandra, saying it's weird of her to take off like this. I'm starting to worry.

I rolled my eyes, then started to type. Honestly, Miranda had to get a grip.

Miranda, you have to relax. We'll talk in the morning. Okay?

I sent her the e-mail, then went back to the instant message box to chat with Henry.

FINEA$$BROTHER: What r u doing? You ARE trying to get rid of me!

ALLABOUTHENRY: Hey, sorry. Had to check an e-mail. And you know I'm not trying to get rid of you! But it IS after midnight. I can hardly keep my eyes open.

FINEA$$BROTHER: So you're not coming over????

ALLABOUTHENRY: You know I want to, but I can't. Tomorrow, okay?

FINEA$$BROTHER: Okay. But you better be in good form tomorrow, ha ha.

ALLABOUTHENRY: Tomorrow, YOU'D better be in good form. What I'll need from you might make you throw out your back!

FINEA$$BROTHER: Promises, promises. I love you. We'll hook up tomorrow.

ALLABOUTHENRY: I love you more! Good night.

I sighed with contentment as I signed off from the instant messenger program. Hallelujah, Henry was back. Really and truly. Once again everything was right with my world.

As I lay on my bed, I pushed all of Miranda's negative words out of my mind. I wasn't going to let her paranoia bring me down. Soon enough, she'd know the truth.

Soon enough, Shandra would show her face.

22

THE SOUND OF Camille's voice roused me from sleep.

"Right now?" she was asking. "Phoebe's still sleeping. All right. I'll get her up."

I rolled over to face Camille. "What is it?" I asked groggily.

"Oh, you're up."

I sat up, yawning as I did. "I am now. Who was on the phone?"

"That was our president. There's an emergency meeting. Right now."

I glanced at the clock. "It's not even seven-thirty yet."

"Katrina said she wanted to make sure she got everyone before we went out to class. We don't have to wear our sorority colors, but she does want us downstairs as soon as possible."

"Did she say what this is about?"

Camille shook her head. "Only that it's starting in fifteen minutes."

Groaning, I got out of bed. As I walked to the closet, I

finger-combed my hair. "I wonder if I should get dressed or just put on a robe?" I stared at my closet, wondering what to do.

"Phoebe."

The urgent tone of Camille's voice made me turn to face her. "Yeah?"

"Aren't you wondering . . . if this is about Shandra?"

"I don't know, but I don't . . . I don't think so." I turned back to my closet.

"Aren't you concerned?"

I was concerned, but I didn't want to admit it. I'd been telling myself that Shandra was alive and well because of how Henry was acting, but a small part of me knew that didn't have to be the reason. The thing was, I wasn't prepared to face the alternative. So in the past day, I'd pretty much blocked it from my mind.

Exasperated, I looked at Camille again. "You know what I don't need? I don't need you and Miranda freaking out, acting like we killed Shandra and dumped her body somewhere. Because that's what people are gonna think if we act all suspicious."

"I think we should call Miranda. Come up with a plan."

"Oh my God, why? So we can look even more guilty?"

"All right," Camille said. "Maybe you have a point. Calling Miranda right now might not be the smartest thing. But what should we say? If this *is* about Shandra?"

"That we don't know what happened to her. Because we don't."

At first, Camille looked doubtful, as though she didn't like my answer. Then her eyes widened as an idea struck her. "My God, what if she's back? What if *that's* the reason for this emergency meeting—because she's gonna tell everyone what we did?"

Panic made my knees wobble. Damn, I hadn't thought of that.

"Now do you see why I'm worried?" Camille asked.

I held up a hand to silence her. I needed to think. "Please, let's not freak out. I can't handle this."

"Fine." Camille threw up both hands as she walked to her own closet.

She was pissed, I knew, but I didn't know what else to do. What else to say.

If we were about to get fried, it was too late to do anything to stop it.

Everyone was in the common room. All our sorors, and all the pledges. Many were in robes and curlers, some sitting on the floor and windowsill because there weren't enough seats for all of us.

I saw everyone—including Cassie—but didn't see Shandra.

"All right," Katrina began. "I'm going to get right to the purpose of this meeting. Has anyone seen Shandra?"

My body shuddered as a breath oozed out of me. I glanced around surreptitiously, trying to see if anyone was staring at me in a weird way. No one was, but every girl was shaking her head in response to Katrina's question.

"When was the last time anyone saw her?" Katrina continued.

When no one spoke, Cassie raised her hand. Katrina nodded to her. "I saw her Sunday night," Cassie said. "Before I had to go home and see my father."

"I saw her in the cafeteria Monday evening," Liz, one of the pledges, said.

"And no one saw her after that? Tuesday? Yesterday?" Katrina went on.

No one said anything.

"Not even our fraternity brothers saw her after Monday," Katrina told us. "And she hasn't been to any of her classes. I called her mother, and she hasn't heard from her."

Oh fuck! I didn't dare look at Miranda and Camille.

"I'll admit, I'm starting to worry," Donna said, taking over for Katrina. "I've already heard a rumor of what might have happened to her."

I tried to swallow but couldn't.

My heart ramming against my rib cage, I waited for Donna to elaborate, but she didn't. What the hell could she have heard, and where?

Camille raised her hand. Inwardly I freaked, but I tried not to show it.

"Yes, Camille?" Katrina said.

"What if . . . what if Shandra's going through something and took off for some space? You know, time to think? All of us have wanted to run away at some time in our lives, haven't we?"

"Yeah," someone else said. "Maybe she's having man trouble."

"I did hear something to that effect," Donna told us.

"I don't think so." Cassie had spoken, and when I looked her way, she was shaking her head. "I mean, I don't think she just took off. I can't say for sure she didn't, but why would she leave without her purse? Without her wallet and her credit cards? Without her cash? She even left her house key in the room."

"Who was she seeing?" Katrina asked. "Going on dates with. Studying with. Someone's got to know."

Because in a sorority house, girls always know about their sorors' private lives, I thought sourly.

Cassie glanced around the room. I looked at her in alarm as her gaze landed on me. She quickly looked away, clearly uncomfortable. Then to my absolute horror she said, "The only guy I ever heard her talk about was Henry Reid."

My mouth almost hit the floor. "Excuse me?"

"It's true," Cassie went on. "And you know it."

"Henry's my *fiancé*."

"I know that, and I'm not trying to be disrespectful, but according to Shandra—"

"According to Shandra, nothing!" I was on my feet in a flash, my heart pounding out of control. "How dare you mention my fiancé as if he's involved with her! Are you trying to say she ran away with him? Because he's still here, by the way." I knew damn well Cassie wasn't saying that, but I had to do damage control. I couldn't have all my sorority sisters thinking that my fiancé didn't love me. "So he obviously didn't take off anywhere with Shandra."

Cassie didn't say anything else, just stared at the ground. But it looked as though she had more on her mind.

As I settled back in my seat, I glanced around the room. Evelyn shot me a curious look.

My conversation with her came back to me in a flash. God, what she must have been thinking right then.

Shit. I never should have talked to her about my frustration with Shandra. If it turned out that Shandra was seriously hurt—or worse—Evelyn would think I had something to do with it.

Unable to face her a moment longer, I turned away. But then I saw Miranda's face, and she looked as if she was going to fall apart. I lowered my gaze to my hands.

"If anyone thinks of anything, at any time, do not hesitate to come to either Donna or myself," Katrina said. "And if there's anything any of you wants to tell us, I'd suggest sooner rather than later is the better option."

23

THOSE WERE OMINOUS words if I'd ever heard any, which only made me wonder about Donna's earlier statement that she'd heard a "rumor." What kind of rumor, or was that just a lie?

I mean, my friends and I had been so careful getting Shandra out of the house. No one had been around when we ushered Shandra out of the building. Who would have told Donna a damn thing?

A buzz of chatter filled the common room as we all filed out. I didn't dare look at Miranda or Camille. I all but ran up the stairs, unable to get to my room fast enough.

A hand clamped down on my shoulder as I made it to the second-floor landing. Gasping, I spun around.

It was Camille. "God, Phoebe—"

"Not *now*," I whispered harshly.

Back in our room, I made sure to lock the door. I walked to my side of the room and plopped onto my bed. The significance of the meeting came crashing down on my shoulders.

"What are we gonna do, Phoebe? Something must have happened to Shandra."

My breathing was shallow, slow. I didn't want to believe that was possible, but ignoring it wouldn't make it go away. "I . . . I don't know. . . ."

"Did you see Miranda's face? I don't think she'll be able to keep quiet for long. And what did Katrina mean by if anyone has anything to say, sooner is better than later?"

"Please keep your voice down. What if someone's listening at the door?"

"We have to go back," Camille continued, ignoring me. "Check the scene for clues."

I frowned as I looked at her. "Like we're a couple of CSIs?"

"Don't you care?"

"Of course I care."

"Then don't you think we have to do something?"

"Yeah." I got off my bed and walked to my closet. "We have to go to class."

"You did *not* just say that."

"What are we supposed to do?" I asked, challenging her. "It's been days. It's not like we'll find Shandra where we left her. She wasn't there when Morgan got there."

"You sound so . . . heartless."

Did I? Maybe I did, but I was afraid. Too afraid to consider the possibility that something really awful had happened to Shandra. "You think I don't care? I'm scared to death right now that she's dead somewhere—*because of what we did*. Don't tell me I'm heartless."

"I'm sorry—"

"I may not have liked her, but I didn't want anything

really bad to happen to her. Can you blame me if I don't want to think about it? I just keep thinking she's gonna show up any minute. I wish she would," I added sadly.

"I know you care. I'm scared, too."

Scared was an understatement. I was terrified.

24

I DON'T KNOW why, but I sensed there was something horribly wrong as I stood outside my door. I thought I was terrified that morning at the house meeting, but what I felt standing outside my dorm-room door was worse than terror. It was a sick chill that started inside my gut and spread throughout my entire body.

My right hand quivered as I put it on the doorknob. And then I hesitated. I almost couldn't do it—turn the knob, as I'd done a million times. Somehow I knew that when I did, my world would change.

It was the sound of voices at the other end of the floor that made me finally open the door and step into my room. When I did, I found Camille and Miranda there. Miranda's eyes were red from tears, while Camille had a look of horror on her face.

"Oh, God," Camille said. "Phoebe . . ."

I dropped my tote bag to the floor. "What?" I all but shrieked.

"This," Camille said. She reached for the remote and

turned on the small television. Then she hit the VCR's PLAY button.

A newscaster appeared on the screen. ". . . found early this morning behind an unoccupied building in downtown Buffalo. The unidentified woman was naked, but police aren't saying yet if she was sexually assaulted. An autopsy is scheduled for later today. This makes the fifty-fourth homicide of the year in Buffalo."

My eyes glued to the TV, I started to shake. This "woman" didn't have a name, but I knew.

Oh, God. I *knew*.

Shandra was dead.

Camille turned off the TV. Miranda softly sobbed.

"What *happened?*" Camille finally asked. "How could this have happened?"

I wanted to reassure Camille and Miranda that it was a mistake, that it was another girl, that it couldn't be Shandra. But I could no longer deny the truth.

"We killed her," Miranda sobbed.

"No." I finally found my voice. "No, we didn't."

"We left her there, and some creep found her—"

"If she had stayed where she was supposed to, Morgan would have picked her up—"

"So this is *her* fault?" Miranda asked incredulously.

"It's no one's fault," I said, hoping desperately to believe my own words. Yes, Shandra had been my least favorite person, but the point that night had been to teach her a lesson—not to get her killed. "It could have happened anywhere."

"But it didn't," Camille said. "*We* took her there that night. And because of that, she's *dead*."

My head started to swim. This couldn't be. It just couldn't be. "I . . . I feel sick." I staggered to my bed and collapsed.

Miranda blew her nose, then asked, "What should we do? We have to make this right."

"We can never make this right," Camille said.

"So we say nothing?" Miranda sounded appalled. "I don't know if I can live with myself. To be responsible for someone's death—"

"I've prayed for her soul," Camille said. "I've been praying for the past few days."

"Maybe we should pray right now," Miranda suggested. "All of us. For forgiveness. And guidance."

"Stop!" I cried. My head was spinning and my stomach lurching, and Miranda and Camille's chattering wasn't helping matters any. "I can't . . ."

"Deal with this?" Camille finished for me. "Well, this is reality. A reality you created."

My stomach continued to lurch as if there were a toxic mix churning inside. I rushed to the wastebasket, barely making it before I threw up.

Several moments passed. Miranda spoke first. "The police are involved. It won't be long before they come here, asking questions."

"We're screwed," Camille said.

"We have to confess," Miranda said. "It's the only way."

I took a few deep breaths as I wiped my mouth with the back of my hand. "We didn't kill her. For God's sake, Miranda, stop acting like we did."

"How can you say that?"

I stalked across the room and gripped Miranda by the shoulders. "Think about what you're saying. If we tell anyone about what we did, they'll feel obligated to go to the police. And if they go to the police, we can all kiss our lives good-bye."

"No." Miranda shook her head. "You said yourself, we didn't kill Shandra. When we tell them that—"

"Wake up!" I yelled, shaking Miranda. I guess I was hoping to shake some sense into her.

Camille grabbed me, pulling me away from Miranda. "Phoebe, stop it! There's no need to lose it with Miranda. She's worried, and rightfully so."

"You think we should confess, too?"

Camille shook her head. "No. I agree with you. If we say we took Shandra there, there's no reason they won't think we killed her. And you have a great motive, Phoebe. Jealousy because she was after Henry."

"It wasn't about jealousy," I protested. But not even I truly believed my words.

Camille rolled her eyes. "Regardless, how do you think others will see it? You hated that she was flirting with your man, and you wanted to get her out of the way. You got into a fight with her at a fraternity party, with dozens of witnesses!"

Damn it all to hell, Camille was right. If word got out that I was involved with this private initiation of Shandra, people would put two and two together and say I was a heartless murderer.

Once again I sank onto my bed. I grabbed Miffy and hugged it to my chest. "I can't believe Shandra's dead."

"I can't, either," Camille said, sitting beside me.

"We can't say anything," I told them. "You hear me, guys? We can't say a word to anyone about what we did."

"It may be too late."

My eyes flew to Miranda's. "What are you talking about?"

"Someone slipped the campus paper under my door yesterday." Miranda pulled it out of her purse. "I didn't mention it before because I was . . . I was scared. It's about Shandra."

My eyes widened. "You don't know who gave this to you?"

"No. But the fact that someone slipped it under the door when I would have seen a copy—"

"Means he or she was trying to make a point," Camille said. "Someone's suspicious."

"Yeah," Miranda said. "It could have been Cheryl. She hates me."

I knew Miranda was having problems with her roommate, but that didn't interest me right then. Instead, my eyes scanned the headline. I froze. A black-and-white picture of Shandra graced the front page, with the caption:

WHAT HAPPENED TO SHANDRA JAMES?

"Damon wrote this," I pointed out.

Miranda only shrugged.

"Are you still seeing him, Miranda?"

"Off and on. I haven't heard from him since yesterday morning, but I think he's just scared to face his feelings for me."

Yeah, right. I thought. But that wasn't important at the moment. "Did you say something to him?" I asked her. "Anything at all?"

"No."

I couldn't tell if Miranda was telling the truth. She wouldn't look me straight in the eye.

"Miranda, you e-mailed me and said that Damon asked about Shandra. . . ."

Still not looking at me, she muttered, "Maybe I said something to him."

"You spoke to Damon about this!" I shrieked.

"I didn't tell him anything specific. Not what we did—"

"What *did* you tell him?"

"Only that we'd taught her a bit of a lesson—"

"What?" Camille and I spoke at the same time.

"I didn't tell him what happened, only that we hadn't hurt her and that it was *before* she went missing—"

I was on my feet in a flash. "Are you crazy?" I demanded. "How could you tell him that? With a guy who obviously wants you for just one thing!"

"I had to tell someone."

"Son of a—" I pounded a fist into the air. I wanted to yell and scream and throw things. But what good would that do me? The damage was done.

God help us, the damage was done.

25

I RAN.

I ran out of the sorority house toward Frontier Road. Pumping my legs as hard as I could, I ran like the devil himself was chasing me. I whizzed around the corner when I reached Frontier, heading right, toward the thicket of trees.

It was the only place I could be invisible.

I sprinted until I reached the path in the Letchworth Woods. My sides hurt, and I was wheezing from running so hard, but I didn't want to stop. I slowed to a jog but could keep that up for only a few more seconds. Finally, exhausted, I collapsed onto the path. It was then that the tears came.

And came.

I couldn't stop crying. Snot poured out of my nose, dripping onto the ground with my tears. I screamed. I dug my fingers into the dirt, picking up handfuls and throwing them. I grabbed at fallen leaves and squeezed. My fingernails broke the skin of my palms.

But that pain was nothing compared with the pain in my heart.

Shandra couldn't be dead.

She couldn't be dead.

"Please, God, she can't be *dead!*"

The word *dead* resounded in the forest around me, making everything more real.

I wiped at my tears, but more came. I thought they would never stop.

The wind swirled around me, picking up leaves. They danced around me in an array of dazzling fall colors.

I gulped in the cool air, trying to calm down. And then something made me whip my head around. My eyes flitted left to right, searching. Had I heard something?

I didn't see anything, but I couldn't shake the overwhelming feeling that I wasn't alone.

My heart thundered as I slowly got to my knees. Dried leaves rustled beneath me, and I momentarily paused. But if someone was out there watching me, I couldn't worry about making noise. I had to find a hiding place, and fast.

I crawled to the trees, looking for the best spot to hide. It was dusk, and while not totally dark, someone could easily be lurking in the shadows, watching my every move.

What was I thinking? Why had I gone out there?

Because it was a place I knew I could hide, because no one would look for me there. I had hoped to feel safe there, but instead I was scared beyond all reason.

"God, please be with me. Let me be okay." I edged my body around the trunk of a large maple tree and hid there for a couple of minutes. In that time, I didn't see anyone or hear anything suspicious other than the rustling of the leaves. Figuring the coast was clear, I slowly made my way from my hiding spot to the path. I started trotting back in the direction I had come.

That's when I thought I saw a shadow moving in the distance, toward the entrance of the path.

Cold fear shot through me. I *knew* I wasn't alone! I backed up, into the cover of the trees. I stood there only a moment before I knew I couldn't stand around like that. I had to run.

So I spun around and sprinted through the trees. My heart was going a mile a minute and I still had a cramp in my side, but I couldn't stop. Not until I reached the road.

There were footsteps. Behind me. Pounding on the path.

My breathing came out in whimpered gasps. I moved as fast as my legs would allow me. I was almost there. Almost at the road . . .

And then a hand clamped down on my shoulder. Before I could scream, another hand came down on my mouth.

And I knew it was over.

26

ADRENALINE KICKED IN. I started to fight.

Grunting as I gathered all my strength, I lifted an elbow and jammed it into my attacker's solar plexus. He moaned and loosened his grip slightly. I was about to elbow him again when I heard a strained, "Phoebe."

In the midst of my fear and adrenaline rush, something clicked in my brain. That sounded like . . .

Morgan?

Without any resistance from my attacker, I was able to turn around. I looked up into Morgan's face, saw him wincing in pain as he held his chest.

"What are you doing?" I screamed. "You—you're *following* me?"

"Relax, Phoebe." Morgan drew in a deep breath and lowered his hand. "I went to your room to see you. Camille said you got dressed like you were going for a run. I knew where you were headed."

My eyes narrowed as I stared at him. And for the first

time since I'd known him, I wasn't sure I should believe him. His story seemed almost too convenient.

"Why are you staring at me like that?" He gave me an odd look. "You're not . . . you're not afraid of me, are you?"

"I heard someone chasing me. Of course I was afraid!"

"I didn't mean to scare you."

A beat passed, then I asked, "Why'd you cover my mouth?"

"Because I thought you were going to scream."

I eyed Morgan warily.

"You don't believe me?" he asked. "What—you think I'm that creep stalking women out here or something?"

"Why would you mention that?" I asked, and to my own ears I sounded suspicious. "Why would you think I would think that?"

"Because someone was raped and murdered here," he replied testily. "Why else, Phoebe?"

I didn't answer, because in truth I didn't know what to believe.

"Why do you think I came out here after you?" Morgan went on. "There's some freak on the loose, yet you love to run on this path regardless of the danger."

My suspicions started to ebb. He was right, of course. But whether it was smart to be out there alone, I'd always found that path a place of solace, where I could be alone with my thoughts. Morgan knew that, because we'd walked out there together a few times when we'd first started to get chummy. And that one time we'd come close to making love, it had been there as well.

I asked, "Why were you looking for me?"

Morgan blew out a weary breath. "Did you hear the news? A woman's body was found downtown."

I closed my eyes. Swayed a little. "Yes. That's why I had to get out of my room. . . ."

"So you think it's Shandra?"

The best I could manage was a nod.

"Fuck," Morgan uttered.

"I'm going crazy, Morgan. This wasn't supposed to happen."

"I didn't get there fast enough. Now she's dead."

"Are you sure you didn't see anything that night? Anything at all?"

"You think I wouldn't tell you if I did?"

"I'm not saying that, but maybe there's something you forgot. Something you saw that didn't register."

"I told you. I saw nothing. I went there, she wasn't there."

I nodded glumly. What had I expected—that he'd seen the killer running to his car?

The thought of Shandra being brutally murdered made me shudder. My God, how horrible it must have been for her to realize that she was about to be killed.

I glanced around warily, feeling unsafe. "Can we get out of here? I'm kinda creeped out."

Morgan nodded. "Yeah, let's go."

I took the lead, walking the short distance to the road. Once there, I stepped onto the asphalt, preferring to walk on the smooth surface of the road rather than the grass. For a couple of minutes neither Morgan nor I spoke, and when he did break the silence, his question shocked me.

"Are you and Henry back together?"

Halting, I looked up at him in surprise. "What?"

"Are you?" His tone sounded almost accusatory.

"Yeah, but—"

"Why?"

I saw headlights coming in the distance, and I hopped back onto the grass.

"You don't want to answer me," Morgan said.

"No, I don't want to get run over." I stopped walking and looked up at him again. "And I don't understand your question. Why, what?"

"Why are you back with him? Acting like he's the perfect boyfriend. You know he was cheating on you."

I bit back my anger. "We've worked things out."

Even in the darkness, I could see the disappointment in Morgan's eyes. He shifted his weight from one foot to the other, all the while shaking his head. "I don't understand you."

"You know how I feel about Henry."

He made a sound of disgust.

"What's your problem?"

"*My* problem?" Morgan gaped at me. "What's *your* problem? You're living in this friggin' fantasy world where Henry's concerned, where you want to pretend everything's perfect. And you know he was fucking around on you. Do you even love him, or is this all about ego?"

"How dare you—"

"Why do you still trust him? Why do you want to put up with more of his bullshit?"

"I think this conversation is over."

"I was hoping you'd finally get it," he pressed on. "That you deserve better. For God's sake, you resorted to torturing Shandra because you knew he was with her. That's not the Phoebe I know. You've become a different person. Can't you see that?"

His words hurt. Made me angry. "I didn't *torture* her. Is that what you're telling people?" I thought of that article in the paper. "Are you the one who talked to Damon? Is that why he wrote that article about Shandra?"

"You think I talked to Damon about this?"

"Did you?"

"You want to believe that, you go ahead."

"Why can't you answer me?"

"If you don't trust me, don't talk to me. Obviously, I'm not as trustworthy as Henry."

"I didn't say that."

Morgan picked up his pace, walking ahead of me. Behind him, I gritted my teeth. Maybe it had been wrong for me to involve him. Clearly he had feelings for me.

I hurried to catch up with him. "Look," I began softly, "I don't know if I'm doing the right thing. With Henry. But things are good between us now, and I have to follow my heart."

"Great. You do that."

"Wait," I said when Morgan sped up.

"Why should I? You don't trust me. I'm no one to you."

"That's not true."

He faced me, gave me a pointed look. "It isn't?"

"No. You do mean something to me."

"Bullshit," he snapped.

The way he said the word, and the icy look he gave me, caused me to flinch. I stared at him, and he at me. I didn't know what to say.

"That's what I thought."

And then Morgan sprinted off, leaving me to walk back to the sorority house on my own. I was away from the woods now and so had no real reason to be afraid, but still.

Morgan wasn't just upset. He was angry with me.

Jealous.

I shivered. I wondered exactly what a jealous man was capable of.

27

I COULD THINK of nothing but Morgan—and jealousy—
on the way back to the sorority house. And it wasn't just
that he'd frightened me. I thought about jealousy and how
it could drive a person to do things she never would have
considered doing before.

Morgan said that I'd changed. And I *had*. Oh, I could
deny to my friends that jealousy had played a part in what
I did to Shandra, but I could no longer deny it to myself.

Jealousy and anger had caused me to cross the line, to
do something I otherwise never would have considered.

Morgan was in love with me. I don't know how I hadn't
figured that out before, but he was. Had jealousy affected
him the way it had me, pushed him to cross his own bound-
aries? Had he hurt Shandra that night as a way to punish
me for not loving him back?

No matter how hard I tried, I couldn't bring myself to
believe that.

I wasn't sure what was real anymore as I stepped into

the Alpha house. The events of the past few days seemed like a dream.

A nightmare.

One that was only beginning.

The moment I walked into the sorority house, I saw Evelyn. She jumped up from her seat on one of the loungers and all but ran across the room to me.

I groaned inwardly. I did not want to talk to Evelyn right then. Or the next day, for that matter. I had a pretty damn good idea what she was going to say.

"Phoebe." Her voice was hushed.

"Hey, Evelyn." I tried to sound upbeat but failed.

"I need you to come to my room for a minute."

"Right now?" I asked.

"This can't wait."

Reluctantly, I followed Evelyn up to the top floor. Like most of the other seniors in the building, she had a single room, which allowed privacy.

She closed the door and got right to it. "Phoebe, what did you do to Shandra?"

I didn't answer right away, debating whether I should. I finally shook my head, saying, "Nothing."

"You don't know what happened to her?" she asked disbelievingly.

"No." I couldn't meet her eye. She had to know I was lying.

She gave me a pointed look. "Are you sure about that?"

"Of course I'm sure."

"I remember what we talked about, Phoebe. About how you could get back at Shandra. Teach her a lesson."

"I know . . . and I know how it must seem . . . but there's no way I would kill her! You have to believe me!"

Evelyn didn't say anything for a few moments. "People

are talking. You've been acting differently the past few days. Hiding out, practically. Why?"

"Are you accusing me of murder?"

"I know what you said to me. I know how much you hated Shandra."

"And you didn't?"

Surprisingly, Evelyn's expression softened. "That's why I'm talking to you now. Because I think that maybe this is my fault."

"How do you figure that?"

"I told you it was a good idea. Hurting Shandra to teach her a lesson. But I never thought . . ." Her voice trailed off. "Look, if you did do something crazy, if you snapped—"

"Evelyn, stop!" I couldn't stand another moment of this. Evelyn actually believed I was a *murderer.*

I opened the door and fled into the hallway. But I knew there was no place I could hide. Not from this.

28

I DREAMED THAT night that Shandra's body had been identified, that police had swarmed the campus, and that Camille, Miranda, and I were arrested. The dream was so real, it had me up from about three-thirty, and I'd only dozed off and on since.

So when the phone rang just before seven, I was already awake. But I didn't get up to answer it. A call at that hour could mean only something bad.

The second ring made Camille jump. Cursing, she threw the covers off and headed to my night table, where the phone was.

"This had better be good," she uttered. Then, "Oh. Yes. Okay. I'll tell her."

I sat up, facing Camille as she hung up the phone.

"That was our housemother. She wants to see us immediately."

Oh my God. Oh my God. Shandra's body had been identified. Our lives were about to end.

I would be expelled from the sorority that meant so much to me. And worse, there would be criminal charges.

"We have to get up, Phoebe. Right now."

I did. I slipped on a robe and my bunny slippers, then went with Camille to the house's top level and the house-mother's door.

Camille rapped on it softly.

The door swung open. Rowena's lips were pulled in a thin line as she faced us. "Good. You're here. Come in."

Rowena, a graduate of UB and one of our sorority sisters, was in her mid-twenties—barely older than the undergrads. Biracial, she was very fair-skinned with brown freckles covering her face and had a mass of wild, curly, auburn-colored hair. Right then she was wearing glasses, but she normally wore contacts. Though she acted as our housemother, a more accurate description of her role was graduate adviser, meaning she looked over the affairs of the undergraduate sorors and reported any questions or reprimand of sorors to the graduate chapter. As graduate adviser, she was the link between the larger chapter and the regional director, as well as the link between the sorority and the campus in terms of rules regarding the sorority's actions and policies.

Rowena had held the position of president on the undergraduate sorority board when that year's seniors had originally pledged, and she and Katrina and Donna had all become friends then. From what I saw of them together, they seemed very close. Rumor had it that Rowena, being a fairly recent grad herself, knew the school administrators very well and knew how to get around some of the school policies. That was helpful with some of the pledging rituals that UB might otherwise frown upon.

As housemother, she oversaw us in a general way. She made sure that we had our schedules, kept us in line if our parties went on too long, and was there for us to talk to if we had tough personal issues we were dealing with and didn't want to speak with anyone on the board about them.

Camille and I entered the room to find Miranda there as well. She was sitting on a chair that faced the house-mother's bed. Two more chairs were placed beside Miranda's, and I couldn't help thinking the chairs were positioned to look like the defendants' chairs in a courtroom.

"Please, have a seat beside Miranda."

Miranda shot us a look of fear as we moved across the room to sit beside her. Camille and I sat on either side of her. As I faced our housemother, I swallowed.

"I apologize for getting you all out of your beds so early, but this is an urgent matter." She paused as she stared at each of us in turn. "It has come to my attention that you might have information about what happened to Shandra."

I tried to swallow again, but now there was a lump in my throat that was making it hard to breathe, much less do anything else.

Rowena faced Miranda. "Someone told me that the night Shandra disappeared, you left your room quite late. This person suggested that Camille and Phoebe were with you."

"I . . . I . . ." Miranda hedged. She glanced my way, as if seeking an answer as to what she should say.

"Does this person have a name?" Camille asked.

"Fair enough. It was your roommate, Miranda. Cheryl."

"Cheryl hates me," Miranda said instantly.

"Enough to make this up?" Rowena asked, but there was a skeptical tone to her voice.

"This is crazy," I said. "You take the word of a girl who's made no attempt to get along with anyone here—"

"It wasn't just Cheryl." Rowena gave me a pointed look.

"Evelyn also spoke to me, which is why I called you all to my room. Evelyn was worried that you'd done something to Shandra."

Evelyn! How dare she?

"Do you know what happened to Shandra?" Rowena asked. "Miranda? You look like you want to say something."

Miranda glanced at us briefly, then cleared her throat. "Well, um. Shandra was—"

I discreetly kicked her leg, and she stopped abruptly.

"Miranda?" Rowena prompted.

I gave my head a slight shake, hoping Miranda would get the point.

"You do know something, don't you?" Rowena asked. When no one answered, she said, "I'm waiting for one of you to tell me what happened."

"Okay, here's the deal," I said, and it was Miranda's turn to look at me in shock. "None of us really likes Shandra, especially not me. I admit it."

"I already know that. I heard from Donna and Katrina that you and Shandra were having problems getting along."

"Maybe the pressure of our problems got to her and she decided to take off."

Rowena's eyes narrowed on me. "Do you think this is a joke?"

"No, ma'am."

"You expect me to believe that you have no idea what happened to Shandra?"

"We have no idea," I answered.

"And what about you, Camille? You haven't said a word."

"I—I have no idea," Camille replied. "Who knows—maybe Shandra had a family emergency."

Rowena paced the floor, not saying a word as she stared

at each of us. Once again her gaze landed on me. "I heard something else," she said. "Very disturbing. Is it true you tried to run Shandra down with your car?"

"What are you talking about?" I asked in total disbelief.

"Last week, outside the Zeta fraternity house?"

"No! I can't believe anyone would say that. Who is telling all these lies?"

Rowena didn't respond, just continued to look at me as if I were some kind of evil creep.

"I filed a missing person's report with the police. Yesterday I learned that a woman's body was found under some bushes behind a building. Shandra's mother is due to arrive in Buffalo later today. She'll be heading to the morgue to possibly identify Shandra's body." Rowena finally took a breath. "There's nothing funny about this. If any of you had anything to do with Shandra's disappearance, I assure you this is very, very serious. I've turned the other way with regard to some of the pledging rituals, but if any of you did something to Shandra, this is a matter that would have to be reported to the regional director, and from there, the national board. Not to mention the criminal ramifications. Do you understand?"

"Yes," we all answered in unison. I added, "Can we go now?"

Rowena glared at me, and for a moment I thought she might throttle me. But she said, "Yes. You can go."

But I'm watching you, she may as well have added.

Because I knew she would be.

29

WE WERE IN deep shit, and it was getting only deeper.

"We should have told her," Miranda said as she paced the floor in my room a short while later. "Told her that we took Shandra out that night but that we didn't kill her. She *knows* we're lying."

"She can't prove it," I pointed out. "That's what matters here."

Camille took a long drag on her cigarette. She'd quit smoking the previous semester, but clearly the stress of the situation had made her start the habit again. "No," she said, "That's *not* what matters here. If Shandra is dead, and they search the scene, maybe they'll find something that connects us to what happened. Forensic evidence and all that good stuff. So if we lie about our part in this, it's going to look like we lied about more than that. Don't you see?"

"Exactly," Miranda agreed. "We admit to the initiation and we'll have to face consequences for that, but it won't be near as bad as being suspected of murder!"

My head was throbbing. Miranda and Camille made

excellent points, but I feared it was too late to come clean. That we'd waited too long, and coming clean now would look only more suspicious.

Of course, I'd never in my wildest dreams expected that Shandra would end up dead, so I hadn't figured we'd need to come clean at all.

"Let me get this straight," I began. "You want us to come clean today—now that we know Shandra's mother may be identifying her body? How's that going to look?"

Miranda and Camille exchanged glances, but neither said a word. They knew I had a point.

"What's this about your trying to run down Shandra?" Camille asked after a moment.

"Yeah," Miranda said. "What was that about?"

Surprised, I looked at both of my friends in turn. How could they ask me that? "I would never—" And then a memory flashed into my mind of slamming on the brakes the day Morgan had been in my car. "Oh my God."

"Phoebe . . ." This from Miranda.

"It was an accident," I said, but I knew how pathetic that sounded.

"Phoebe!" Camille exclaimed.

"No, honestly, it was an accident. I didn't even remember it until now. I was driving away from the fraternity house and she came out of nowhere. But I wasn't trying to kill her! I hit the brakes to avoid hurting her. Morgan was with me."

"Morgan?" Camille asked.

"Yeah. I'd picked him up and was taking him to dinner. . . ."

Oh my God. Morgan!

Miranda's eyes widened with concern. "You think he's the one who's saying this?"

"No," I said halfheartedly. "Oh hell, maybe." I blew out

a huff of air. "He's mad because I'm back with Henry. But still, I can't imagine him doing something like this."

"Then who would?" Camille asked. "Who else saw you nearly hit Shandra?"

"I don't know who else was there. Other than Shandra. She could have said something to Katrina."

Camille finished off the cigarette and immediately started another one. Then she reached for her half-eaten bag of Doritos. "I feel like I can't be around here this weekend. You think Rowena's the only one who's suspicious? And with Shandra's mother getting into town today . . . I do not want to know if that's Shandra's body."

"You're gonna leave?" I asked her. I didn't want her to. I couldn't handle being in my room alone.

"I don't know," Camille replied.

"I'm working tonight, and all weekend—thank God," Miranda said. "I hate that shit job, but at least it will get me out of here for a while."

"I think I'll head home to Rochester," Camille said. "My mother keeps calling, saying that she misses me. She's in remission, but still I worry about her. I need to spend more time with her."

If Miranda and Camille weren't going to be around, then neither was I. "I guess I'll spend time with Henry." Maybe I could even persuade him to go away for the weekend.

"I still think we should come clean now," Miranda said. "Not later."

"No." I shook my head vehemently. "It's too late for that now."

"Phoebe—"

"No, Miranda. I mean it. And please tell me you didn't tell Damon that we took Shandra to that building." I gave her a hard stare. "Did you?"

She shook her head. "I already told you, I gave him only a couple of small details."

"So he can't screw with this?" I asked.

"No."

"All right." I had no choice but to believe her. "Like it or not," I began slowly, "we've got to stick to the story that we were never involved. I think it's a good idea if we keep a low profile this weekend. So, yeah, you go home, Camille. Your mother's ill. No one will question that. And Miranda—you go to work as usual."

They both nodded. Camille blew out a smoke ring. I felt bad that she was smoking again, after she'd tried so hard to quit. Her mother's cancer had scared her into coming to her senses, and now this.

"And on Monday?" Miranda asked. "What do we do when we have to stop hiding?"

"On Monday," I started, "if the news is bad, we'll deal with it then."

Not a bright plan, I knew, but it was the best I had to offer.

30

ALONG WITH MY books for the day's classes, I packed a weekend bag, not planning to return to my dorm room. I didn't eat lunch or dinner in either of the campus cafeterias, opting to drive off campus to get something to eat elsewhere.

It was a day full of anxiety and overwhelming emotions. Class after class, I couldn't concentrate on my studies. All I could think about was the likelihood that Shandra's body would soon be officially identified, and how the heat was about to really come down on us.

I thought my solitude would be comforting, but it gave me too much time to think. Not even the idea of shopping put me in a good mood. So after grabbing a quick bite for dinner, I headed back to campus and the Zeta house.

I called Henry's cell along the way. "Hey, sweetie. Where are you?"

"In my room. Studying for my statistics exam."

"Can I come over?" I was counting on the fact that he

wouldn't say no. "There's a whole lot of shit going down with Shandra—"

"I know. Yeah, come over."

Twenty minutes later I was in Henry's room, walking into his embrace. "She's dead," he said to me.

I pulled back to gape at him. "Her body—" I gulped. "It's been identified?"

Henry shook his head. "No. But I hear her mother's in town. The fact that she's here—don't you think that means . . ."

"I know, Henry. God, I know."

And despite the grim reality of Shandra's likely demise, something made my heart lift a little. If Shandra was indeed dead and not hiding out, that meant she couldn't have told Henry what happened the night of the initiation, and therefore he was being nicer to me because that's what he felt in his heart.

I know it didn't make sense, to be so happy with the knowledge that Henry loved me right then, but I was. It was like a ray of hope shining through a dark cloud.

"Maybe we should turn on the TV," I said after a moment. "The six o'clock news will start any minute. There could be an update." I needed to know for sure. "Where's the remote?"

"Somewhere on the bed."

I searched the rumpled sheets and found the remote control. Then I turned on the television and flipped around until I hit Channel 7. The six o'clock news would be starting in four minutes.

The first story was about the murder of a policeman. The second about some tax bill for the state of New York. I was about to breathe a sigh of relief—still hanging on to some hope—but then the third story began, and a chill swept over me.

"And now to a case we first told you about yesterday. The body of a young woman found behind an abandoned building in downtown Buffalo has now been identified as missing University of Buffalo student Shandra James."

I gasped sharply. "Oh my God, it's true."

". . . was last seen Monday evening . . ."

I felt Henry's hands on my shoulders, but I didn't turn to look at him. "Holy crap," he whispered.

"Shandra James was naked when discovered early yesterday morning, leading to speculations of sexual assualt. . . . ," the newscaster went on.

"She's dead. Really dead." *And, God help me, this is my fault.*

". . . investigation is ongoing . . ."

"I can't fucking believe this," Henry said. "What the hell was she doing in downtown Buffalo?"

A sob escaping me, I turned toward Henry, buried my face in his chest, and started to cry.

I cried against Henry's chest for a long time. Then he left me alone to go downstairs and break the news to the rest of the guys. I called Miranda then. Her voice mail picked up, so I said, "Miranda, it's Phoebe. Call me as soon as you get this message. I just got some news. Shandra—" I burst into tears. "You just need to call me."

I collected myself and made another phone call, this time to Camille's cell. "Camille, it's me. Are you on a bus to Rochester?"

"No, I'm at the Galleria Mall."

"I thought you were heading home."

"So did I. But I called my mother, and she's got some new boyfriend over for the weekend, so I decided not to head there. I can't believe it. She's fighting cancer, for God's sake, and she's still out finding new guys."

Her mother's love life had always been a bone of contention for Camille—the fact that she went through a lot of guys. She'd been married four times in her fifty years. Of course, Camille didn't realize she was a lot like her mother in that way, who also seemed to have serious commitment issues after her husband and Camille's father left their lives without a trace.

All that was completely unimportant now. "There's news, Cam. Shandra—they identified her body. She really is dead."

Camille gasped sharply. "No, Phoebe! Oh my God, no. Please . . ." Camille began to sob.

"It's true." My voice caught in my throat.

Camille continued to cry, and I had to swallow a few times so I wouldn't start crying myself. "I think . . . I know what we said before, that we should keep a low profile for the next few days, but I think we need to be around this weekend. To be away right now, I don't know. I just think . . ." I could hardly form a coherent thought.

"Yeah. You—you're right." Camille paused for a moment, and I no longer heard her sobs. "Phoebe, I'm shaking."

"I am, too. I left a message for Miranda, but I guess she's at work."

"She's gonna be devastated."

"I know. We all are." I drew in a shaky breath. "See you soon, okay?"

"Okay."

Despite my numbed haze when I entered the Alpha Sigma Pi house, I instantly sensed a different mood in the place. It was eerily quiet as I stepped into the main hallway.

I took tentative steps farther into the house, toward the common room. And that's when I saw everyone. The common room resembled a funeral parlor, with the way girls were huddled together in small groups, hugging one another, wiping their eyes. Some were softly crying.

The ground swayed beneath me.

I gulped in air and continued walking. I didn't know what to do. Head into the common room and ask what was wrong? Or ignore that there was a roomful of distraught women and simply head upstairs?

Obviously, I had no choice. I remembered Evelyn's words, that I'd been acting strange by not being around much, and I knew that if I headed straight upstairs, I'd look guilty as hell. So, my legs wobbling, I walked into the common room, trying to fake a look of shock.

"Hey." My voice was shaky. "What's going on?"

Amanda and Carla, two of the current pledges, looked up from their spot on the armchair. Sitting side by side, they had their arms wrapped around each other for support.

"It's awful," Carla said. "Shandra's body was found."

I gasped. Covered my mouth.

"I know," Amanda said. "It's so hard to believe. But it's true. We got the news about two hours ago."

My tears came naturally. "H-how?"

"We don't know. But I think the police are gonna come by to ask some questions."

"Oh." I could hardly get the word out. "I guess, uh, I guess, yeah." My armpits were getting damp. "Do they think someone here did it? Wasn't she found downtown?"

Carla's eyes narrowed quizzically. "How'd you know she was found downtown?"

Oh, shit! "I . . . I just assumed." My brain scrambled for—and found—the plausible answer. "I heard a couple of days ago that a woman's body was found downtown somewhere."

I could almost see the lightbulb going on in Carla's head, and was thankful that quick thinking had saved my ass. Panicking under pressure could be my downfall.

"That's right," she said. "I heard about that, but I didn't want to think . . ."

"I know." I rubbed her back. "None of us did."

I gave Carla and Amanda hugs, because they looked as if they needed one. Then I glanced somberly at the rest of the girls. Absorbed in their grief, they didn't much notice me, so I backed away from the common room. I wanted to sprint out of there, but my legs wouldn't cooperate. They felt like cement blocks.

Somehow I made it to the stairs. As I ascended, I could hear voices. They were heated, I realized.

Reaching the first landing, I spotted Angelina and Rowena. Seeing me, Rowena quickly stepped backward. Then she glared at me and headed down the stairs. I craned my neck to look at her, but she didn't glance back at me, just pounded down the steps.

I turned to face Angelina, who was wiping at a tear. "Hey, Angie," I greeted her in a solemn tone. "Everything okay?"

"Okay?" Her eyebrows shot up in disbelief. "Shandra's dead!"

"I—I know. I just heard the news."

Her eyes narrowed on me. "Did you do this?"

Shock made me reel backward. "What?"

"Did you kill Shandra?"

"No! Oh my God. I can't believe you would ask me that."

"You hated her because she was after your fiancé."

"And you think I *killed* her? My God, Angie—I would never kill anyone!" I gripped her hand. "You know me! I can't believe anyone would say that!"

Her hard expression softened. Then she hugged me

tightly. "I'm sorry. I guess I'm just so shocked about all this, and I'd heard that you hated her so much. . . ."

"It's okay." Who the hell was talking about me? Rowena?

"No, it's not okay. We have to live in fear."

"Whoever did this, I'm sure the police will catch the creep."

Angelina and I pulled apart. She was gnawing on her bottom lip. I supposed out of stress. Or fear. Or both.

"You want to get coffee or something?" I asked. "Maybe we can talk about what's happened. I think we all need to get what we feel off our chest."

Angelina shook her head. "I'm gonna head out of here. See my boyfriend. I need to be with him now."

The one thing about Angelina—which was in part what shocked me so much about her question—was that despite her gorgeous looks, she was a down-to-earth person with a warm heart. Her boyfriend wasn't in a fraternity, which many of our sorors frowned upon. I didn't understand why. Some were cruel enough to call him a dork. I'd met Ned and he was as nice as she. He was a teaching assistant who lived in the adult complex of apartments on campus.

"You sure?" I asked.

"Yeah. I need to get out of here. I'm starting to wonder who I can trust."

"Meaning me?" I asked, my stomach sinking.

"No. No, of course not."

"Then what did you mean by that?"

"I'm sorry. I have to go."

"Angie—"

But she was already breezing past me and down the stairs.

Well, shit.

Angelina couldn't get away from me fast enough. It was obvious, despite what she'd said, that she was afraid of me.

It was no doubt imperative that I become more available, in order to appear less suspicious than I apparently did. Perhaps not having gone to lunch with Angelina that day had fueled her doubts about me once the rumors started circulating.

I ran to my room. Camille was already inside. We walked into each other's arms and held each other. Neither of us said a thing.

Words were pointless.

31

LATER THAT NIGHT, shortly after ten, most of us were gathered in the common room for an emergency sorority meeting, where the news about Shandra's murder was formally announced.

"This is obviously a very awful time," Katrina said. "We're all very emotional about this. And one way or another, we will get to the bottom of what happened."

I was surprised that Rowena wasn't in the room. What could keep her from so important a meeting? Of course, she could have had a meeting with the graduate chapter or even have had a class. She was obtaining a master's in English and often had night classes.

"We want you to know that the board is here for you if you need to talk," Katrina went on. "This is obviously very trying for all of us, and we're going to need support. Grief counselors will also be coming to our house in the next couple of days."

I was relieved that Donna and Katrina didn't single out

me, Camille, or Miranda. But the looks Donna kept throwing in my direction said everything.

She thought I'd killed Shandra.

"In light of some disturbing allegations—and the many questions about what Shandra was doing in downtown Buffalo—the police will be questioning every one of us." Katrina scanned the room. "I'm sure you all will have no problem cooperating."

Her gaze landed on me. I looked away just as a scream sounded, followed by the slamming of a door.

All of us jumped to our feet, some of the girls screaming and moving to hide behind sofas and lamps. The scream came again, a horrified shrill, and I moved into action. Katrina and Donna were hot on my trail as I sprinted to the front door.

I drew up short when I saw a woman standing there. Her hair was a tangled mess, with twigs and dried leaves caught in the strands. There was blood covering half her face, and I almost expected to see a butcher knife in her hand— as if this were the scene from a horror movie.

But then I recognized her eyes. . . . I'd know those wide brown eyes anywhere.

Angelina!

Her body shaking, she was alternately screaming and making ghastly sounds.

"Angie!" I exclaimed. I charged toward her. "Oh my God!"

"What happened?" someone else asked.

I wrapped my arms around her trembling shoulders, then slowly led her to the common room. Everyone gathered around us, both concerned and frightened.

Katrina reached for Angelina, and she jerked a hand back reflexively.

"She's completely terrified," I said, stating the obvious.

Then I sat Angelina on one of the sofas. "Angie, what happened?"

"S-someone . . . someone a-attacked . . . me . . ."

There was a buzz of excited chatter around us, many questions flying out at once. I raised a hand to quiet my sorors.

I smoothed her tangled hair. "Go on."

"I w-went to see Ned. We had a f-fight and I—I left." She paused, gulping in air. "I took the shortcut through the woods to head back here. And then someone . . . attacked me. Just ran out of the trees."

The news hit me like a forceful slap in the face. Just a couple of nights before I'd been on that same path and thought someone was following me. Until Morgan appeared.

"Were you raped?" someone asked.

Angelina shook her head. "No. I fought him. But he grabbed a rock . . . hit me." She fingered the area where she was bleeding. "I kneed him in the groin, then I started running. I think, I think he ran off. Into the trees."

"It's that rapist and murderer," I said softly, a heavy chill settling over me.

"Why would you go out there alone?" Katrina asked. "You know it's not safe."

Angelina started to cry again.

I glared at Katrina over my shoulder. "Obviously she made a mistake. But she's not the only one who uses that path. I was on it a couple of nights ago, and I thought someone was following me, too."

Gasps erupted around me.

"As of right now," Katrina announced, "no one goes on that path alone. You hear me?"

I squeezed Angelina's hands. "We have to call the police."

She nodded jerkily. "I'm sorry I said what I did earlier. I know you're not capable of anything so . . . so awful."

"It's okay. I'm gonna go to the phone."

"No!" Angelina exclaimed. "Please—I want you to stay with me, Phoebe." Her eyes implored me not to leave her side.

Odd.

But if she wanted me near her, that's where I would be. I threw a look over my shoulder and faced the girls. "Someone—someone call the police."

Katrina's gaze lingered on mine for a moment before flitting to Angelina. What—didn't she trust me to be near her? Did she think I was going to strangle Angelina in a room full of my sorors?

"You heard Phoebe," Katrina said, facing the crowd. "Who's got their cell phone?"

Angelina squeezed my hand. "Phoebe?"

"Yes?"

"I—"

Katrina knelt beside me and patted Angelina's arm. "You're gonna be okay, Angie."

What did Angelina want to tell me? "What is it, Angie? Did you get a look at who did this to you?"

She brusquely shook her head. "No, but . . ."

"But what?"

She hesitated before speaking. "I just wanted you to know. Whoever attacked me . . . I think he's the one who attacked Shandra, too. In fact, I'd bet money on it. But she wasn't so lucky."

God help me, Angelina was probably right.

I'd likely had my own near brush with a killer and hadn't even known it.

32

THE ATTACK ON Angelina was all any of us could talk about that night and the next morning. That and Shandra's murder.

Camille and I only went out for breakfast, then returned to our room, where we hoped not to be disturbed. I'd called Miranda again, but once again got her voice mail.

"Maybe there is some creep stalking women on campus," Camille said as she lay on her back, staring at the ceiling. "What if he saw us that night, followed us, killed Shandra?"

"I'm really scared," I admitted. "A couple of nights before Angie was attacked, I thought someone was following me. I could be dead right now." I refrained from telling her that Morgan had grabbed me that night, scaring me to death.

The knock on our door made us both jump. We exchanged nervous glances.

"Do you think it's the cops?" Camille whispered, her eyes filled with fear.

"I don't know."

There was another knock, and I knew there was no point in ignoring it. Short of being in Mexico, one way or another we'd have to deal with the cops.

I hopped off my bed and crossed the room to the door. Donna and Katrina stood outside.

"We need to talk to both of you," Donna said without preamble. "Separately."

"Why?" I asked. When you had a father who was a lawyer, you weren't easily bullied.

"You know why," Donna said. She and Katrina stepped uninvited into the room.

Behind me, I heard Camille whimper.

I shot her a look that said, "Don't freak out." To Donna I said, "I don't understand."

"We need to talk to you—before the police arrive. I'll talk to you here, Phoebe. Camille, you go with Katrina."

"What are you hoping to accomplish?" I asked.

Donna was a few inches shorter than I was, but she stared into my eyes as though she'd routinely gone to battle with people twice my height and weight. "We want to find out what happened to Shandra."

"Are you questioning everyone—or just us?"

"Phoebe," Camille said, placing a hand on my arm, "it's okay."

"No, it's not okay. Isn't it obvious? Angelina was attacked last night. I was followed a couple of nights before that. Clearly there's some sicko out there, preying on us. We're all Alphas. Even Carmen Young had applied to this sorority."

Donna seemed unaffected by my display of dramatics.

I looked to Katrina, hoping she would get the significance of my statement. "It makes sense, don't you think? Holy shit, I'm surprised no one made the connection before now. Someone is out to get members of our sorority. Now we have to figure out why."

"We still need to talk to you," Donna said matter-of-factly.

Annoyed, I rolled my eyes in Donna's direction, then looked hopefully at Katrina. Her eyes were hard, unwavering. Clearly she didn't believe my theory had merit.

"Camille," Katrina prompted.

"What, you both are cops now?" I couldn't help asking.

"Phoebe," Camille said firmly. Then she went to the door with Katrina, and I wanted to scream. But they were already walking out of the room, and I knew that if I kept protesting, I would seem even more guilty in the court of public opinion.

The sound of the door clicking shut behind Katrina and Camille was akin to a gun cocking, as far as I was concerned. Because as the door shut in my room, I knew I was about to face a firing squad. Camille would no doubt face the same in Katrina's room.

"Have you talked to Angelina about what happened to her?" I asked Donna when she faced me. "She was attacked and survived. She might be able to recognize the killer, even if she doesn't know it."

"Angelina spoke with the cops before she left. I'm sure she told them everything she knows."

"Wait a second. She left? Where'd she go?"

"She went home."

"Home!" I exclaimed, totally stunned. "As in Kentucky?"

"Yes. And it sounds like she might not be coming back."

"Whoa, whoa, whoa. When you say not coming back, do you mean like *ever?*"

"She's terrified, Phoebe. Look, enough about Angelina. You know damn well I'm not here to discuss her."

I'm not sure why I was so rattled by the news of Angelina's leaving, except that I was sure she had wanted to tell me something. I understood she was scared, but to leave and not be planning to come back? That was a little extreme.

Donna folded her arms over her chest. "What happened on Monday night?"

"I didn't kill Shandra."

"You and Shandra had a long-standing feud over your boyfriend."

"My fiancé."

"Your fiancé. Your man. Your sugar pie. Whatever you want to call him. The point is, you were fighting over him."

"And you think I decided to kill the competition? I'm not that insecure." I used my left hand to tuck a strand of my hair behind my ear—and to show off my two-carat rock.

"Why are you so angry?" Donna asked. "If you had nothing to do with Shandra's murder—"

"How would you like to be accused of something like that? And now some of my sorors are asking me if I'm a *killer?* This is your fault. You're the one making it seem to everyone like I had motive and means. The truth be damned."

"Don't blame me for what you've gotten yourself into."

"Are you gonna deny you're talking about me? Nosing around, asking suggestive questions?"

Donna looked at me long and hard before saying, "All right. Let's start over. Do you have any idea what could have happened to Shandra on the night she disappeared?"

I hesitated slightly, then said, "No. I don't know who could have done this to her."

"That wasn't exactly what I asked you."

I didn't respond.

"All right," Donna said in an exasperated tone. "If you

have nothing to hide, I'm sure you'll have no problem talking to the police when they come by later."

"Of course not."

"And if they need to search your car, you'll cooperate with that, too?"

The air in the room was suddenly difficult to breathe. I hadn't considered that the police might want to search my car. And if they wanted to search my car, they'd no doubt want to search Miranda's.

"Phoebe?"

"Um, yes. Sure."

"All right," Donna said, but she sounded skeptical. If she was so interested in law enforcement, why was she studying pre-med?

She turned and headed to the door, but stopped before opening it. "For your sake, I hope you're being completely honest with me."

I didn't say a word. She might not be a cop, but the real ones did scare me. With forensics and crime-scene investigators, there was invisible evidence the cops could find in Miranda's car to link us to Shandra.

We were so screwed.

"What did she say?" I asked Camille when she returned to the room twenty minutes later.

Camille rolled her eyes. "She started with this 'I've always liked you' spiel. 'You're smart, have a lot going for you.' Then she immediately asked me if I'd killed Shandra. I told her I was shocked she would even ask me that. But this is the worst part, Phoebe. She said she already talked to Miranda, and that Miranda told her we were involved and that what happened was an accident."

"Miranda said that?"

"That's exactly what I asked her. She went on to say that Miranda said we didn't meant to do it, but when I pressed her about what else she said, then she asks me to tell her my version of the story. That's when I realized she was trying to bait me. Using Miranda to try to get me to talk."

"Obviously. Who does she think she is? Sherlock Holmes?"

Camille plopped onto the bed. "I doubt Katrina even talked to Miranda. I think she's been working pretty steadily since yesterday."

"And she could be staying at her mother's house this weekend, given that we talked about keeping a low profile."

"I wonder if she even knows what happened."

"I called her cell, left a message."

A beat passed. Camille took a deep breath and said, "Look, Phoebe. It gets worse."

"Worse? How could it get any worse?"

"Someone saw us that night, dressed in black, coming in late."

"What?"

"That's the story. And given that it's true, I'm sure it's credible."

Seconds passed. Neither of us spoke.

Finally Camille broke the silence. "I think it had to be Cheryl, don't you? When Miranda got back to her room that night? Maybe she wasn't sleeping."

"It had to be," I agreed. But I wasn't sure.

What if it had been someone else?

33

MIRANDA FINALLY CALLED me back in the early afternoon. As I suspected, she was at her mother's house and had just checked her messages. I told her about Angelina's attack as well and my own near brush with the killer, and said that she needed to come back to the sorority house right away.

Less than an hour later she came into our room.

"So it's true," she said sadly. "Shandra's dead. And Angelina was attacked?"

"Yeah," I said softly. "Angelina was so freaked, she went back to Kentucky. Could things be crazier?"

"By any chance have you talked to Katrina or Donna?" Camille asked, getting to the reason why we wanted to see Miranda.

She shook her head. "But Katrina left me a message on my cell. She said she needed to talk to me right away."

"But you haven't spoken to her yet, right?" I wanted to be sure.

"No. I wanted to come to your room first."

"They're trying to break us," Camille said. "They got to me and Phoebe earlier. Now more than ever we have to be united."

"With Angelina's attack, it should be obvious that Shandra was killed because of some sicko's depraved desires, not because of us," I added. "Maybe even someone who has it in for sorority girls. I mean, look who's been—"

"I can't keep lying." Miranda shook her head. "I'm dying inside."

"I know I agreed with you before," Camille said. "But I've thought about it. If we say we hurt Shandra, we'll risk going to jail. Jail! I can't get locked up, Miranda."

"They're not looking to nail anyone for hazing Shandra," I pointed out. "They're trying to find who *killed* her."

"That's why we admit what we did. Tell them that we just wanted to teach her a lesson. Why would they send us to jail for that? They'll believe us."

I gaped at Miranda. "Oh, you think so?"

"Yes, I think so—"

"Maybe in your nothing-goes-wrong world, but this is the real world, Miranda. You can't be so naive!"

"Stop!" Camille held up both hands.

I looked at her, wondering if she'd suddenly switched sides. She angled her head toward the door.

I whipped my head around. Strained to hear sound. I thought I saw the shadow of feet outside our door.

"Great." I cursed under my breath. "If we're going to talk, we have to get out of here."

We gathered our jackets and headed to the door. I yanked it open, prepared to catch a spy, but saw no one standing there. So I made my way into the hallway, trying to act as casual as possible.

I knew Miranda was scared, and so was I, but the attack on Angelina would only work in our benefit. And I wasn't thinking in a callous way. I certainly wasn't happy about Angelina's ordeal—far from it. But it offered a plausible explanation for what happened to Shandra, and would take the focus off us.

Like Miranda, I wished we could admit that we'd been involved in a hazing incident and nothing more; but given the timing, it would look too suspicious.

"Where are we going?" Miranda asked.

"Anywhere but here," I told her.

"I'm hardly eating," Miranda went on. "I can't eat when I'm so stressed."

"Miranda, please. Can you wait till we get out of the building to talk?"

My feet were about to hit the first floor, but looking across the room, I stopped abruptly. Unprepared for my sudden halting, Miranda bumped into my back.

"Oh my God," I said.

"What?" Camille asked.

I gripped her hand, saying, "Those men in suits . . . they must be cops."

"Oh, hell," Camille whispered. "What do we do?"

"I'm not sticking around."

The detectives were talking to some of the girls and didn't see us where we were standing. I quickly spun around and hustled back up the stairs. I crossed the second floor to the end of that hallway, hurrying for the back stairs.

"Is this what we're gonna do?" Miranda asked when we were in the stairwell. "Run from this like we're criminals?"

"If we have to, yes!"

"You really think that's helping?"

Camille stepped between us. "If you two are gonna argue, you better realize that the sound carries in a stairwell. The cops can charge in here in seconds flat."

It seemed like forever before we hit the exit and stepped

outside. "We can't hide from the cops forever," Miranda said. "We can't hide from this."

She was no doubt right, but I still wasn't ready to face reality. "Maybe not forever, but for now we can."

34

WHILE WE ATE dinner, we bickered over what to do. Miranda finally agreed that she'd stay quiet, that we'd deal with the consequences of hazing should it ever come to that.

We watched a movie to pass the time, a comedy with Will Smith, but I didn't laugh once. I felt that I was a prisoner on death row who'd been given a stay of execution but would have to face my day of reckoning sooner rather than later.

And, I admit, maybe things had spiraled out of control a bit, and the blame for that was squarely on my shoulders. But what could we do that wouldn't make us seem guiltier than hell?

The sorority house was quiet when we returned. Camille and I went upstairs, where I dressed in my pj's and went to bed. She turned on the television and started to watch a rerun of *The Simpsons*. It was just as well. We were all talked out over what to do and what not to do.

Hours later, I still couldn't sleep. I realized then that I

hadn't talked to Henry. I'd turned off my cell, not wanting to be reached by anyone. Well, not wanting to be reached by Katrina or Donna or our housemother, telling us the cops were looking for us.

I wanted to be with Henry, snuggled beside him in bed.

I gave him a quick call. "Henry, I'm coming over."

"Now?"

"Yes." I hung up, not giving him the chance to say no.

Quietly I got dressed in jeans and a pullover sweater, then threw on a leather jacket and left the room.

Feeling like a thief in the night, I cut across the grass in the shadows.

Worse, I felt like a woman on the run.

I saw Evelyn a distance off near the Zeta house, heading down the front path. I turned my head hoping she wouldn't notice me on the grass. As far as I was concerned, she had betrayed me and I had nothing to say to her.

Moments later I tiptoed into the fraternity house. A couple of guys were downstairs, and I gave them a wave as I made my way to the stairs.

The lights were off inside Henry's room, but the light from the full moon enabled me to see. I got under the covers with him and slid my hands up his naked chest. I whispered, "I missed you."

"What happened to you today?"

"Hmm?"

"My game. You said you were heading to Kent State to watch me play."

"Oh, God. I totally forgot." How had I forgotten? "I'm sorry."

He sighed softly. "It's okay."

"Did you win?"

"Had our asses kicked. You would have driven all that way for nothing. I tried calling you all day. Before the game and after."

"I turned off my cell, and I unplugged my room phone."

"Why?"

"It's a long story." I pressed my lips against Henry's warm shoulder—and then had an awful feeling. Did I smell the scent of sex?

"Does this story have to do with Shandra?"

Maybe it wasn't sex I smelled, but sweat. I pushed the thought out of my mind. "There was an emergency house meeting about her murder, and a couple of detectives showed up."

Henry sat up. "Phoebe, I've been hearing all kinds of things."

"I'm not surprised, baby."

Henry lowered his voice to a whisper. "Did you . . . did you do this to Shandra?"

"Are you serious?"

"If you were hearing what I was hearing, you'd ask too."

My stomach sank. One minute you're a popular person on campus. The next, everyone is talking behind your back. It took only one person to tell another person a theory before wild stories spread. "I don't think I want to know what people are saying, but tell me anyway."

"Word is, you and your friends strangled Shandra and dumped her body. I'm taking a lot of heat from the guys here."

I was too stunned to speak. Then anger took root inside me. "I thought I was part of a civilized sorority. Yet people are spewing lies without even thinking about how they can hurt people.

"I knew people were talking," I went on, "but, Henry, how could you ask me that?"

"I didn't say I believed it." Henry lowered himself next to me once again and brushed his lips against my cheek. "But it's no secret that you and Shandra hated each other."

"Because of you," I pointed out. "Quite frankly, it's

about time you take some of this heat. Do you know how much bullshit I've had to deal with because of you?"

"So you're gonna start that again—"

"I'm not starting anything. But you know damn well our issues were because of you and your *flirtation* with Shandra." I thought of the odd smell in his room and wondered if he was cheating on me again. I sat up. "That's the reason people are saying I killed her. Reality check, Henry—this is all your fault!"

"I'm gonna pretend you didn't just say that and go to sleep."

God, he pissed me off sometimes! Yeah, we were trying to work past our problems, but I couldn't help wondering if it was worth it. He'd given me so much grief recently, and now Shandra was dead and my life could be over because of him.

I was contemplating getting out of bed and taking off when Henry reached for my hand. "Are we ever gonna put this behind us?" he asked.

Drawing in a shaky breath, I lay beside Henry once more. "I do want to, baby. But you have to understand how I feel. . . . When you get mad at me . . ."

"I'm not mad, baby. Just tired."

He hugged me tight, and I let him. I needed his strength right now.

"I was in the Letchworth Woods a few nights ago," I told him. "On the path. Someone was following me."

Henry pulled back and I saw the shock on his face. "What?"

"I know it was crazy." I paused. "Henry, I was so scared. Did you hear about Angelina, how she was attacked?"

"No."

"Last night. Along that same path. She had a gaping hole on her forehead."

"Holy shit."

"Yeah." I snuggled closer to him. "She had to get six stitches. She'll be okay, thank God. But she's so scared, she went home to Kentucky."

"Phoebe, I don't want you out there alone. You hear me?"

"I know." I sighed. "The person who followed me, who attacked Angelina—what if he killed Shandra? I think that's what happened." I stopped short of sharing my theory that maybe the killer was after sorority girls.

"That creep won't stop till he's caught."

"Exactly. Maybe none of us are safe, Henry. Not with a crazy person like that out there."

35

ORIGINALLY I'D PLANNED to return to the sorority house on Sunday night, but I stayed with Henry until Monday morning. I wasn't so much hiding out now as that I was scared there might be a total creep out there trying to prey on us. The more time I spent with Henry, the safer I'd be.

Miranda and Camille had both called my cell. Even though their messages sounded urgent, I didn't call them back. I needed a couple of days away from the craziness. I wanted it to just be me and Henry and nothing else.

Thankfully, my first class on Monday wasn't until eleven. Henry, bless his heart, had picked me up a bagel and some juice from the cafeteria earlier. He had given me a kiss and told me that he loved me before heading out to class.

It's weird—for the first time, his telling me that didn't make me all warm and woozy. I didn't know why.

Maybe it was the lingering questions about the possible smell of sex on his sheets Saturday night. Or maybe it was the realization that Morgan was right—I'd never be able to trust him.

My morning class was uneventful, as was my entrance into Putnam's for lunch. Only a few people seemed to take notice of me. It wasn't a crowd that I knew. Thankfully. I didn't want to deal with the whispers and finger-pointing.

I headed to my right and the far end of the cafeteria, where there were empty tables. Not wanting to be bothered by anyone, I dug a textbook out of my tote and stuck my nose in it while I nibbled on some french fries.

Not more than five minutes later I looked up when someone sat to my immediate left. I whipped my head in that direction, wondering who had the nerve.

My stomach fluttered with a mix of desire and fear. Every time I saw Morgan, something inside me came alive in a strange way. It was a little scary.

I washed down the tasteless burger in my mouth with a swallow of grape juice. "Morgan. Hi."

"How you doin'?"

"You still mad at me?" I asked cautiously.

He shook his head. A smile lifted my lips.

"You know I think the world of you," he went on. "I can't be mad at you for long."

I felt a rush of emotion, the kind that almost had me crying. I guess I needed to hear that. "That means a lot. Really. With all that's happening right now."

"Sounds like things are about to get real freaky."

"That's the understatement of the year. My life . . ." My voice trailed off as I shook my head.

"What, Phoebe? What were you going to say?"

"Truthfully, my life's about to be ruined. All because of . . ."

Because of Shandra James. That's what I'd been about to say. But something—the realization of how horribly unfair that thought was—made me hold my thought in check.

If anyone had ruined my life, *I* had. Or Henry, who had driven me to hurt Shandra. Had Shandra asked to be murdered, discarded behind a dark building as if she were trash? Could I be crazy enough to blame her for my problems? I was the one who'd handled the situation badly.

"Phoebe?"

I whipped my gaze to Morgan's. "Yeah?"

"You were saying . . ."

I pushed my plate away. I couldn't eat another bite. "Shandra," I whispered. "I feel awful about everything. If I hadn't set up that initiation . . ." And then I started crying. Little sobs, because I couldn't allow myself more than that there. But I wanted to bawl, cry my eyes out and never stop.

"If I knew, I *never* would have done that. I never wanted anything bad to happen to her!"

Morgan gathered me in his arms. "I know you didn't."

I let him hold me. I rested my head against his chest, not caring who saw us. Right then, I needed his comfort and strength.

"Some people think I did, Morgan. They actually believe I'd snuff the life out of someone. And that hurts. My God, it hurts so much."

"It's okay," Morgan murmured, rubbing my back.

Brushing my tears, I lifted my head and stared into his eyes. Then an idea struck me. "You can help me."

He gave me a questioning look. "How?"

"You know I didn't murder Shandra. I mean, if I had, I wouldn't have asked you to pick her up."

"Yeah?"

"So you have to tell the cops." After listening to Miranda's messages—and wrestling with my own conscience—I'd been thinking about coming clean about the initiation.

I knew the timing sucked, but I feared the truth would come out whether I wanted it to or not.

Morgan looked at me as if I'd grown a second head. "Tell the cops?"

"It makes sense. Don't you see? You tell them I called you, that you went to the scene and—"

"Whoa." Morgan held up a hand.

"What?"

"I—" He hesitated. "I don't really want to be involved."

I stared at him in disbelief. "Why not?"

"You want me to say I went to the scene—the last place Shandra was probably alive?"

"You wouldn't be implicated. In fact, they'd think you were the good guy—since you were going there to pick her up."

"I don't know about that," Morgan said doubtfully.

I placed a hand on his and gently squeezed it. "You know the truth, Morgan. I need you. I can say I didn't kill Shandra until I'm blue in the face, but who's gonna believe me without proof?"

Morgan glanced down at our joined hands before meeting my eye again. A moment passed. I felt a flash of heat. "You know I'd do anything for you," he said.

Relief washed over me in waves. "I appreciate it, Morgan."

"Not like some other guys."

I ignored his comment because I knew what he was getting at. I also ignored it because he was right. And that was something I didn't want to deal with right then. I had enough on my plate.

Morgan chewed and swallowed a mouthful of fries before asking, "You sure you want Henry freaking out about us? Because he will, you know. If I tell the cops you called me to get Shandra that night."

I groaned. Morgan was no doubt right. Henry would

likely blow a gasket. But for some reason I wasn't as concerned about that as I would have been a week earlier. Even a couple of days earlier.

That's what happens when a possible murder charge is hanging over you. You reassess your priorities.

"Did you think about that?" he asked.

"It's not like I have much choice," I answered. "I'd rather Henry know the truth than go to jail. Besides, he knows you're my friend."

"Then why's he been getting up in my face, telling me to stay away from you?"

"He has?"

"Hell, yeah. He's acting crazy. Been doggin' me since he saw us that day we went to Applebee's. He has to have asked me a million times if I fucked you."

I hadn't known. And I suddenly wondered if that was why Henry was being so lovey-dovey with me again. Because he sensed he had some competition rather than because he'd come to the conclusion that I was the one for him, as he'd said.

The reality settled over me like a cold, wet blanket.

"I don't know what to say, Morgan. I'm sorry."

"Hey, I can handle myself. I'm just letting you know because he might lose it if he finds out you called me to help you that night. And an angry Henry—that isn't a pretty picture."

The memory of Henry's rage in Applebee's hit me then. I found myself wondering what he was capable of.

"If I were you," Morgan continued, "I'd hold off mentioning me to the cops. Seriously, I worry about Henry hurting you."

"Right," I said. But was Morgan really so concerned about me, as he said, or was he thinking of himself? Was there another reason he didn't want me to go to the cops?

That day in the woods . . . had Morgan really found me there, or had he been lurking?

My stomach kotted with nervous tension. Glancing at my watch, I jumped up. "Shit, I have a class in two minutes. Look, I haven't talked to the cops yet, but that's only a matter of time. Why don't I let you know how I think things go after that? Then we can decide if it's better to bring you into it."

Morgan nodded as he chewed.

"All right." I pushed my chair beneath the table. "I've got to run. I'll talk to you later, okay?"

"Phoebe, wait."

I hesitated. "What is it? I really have to go."

"There's something I haven't told you. Something that might be important."

"How important?"

"It's about Henry."

"You think he slept with Shandra. I know that."

"That's not what I was gonna say."

"Then what?"

Morgan glanced around, then looked me dead in the eye. In a low voice he said, "I think maybe he killed her."

36

I STOOD THERE, dumbfounded.

"Sit down," Morgan instructed in a hushed tone. "Please."

I pulled out a chair and plopped into it. Suddenly it was hard to breathe.

"I know. That's the last thing you want to think—"

"Why—why would you say that?"

Morgan's eyes did a sweep of the room before speaking, as though making sure no one was within earshot. "You said if I thought of anything new about that night, I should tell you."

"I did. You told me you didn't see anything."

"How well do you know Henry?" Morgan asked.

"Will you stop beating around the bush? You drop a bomb like that and you don't want to give me details?"

"I'm just trying to get you to think. You thought you knew him, but you didn't think he would cheat on you. How do you know—"

I shot to my feet. "I thought you said you remembered something. I don't have time to listen to you bash Henry."

Morgan grabbed my wrist. "Sit."

The firm tone of his voice and his rough touch unnerved me, so I sat back down, but not before glancing around the cafeteria. Curious eyes were on me, watching my interaction with Morgan.

"I have a class—"

"I think I saw Henry that night," Morgan whispered.

It took a moment for his words to register. "The night of October second? Well, I guess it was actually early-morning October third . . ."

"Yes, Phoebe. *That* night."

"Where?" I was confused. "You saw him where?"

"Near where you told me to pick her up. I was driving, and I saw a green BMW—"

"You saw Henry?" I asked disbelievingly. That didn't make sense. "If you did, then why didn't you say so before?"

"Because I didn't realize it at the time."

"How could you not realize it? Either you saw him or you didn't."

Morgan exhaled loudly. "Look, I can't definitely say it was him. But the car sure looked like his."

"And this car . . . did it stop?"

"No. We just drove by each other near the gas station."

"Then, why are you telling me this?" My voice rose, my patience wearing thin.

"Because I want you to think, Phoebe. Think about the possibility."

"You know what, Morgan? I've heard enough of this." I scrambled out of my chair.

"Phoebe—"

"No, don't say another word." People were staring at us,

but I didn't care. "I would ask you why you're trying to slander Henry's name, but it's obvious. You think that by bad-mouthing him I'm going to jump into bed with you?"

"That's not—"

"Bullshit. Maybe it's a mistake, our being friends."

I stomped away from the table.

"Phoebe. Phoebe!"

I didn't stop.

I was pissed off at Morgan all during my sociology class. It was an emotion I was experiencing a lot lately. That and fear.

Morgan had to be lying.

Wasn't he?

Or at least mistaken. There were a lot of BMWs on the road, a lot of green ones. Driving past a car in the dark—how sure could you be of who was in it?

As I headed back to my sorority house, I decided to forget about what Morgan had said. It was entirely possible he hadn't been lying, but that didn't mean he'd seen Henry's car. I certainly wasn't going to worry about his words when there was no plausible evidence to link Henry to Shandra's murder.

I *knew* Henry. Maybe he wasn't a saint, but he wasn't a killer.

Still, what Morgan told me had my head throbbing, and I was looking forward to getting to my room and passing out for at least an hour.

But when I got to my room and opened the door, I froze with fear.

Because Camille was sitting on her bed, tears streaming down her face, while a man in a suit with a notebook open stood on the floor in front of her.

A cop.

Oh, fuck.

37

THE DETECTIVE WAS an attractive black man, about six foot two and lean, probably in his mid-thirties.

He smiled at me, but it was an official kind of smile that didn't put me at ease.

"You must be Phoebe Matthews," he said.

I stood rooted to the spot, fear coursing through my veins.

"I've been wanting to talk to you. Come in."

I walked into the room with trepidation.

The man walked toward me. "I'm Detective Longhorne of the Buffalo Police."

He extended a hand. I reached for it, my own hand shaking.

"I'd like to ask you a few questions," he went on. Then he turned to Camille. "I think I have enough from you, thanks. Do you mind excusing me and Phoebe for a moment?"

Wiping her tears, Camille got off the bed. As she passed me, she said, "I'm sorry, Phoebe."

My bladder suddenly got weak. I had to press my legs together not to piss my pants.

"I'm here investigating the murder of Shandra James," Detective Longhorne told me when Camille left the room.

"Uh-huh."

"I'd like to ask you a few questions about the deceased."

"O-okay."

"You look a little . . . uneasy. Would you like to sit?"

It's over, I thought. *Camille apologized to me. That means she told this cop everything!*

"Um, sure."

The detective gestured to the seat at my desk, but I opted for my bed. Instinctively, I pulled my teddy bear onto my lap.

The detective opened his notebook and asked, "You knew Shandra James, correct?"

"Yes."

"Would you say she was a friend of yours?"

"No."

"An enemy?"

I hesitated. "No. Just not a friend."

The detective paused as he looked down at me. Or was he glaring? "Did you have anything to do with Shandra's murder?"

I nearly choked on my saliva. I cleared my throat and asked, "Do I need a lawyer?"

"I don't know. Do you?"

Idiot—that was the wrong thing to say! "Not because I'm guilty," I quickly said, "if that's what you're implying."

"I'm not implying anything. I'm here to ask questions. Is that okay?"

I squeezed my teddy bear. I wasn't sure if that was a trick question. I nodded jerkily.

Detective Longhorne drew in a soft breath and shut his notebook. He pulled out the chair from the desk and placed it near my bed, then sat.

"I know this is stressful. I understand that. But I'm going to tell you right now, you'll make it easier on yourself if you come clean."

"I didn't kill Shandra."

"Your friend said it was an accident."

"That's a lie. Camille would never say that, because we didn't kill anyone!"

"Calm down, Phoebe."

"How can I calm down? You want to accuse me of murder—how am I supposed to be calm?"

"I'm not accusing you of murder. Look, I know something happened that night. So do your sorority sisters. They're the ones who gave me your name. Whether what happened is criminal or not is what I'm trying to determine. But I can't figure that out if you don't talk to me."

I realized then that I was shaking.

"Let me help you."

The detective's words sounded sincere. And he had caring eyes, not what I'd have expected of a guy in his position.

"Hazing is one thing. Murder is another. What happened, Phoebe?"

I was pretty sure Camille had told this man everything, but still I couldn't speak. I was scared, yes, but as the daughter of a lawyer, I knew how easily people could be screwed when they spoke to the cops without a lawyer present.

There was no way I would admit to "hazing." For all I knew, hazing could be the equivalent of assault in the eyes of the law. "I didn't *haze* anyone."

The detective's lips tightened. The look said he was

frustrated with me, and had me thinking his whole "I'm a nice cop, you can talk to me" thing was just an act.

"I understand you and the victim had a rivalry," he said.

"Rivalry? That's a strong word. We had more of a . . . a disagreement."

"Over a man?"

Fleetingly, I wondered who had blabbed my personal business to this cop. Probably everyone. What had happened to Shandra—and my involvement in it—would make for good gossip for only God knew how long.

I glanced down. Saw that I was squeezing my teddy bear's head as though I were some psychopath. Great. I could just picture it in a courtroom—Detective Longhorne talking about all the pent-up anger I was taking out on my stuffed animal and how that proved I was a killer.

"Phoebe?"

"Oh, sorry. I just . . . can you repeat the question? I'm a bit nervous."

The detective opened his notebook again. "Were you and Shandra fighting over a man?"

Quick breath. "You could *sort* of say it was over a man. Shandra was infatuated with my boyfriend."

"Hmm." The cop scribbled notes.

"That doesn't mean I wanted her dead," I quickly added.

"But you did want to hurt her?"

The way he said the words sounded truly awful. "I wanted her to respect my relationship—"

"And is that why you took her to an abandoned building in downtown Buffalo during the early-morning hours of October third?"

"That night was about an initiation. Initiations are routine for women trying to get into our sorority."

"I am aware of that, Phoebe. I'm also aware that no other pledge was involved in this particular initiation. Why is it that Shandra James was the only one being hazed?"

Hazed. I hated that word. "At our discretion, we can initiate anyone we want in any way we see fit."

The detective glanced at some notes. "And that included stripping her down and making her bark like a dog?"

Damn, Camille! Did she have to tell the man that part?

"Camille told me everything," he said, as if in answer to my unspoken question.

"My friend is grossly exaggerating the situation."

"That's why I'm speaking to you. To get your side of the story." He paused. "Now, Camille says that once you were through with Shandra that night, you left her to fend for herself. Is that how it happened?"

"Not exactly."

"No?"

"It was stupid, I know. I wish we never did it. We didn't hurt her, just humiliated her. It was just to scare her, because she wouldn't stop hitting on my man. . . ."

"So you left Shandra behind the building?" the detective asked again.

I wanted to cry. The simple questions made me seem like the cruelest person alive. "Yes, we left her. But it's not what you think. We were going back to get her in a few minutes, but we blew a tire. So I called someone, and he was on the way to get her right after that. Many of the initiations are about testing strength of character. . . ."

And that is when I really started to sweat. It was subtle, but I saw it nonetheless. The look of doubt.

I spoke faster then, as if afraid I'd be handcuffed any second. "I have a friend. Morgan Davis. He was supposed to pick Shandra up after we left her there. He's part of our brother fraternity, the Zeta Omega Beta fraternity. Contact him. He'll tell you what happened. Obviously, if I called someone to pick her up, I wouldn't have killed her—right?"

The detective didn't answer, just scribbled notes.

"You see my point, don't you?" I asked.

The detective ignored me, saying, "I was also informed that Shandra James complained to your sorority president that you had tried to run her down with your car."

"That is a bald-faced lie."

The detective eyed me with an uncompromising gaze. Yeah, he'd only been pretending to be the understanding sort. "You're saying that was a complete fabrication?"

I debated whether I should answer him, given that it sounded as though he'd made up his mind, anyway. I didn't like the direction this conversation was headed. I found myself saying, "Should I be retaining a lawyer?"

"If you feel you need one."

Jerk, I thought. *Yeah, right, you want the truth.*

"Was there more to the 'initiation' of Shandra James other than stripping her naked and subjecting her to humiliation?"

Despite my frazzled nerves, I managed to speak calmly. "So you know, my father's a lawyer. I'm getting this feeling that he would tell me not to say anything else until I've spoken to him or retained other legal counsel." There. That sounded official. Thanks to my father, I knew how to talk the talk.

"You'll only speak to me with a lawyer present?" the detective asked for clarification.

"I think that's the smartest thing to do."

The detective slowly closed his notebook and reached into his jacket pocket. He produced a business card and handed it to me. I stared down at his name on the card. It looked so official.

"Why don't we do this," he began. "When you've retained a lawyer, give me a call, and we can arrange for you to come to the station for further questioning. I think I have what I need for now, anyway."

Exactly what did that mean? My heart spasmed.

"Thank you for your time," Detective Longhorne said. "I'll be in touch."

I knew he would be.

I felt sick.

38

WHILE THE REST of the women of the Alpha Sigma Pi sorority headed into downtown Buffalo to volunteer at a soup kitchen for the evening, I stayed behind in the house with Camille and Miranda. When we were sure that the coast was clear, we headed out to my car and drove to a nearby steakhouse. We could have talked freely at the sorority house, but at least in the restaurant we didn't expect the cops to show up.

I wasn't sure how I felt about the day's events, but I certainly wasn't happy. Camille had told the cop too much. Apology or not, she'd screwed up royally.

"I just want to know one thing, Camille," I said from our secluded booth at the back of the restaurant. "Why'd you tell that detective so much?"

"I couldn't lie, Phoebe. That was a *detective*."

"I know who he was. But you didn't have—"

"We've played this your way, Phoebe, and it's just not working. People know we have something to hide. Besides, you've heard of obstruction of justice, haven't you? Do you think I want to go to jail?"

"The police can't just throw you in jail without evidence."

"Spoken like a spoiled girl from a privileged family."

My mouth fell open.

"You thought if we stayed quiet, everything would be fine," she continued. "But it isn't fine. Nothing's fine! Somehow, we fucked up, because someone saw us that night with Shandra, and the more we've been denying the truth, the guiltier we've looked. So, yeah, I told the cop what we did. Because I'm not about to take my chances with getting charged for murder!"

Miranda eyed me, saying, "She's right."

I didn't answer. A moment later the waitress appeared with our soft drinks and Caesar salads.

Miranda fiddled for a short time with her straw. "Have you talked to Katrina yet?" she asked me. "Today, I mean."

I shook my head. "No. Why?"

"She said I should tell you—we have to see Dean Moratti tomorrow. Bright and early."

"You know if she's gone to the dean, she'll be talking to the Panhellenic Committee next." Camille buried her face in her hands. "We're gonna get kicked out of our sorority, kicked out of school. And maybe even go to jail."

"No one is going to jail," I told her. "At least, none of us is."

"I'd love to trust you, Phoebe. But I trusted you that night we took Shandra downtown, and look what's happened."

I gaped at Camille. "So this is my fault?"

"You think it's mine?"

Anger boiled inside me. "You're so smart. You should know what the word *accomplice* means. At least in the eyes of the law."

Miranda stood. "You two want to argue, go ahead. I'm out of here. We've argued too much already. Maybe we shouldn't hang out together anymore."

I groaned as she started to walk away. Camille went after her.

Nothing was easy anymore. I wondered if it ever would be.

I watched Camille and Miranda. They were several feet away from me. Miranda was animated, moving her hands as she spoke. I couldn't hear what she was saying, but I read "frustrated as hell" in her body language.

She said something, looked my way. Camille glanced at me as well. Then they both quickly turned away.

I don't know why, but I got a weird vibe. Seeing the two of them there, standing together, while I was alone. Them against me.

It seemed like forever before they returned to the table. Miranda said, "I didn't mean what I said, Phoebe. I'm stressed out. We all are."

"I know." I sighed wearily. "And you're probably both mad at me—with good reason. I'm the one who got you into this. I wish I could take it back. I really do."

"Yeah. Sure." But Miranda's tone said she didn't entirely believe me.

"You don't believe me?" I asked. "You don't think I'd do things differently if I could go back in time?"

She didn't answer.

I went on, changing the subject. "We need to figure out a game plan. Like what we tell Dean Moratti tomorrow."

"I'm not looking forward to getting expelled," Camille muttered.

"We won't be expelled. Not if we come up with a plausible story and stick to it." I bit down on my lip, thinking. "I don't know. . . . Something about how Shandra was a difficult pledge, and that's why we planned an initiation just for her."

"In other words, keep making excuses?" Camille asked skeptically.

"It's the truth," I said.

"And no one will ever think we're sorry if we say she had it coming." Camille gave me a pointed look. "I say we fess up with the dean, with the Panhellenic Committee. Say we're extremely sorry for what we did. The more repentant we appear, the better."

"No one can prove that this was anything other than a routine initiation," I stressed.

"You think Detective Longhorne believes that?" Camille asked.

I stared at Camille. She held my gaze, her eyes unwavering.

"What you need to do, Phoebe," Miranda began, "is realize that there are three of us in this. We each have an opinion. And in this case, Camille's right. No one thinks we took Shandra out for anything remotely *routine*. They know this was personal."

"I don't care what people think. I don't care what the detective thinks. I need you guys with me on this." My voice broke. "Why are you making this so hard?"

"Because we put our asses on the line for you so you could get revenge," Camille said.

"I *never* thought this was a good idea." Miranda stressed.

The mutiny had started. I jabbed the lemon wedge at the bottom of my Coke with a straw.

"I'm not going to lie anymore," Camille said. "I'm sick of it."

"You both are turning on me. You're my best friends!" Tears filled my eyes.

"No one's turning on you," Miranda assured me. "We

have to tell the truth." She hesitated, looking at Camille first, then back at me. "But maybe you're right—we tell the truth with a slant. That Shandra was a particularly difficult pledge, so we planned a different initiation for her. People might buy that. And we have to be sorry—not defensive."

I sniffled. "I hope this works."

"It's the only chance we've got," Miranda said. "I've been thinking about this for a while—I can't think of anything else—and I'm sure it's the only way to get out of this without charges."

"Maybe," I conceded reluctantly.

"We can't keep our heads up our asses and pretend this will go away," Camille pointed out.

Silence fell over us. We ate for a few minutes in uncomfortable silence.

"Phoebe, have you called your father?" Miranda asked. "Maybe he can talk to the police on our behalf. Point out that we are young and stupid and made a mistake but that we've learned from it. Hell, maybe we can do some community service to show just how sorry—"

"No!" I protested. "I'm not calling my father. I don't want him knowing about this."

"You think word's not gonna get to him?" Miranda asked me. "I had to tell my mom and my aunt about this just a couple of days ago. I was worried to death, but they offered me their total support."

"I am *not* calling my father for help. I can't."

"I'm so tired of talking about this. We aren't solving a damn thing." Miranda groaned, reached into her purse, and threw ten bucks onto the table. "Can we go now?"

Miranda closed her eyes and rubbed her temples. I stared at her for a moment, debating what to do. I finally tossed a ten onto the table as well.

Miranda was right. We were getting nowhere.

39

I WENT TO the Lockwood Memorial Library after dropping off Camille and Miranda. I was in no mood to head back to my room.

Aside from the fact that I didn't want to deal with any of my sorors, I was pissed at Camille and Miranda. They were turning on me. God only knew what they'd say to the dean the next morning.

I spent nearly five hours at the library, using the time to research my humanism paper. I also caught up on some sleep in the cubicle where I had locked myself.

When the library closed at midnight, I still wasn't ready to go to my room. So instead of heading to the Alpha Sigma Pi house, I went to the Zeta house to see Henry.

Alex and Tony, two seniors, were in the common room when I entered. Whatever they were talking about, they quickly stopped when they saw me. And they stared—making me realize that the fraternity house wasn't a safe haven for me, either. The guys here would be talking about

me and what had happened to Shandra just as much as my
sorority sisters were.

Nevertheless, I gave them a bright smile and carefree
wave before heading up the staircase to the third floor. Seconds later I was turning the knob to Henry's door.

It was locked.

Shit, I didn't have my key. It was on the second key ring
I had, back in the drawer in my room. But Henry had to
be in there.

I rapped softly on the door. Henry didn't answer. I
knocked louder this time and listened for sounds inside.
I heard none.

I knocked again. "Henry."

Still no answer.

I dug my cell phone out of my purse and called him.
I could hear the phone in his room ringing.

"Hello?" he said groggily as he answered.

I smiled, relieved. "Hi, baby. I'm sorry to call you this
late. I'm outside your door. I forgot my key."

Henry groaned, as though he'd been in a deep sleep.
"Baby, I'm really tired."

"I promise I won't keep you up."

"No, I'm *really* tired. Let's hook up tomorrow, okay?"

My stomach took a nosedive. Was Henry actually saying he wasn't going to let me in?

"Henry, why don't you come and talk to me. I'm right
outside your door."

There was a pause. After a moment he said, "All right."

Seconds later I heard the sound of a chair scraping
across the floor and, confused, I narrowed my eyes. A
chair? Henry had pushed a chair up to the door?

The door opened a crack. The room was shrouded in
darkness. Henry squinted down at me.

"Henry, what's going on?"

"I'm gonna have to see you tomorrow." Henry sounded as if he had a frog in his throat.

"I don't understand why you won't let me in."

"Because I'm sick," he told me, and coughed. "I don't want to give you whatever I've got."

"Oh. Okay. But I don't care about that." I grinned at him. "I can take care of you."

"No, baby. Really. We'll hook up tomorrow, okay?"

I stared at him in disbelief. "You're serious."

"Yeah, baby." He coughed again. "Tomorrow, okay?"

I stood there like a fool, so shocked that I didn't know what to say. "Okay. I lo—"

Henry quickly shut the door. I flinched.

What the hell had just happened?

40

I GUESS YOU could call that my moment of epiphany. The moment when everything became crystal clear.

I didn't have to see it to know that Henry was with another woman. The same way that I now knew, without a doubt, that he'd slept with Shandra. Oh, I knew it before, in my heart, but couldn't admit the truth to myself. I didn't know if it was just sex with Shandra or something deeper, as she'd implied. I didn't know if Henry even loved me anymore. Maybe I was the girl in his heart, but he still wanted fresh pussy.

Whatever the case, at that moment I hated him. Hated him for cheating on me, deceiving me, for making me become a person I never thought I'd be. I hated him for pushing me over the edge where Shandra was concerned. Because of him, I no longer knew if I had a future.

As I walked slowly down the hallway, I remembered Morgan's question—his asking me how well I knew Henry. I knew I needed to talk to Morgan then.

At least that's what I told myself.

Despite the late hour, I knocked on his door. I leaned against the doorframe and waited.

I was about to walk away when I thought I heard a sound inside his room. A couple of moments later the door swung open. He looked at me in surprise.

"Hi," I said softly.

A beat passed, then he stepped back and opened the door for me. I walked into the room.

"I'm sorry I woke you up." His heavy eyelids told me he'd been sleeping.

"It's all right." His voice was groggy. "What's up?"

I closed the door behind me, then walked to him and put my arms around his torso. He had to be surprised, because he stiffened. If he had any question as to my intentions, I made them clear when I pressed my mouth against his warm chest.

"Phoebe . . ."

"No, don't talk." I put a finger against his mouth. "I don't want to talk."

Curling my arms around his neck, I pressed my body against his. His penis grew hard against me.

"Don't . . . don't tease me . . ."

"What if I told you to drop your boxers? Would you think I was trying to tease you?"

"I'd think you hit your head or something."

"Or something." I slipped out of my sweater jacket and dropped it on the floor. Next, I pulled my shirt over my head and tossed it on top of my jacket.

The room's lighting was dim, but I could still see the guarded look in Morgan's eyes.

Holding his gaze, I dragged my jeans over my hips, making it clear exactly what I wanted.

Morgan turned the lock on the door.

I smiled. "Drop your boxers."

"I know I should ask—"

"No, I don't want you to ask anything. I just want you to get naked."

Morgan pulled me into his arms. A little gasp escaped me just before he brought his mouth down on mine. Hard.

A surge of electricity shot through me, making my nerve endings tingle. My body came alive in a way it hadn't for a very long time.

Morgan gripped my butt, urging me upward. I wrapped my legs around his waist and he walked with me that way to his bed. We landed uneasily, but we didn't pull our lips apart. I reached for his erection, stroking it through his boxers. It wasn't enough. Slipping my fingers beneath the waistband, I shimmied them off his hips.

"Fuck, Phoebe." Morgan groaned in pleasure when I touched him.

His hands roamed my body hungrily, one pushing my bra up while the other slipped beneath my panties. Back and forth, he ran his thumb against me, making me wet. Making me pant.

He hastily moved his body downward. "I want to taste you so badly."

"Mmm." I arched my hips.

He shoved my panties aside and immediately brought his hot tongue down on me. I bucked from a jolt of white-hot pleasure.

Morgan worked his tongue over me skillfully, leaving me gasping for breath. "Morgan . . . oh, that feels *so* good!"

Moments later I was coming, my body shattering into a million blissful pieces. Morgan held me, not letting up the pressure of his tongue, and I came again.

When he was through with me, my body was a mass of quivering muscles. Morgan climbed over me. I thought he was going to spread my legs, but he kissed me instead. A gentle kiss.

I hadn't expected that, his gentleness. It endeared me

to him, made what we were doing deeper. I liked that. I didn't want to think it was just about sex.

I bit his earlobe lightly and whispered, "Do me." I spread my legs around him and reached for his penis. "Make love to me. . . ."

"Oh, I'm going to. All." He kissed one cheek. "Night." He kissed the other cheek. "Long."

41

". . . VERY DISTURBED BY the turn of events . . ."

I was conscious only of some of what Dean Moratti was saying. I was far too stressed and was doing my best to zone out. I thought of the incredible night I'd spent with Morgan, how easily we'd connected between the sheets.

". . . take hazing *very* seriously here."

Morgan's mouth on my inner thighs, his hot, wet tongue . . .

". . . there's no excuse . . ."

Morgan doing me from behind . . .

". . . shame and disgrace to this university . . ."

I lifted my gaze when I sensed movement. Dean Moratti was standing now, staring down at us. He looked a lot like Tony Soprano, and right then I could imagine his wanting to whack us all.

"Camille."

I shot a look at her. She looked as if she were about to pee in her pants as her eyes flew to the dean's. "Y-yes?"

"Are you listening to me?"

"Of course."

"I asked you if you understand the seriousness of what you've done."

"I do. Yes, I do. A-and I'm sorry. I really am."

"You are all good students, which makes what I have to do even harder. But this type of act cannot go unpunished. I have no choice but to take disciplinary action against you girls."

"You're expelling us?" Camille whined.

Expulsion! How was I ever going to explain this to my parents?

"I have no choice," Dean Moratti explained. "With the investigation—"

"You can't expel me," Camille complained. "This was Phoebe's idea. *Her* plan to get even with Shandra."

"Camille!" I shrieked.

"It's true—isn't it, Miranda?"

"Well, yes," Miranda agreed. "But—"

"Miranda and I only went along to help you. We shouldn't have to be punished—"

"Does that matter?" Miranda asked Camille. "We didn't have to go along with the plan, but we did."

I was surprised—and touched—by Miranda's comment.

"We have to stick together now," Miranda continued. "Shandra was a difficult pledge. Phoebe thought of a way to . . . deal with her, so to speak. The pledge process is often humiliating, Dean Moratti. You must know that. I think we're in your office right now because Shandra was tragically murdered—*not* because of the initiation."

"And we didn't kill her," I said, enunciating each word. "Do you really think we did, Dean Moratti?"

He didn't answer me.

"I'm sorry for what we did," I went on. "But you want to punish us because you think we had something to do with Shandra's death. We didn't. Isn't that what matters here?"

"I'm not going to negotiate with you." He looked at Miranda and me in turn. "The university has a strict no-hazing policy. My decision stands."

I knew that it would do no good to argue with the dean. Besides, we had bigger worries. Getting expelled "until the situation was resolved" was one thing. Getting charged with murder would be another matter entirely.

As we left the room, I wondered if Dean Moratti really thought us guilty of murder. Maybe he didn't, but he probably had his doubts. As did most everyone.

I wasn't a fool. I knew that many innocent people got wrongfully convicted of crimes, if circumstances made them seem guilty. If public opinion wasn't in their favor.

We had to do whatever was necessary to make sure we didn't get charged with murder.

Even if that meant trying to solve the crime ourselves.

42

"CAMILLE DOESN'T LOOK so good," Miranda told me as we walked across the marble floor outside the dean's office.

I looked at her then. Camille's forehead was beaded with sweat, and her eyes were glazed. She continued to walk on her own but started to wobble.

I shot an arm around Camille's waist just before she collapsed. As Camille's weight dragged me down, I asked for Miranda's help with her. Miranda went to Camille's other side and began to lift her.

"It's okay, Camille," I told her. "We're gonna get you back to the room."

Camille didn't say anything, but she started to move her feet, which was good. She was aware of what was going on, even if she was having some kind of panic attack.

Miranda and I on either side of her, we slowly made our way to the building's front door. Miranda pushed the heavy door open with her shoulder. The next moment a series of flashes blinded me. I didn't realize what was happening until I heard the first question.

"Girls, was this an initiation gone bad?"

"Is it true that you wanted to teach Shandra James a lesson?"

"Which one of you strangled Shandra James?"

Camille started, then froze. I urged her forward, saying, "Move, Camille!"

From every which way, microphones and cameras were shoved in our faces. A sea of reporters blocked our path.

"Tell us *something*," a male reporter demanded.

"We have nothing to say," Miranda retorted.

"We understand that Shandra was ten weeks pregnant," a female reporter said. "Was it your boyfriend's baby, Phoebe?"

I was trying to get Camille to move, and now I stopped cold. An odd pricking sensation, as if I were being stabbed by a thousand needles, spread over my entire body. My eyes landed on the female reporter who had a microphone shoved in my face.

"Is that why you killed her?" the woman pressed.

My body swayed. No, this couldn't be true. It was an awful, awful lie.

Shandra *pregnant?*

The news was devastating, and I couldn't deal with it there. "Get out of our way!" I yelled, pushing forward. "Can't you see my friend is sick?"

Finally the throng of reporters parted like the Red Sea, and we forged ahead. I thought we were home free until a tall woman blocked our path.

Fuming, I looked up at her. Irritation quickly turned to horror as I checked out the woman's face. In an instant I knew who she was.

The woman had the same honey-brown complexion, the same bright hazel eyes. Her hair wasn't the blond-brown shade that Shandra had favored, but a deep onyx black cut short in a conservative style. Except for the height and the hair, I would almost think that Shandra had come back from the dead.

Louisa James. Shandra's mother.

God help us.

"So you're the ones," she began, her eyes narrowing into angry slits. "You're the ones who murdered my daughter!"

Louisa James seemed to tower over us, though in reality she couldn't have been more than a couple of inches taller than I was. But her presence, the wrath in her gaze . . . it was overwhelming.

"We—we—" Miranda sputtered.

I looked away, moved to my right. I couldn't face Mrs. James. "Come on," I urged. Thank God, Camille started to move faster.

Heavy silence surrounded us as we made our escape.

"You can run," Mrs. James called after us. "But mark my words, I'll see that you face justice."

I let go of Camille and broke into a run. I didn't stop until I reached my car. Miranda and Camille were right behind me. When we were all inside and the doors locked, I finally looked in the direction of the reporters. I expected to see Mrs. James running after us, but she stood in the middle of the reporters, no doubt giving them an earful. I could only imagine how awful the six o'clock news would be that night.

"Shandra's mother!" I exclaimed as I started the car. "Oh my God!"

"I need to get out of here," Camille said, surprising both me and Miranda.

"We're leaving." I burned rubber as I peeled away from the curb.

"Pregnant?" Miranda asked, her tone laced with shock. "Phoebe, did you know anything about that?"

"No! You think I wouldn't tell you if I knew?"

"You think it's true?" Miranda continued.

The medical examiner would have done an autopsy. Undoubtedly, that's where the reporters had gotten their information. "I don't know," I replied. "But I bet they'll try to say it was Henry's baby. . . ."

"Do you think it was?" Miranda asked.

"I don't know!"

"Phoebe, take me to the bus station."

I threw a quick glance over my shoulder at Camille, who was chewing furiously on a nail. "What?"

"The bus station. I'm gonna head to Rochester."

"You're going home?"

"I can't stay here. Not right now. And I have nowhere else to go."

"Camille, you're gonna leave us?" Miranda asked.

"If I don't get out of here, I'm gonna have a nervous breakdown!"

We stopped talking, and the only sound in the car was some hip-hop tune on WBLK. The pounding bass was like a sledgehammer pounding on my skull. I shut it off.

"What about the cops?" Miranda asked. "Are you supposed to leave in the middle of an investigation?"

"I don't care," Camille said. "I really don't." And then she started to cry.

It was another moment of clarity for me. I'd fucked things up royally. My friends, who'd supported me in my quest for revenge, were stuck in this because of me. I had to fix this.

It was my job to make things right.

43

I DROPPED CAMILLE at the bus station. All three of us huddled together, holding on tight, as though we thought we'd never see one another again.

Then Camille got on the bus for Rochester, and I hoped she'd be okay.

"Did you ever think this would happen to us?" Miranda asked as we drove back to UB. "That this would become our lives?"

My chest was heavy as I faced her. "I know you blame me. How can you not?"

"Actually, I don't. Not anymore. I meant what I said in Dean Moratti's office. We had a choice, Phoebe. We chose to get involved that night. We're all to blame."

I smiled softly. "Thanks."

Miranda gave my hand a squeeze.

"I don't really feel like going back to our house," I told her. "I'll just drop you off, okay?"

"Where are you going?"

"To talk to Henry."

Miranda nodded. "Right. Do you think—"

"I don't know what to think. That's why I have to talk to him."

Miranda leaned her head against the headrest. "Who do you think sent the media to the dean's office?"

"Katrina, probably. Or Donna. Who knows? I guess it doesn't really matter."

"This is gonna be all over the news."

"I know."

"There's no way anyone will believe we're innocent," Miranda continued. "Once your face starts hitting the news—"

"I know that. Please stop reminding me." I rubbed a temple with one hand while handling the steering wheel with the other.

"I don't really feel like going back to my room, either. I'll go with you to the fraternity house. I want to see Damon."

"What'd he say about that article?"

"That he had an obligation to write something. That the paper's editor was going to write something much worse if he didn't."

"How do you feel about that?" I asked. I still wasn't sure I liked the guy.

Miranda shook her head. "I'm not sure. But I do think that maybe I can use him to our advantage."

"How?"

"He can write another article for the paper. This time, tell *our* story."

"Oh, Miranda. That's a *great* idea!"

"I'll see if he goes for it. He owes me that much."

Silence filled the car as I made a series of turns, getting back to Greek Row.

"Phoebe, stop," Miranda suddenly said. "There's Damon."

I quickly pulled the car up to the curb.

"Toot the horn," Miranda instructed.

I did, and Damon—as well as other students—started to turn. Miranda rolled down the window and started to wave. "Damon!"

Damon, who was walking with a male friend, turned at the sound of his name. When he saw Miranda, he smiled.

I saw warmth in that smile, which made me wonder if I was wrong about him. Maybe he hadn't just been into Miranda for the sex.

Not that I had the right to judge anyone, given the way Henry—who was my fiancé—had betrayed me.

Miranda sighed wistfully as she watched Damon approach the car. Had they worked out their issues? Lord, I didn't even know what was going on in my friend's personal life anymore. Before, we used to have so much time to chat about our love lives, but now that seemed like ancient history.

"Hang in there." Miranda gave me a quick kiss on the cheek. "Let me know how it goes with Henry."

"Yeah. Thanks."

As Miranda disappeared, my stomach filled with dread. My feelings for Henry had changed—I knew that now— but I still wasn't looking forward to talking to him about what I'd learned.

I was scared, I suddenly realized.

Oh my God. I understood now. What Morgan had said, it all made sense now.

How well do you know Henry?

Henry and I, we're closer than you know.

Shandra had told me that, even as we'd humiliated her. Now I wondered if her pregnancy was a motive for murder.

44

DESPITE HOW SCARED I was, how sick to my stomach, I still went to Henry's room.

Ten weeks pregnant.

Is that why you killed her?

The reporter's words continued to sound in my head, contributing to the stabbing pain in my temples.

I needed answers. Henry was damn well going to give them to me.

I knocked on his door. And waited.

No response.

Now I pounded. "Henry, if you're in there . . ."

Again, there was no answer.

I dug my cell out of my Gucci tote and punched in Henry's number. He answered on the first ring.

"Where are you?" I demanded.

"Who is this?"

"Who do you think it is?"

"Oh, Phoebe. Sorry. I'm with Coach Rawlins right now."

"I need to talk to you."

"I'll call you when I finish here."

Would he? "Listen, this is important. It's about Shandra."

Henry lowered his voice. "I know her mother's here. We'll talk about everything . . . later."

Then he hung up.

I wiped at a stray tear. Why was I crying? I knew I didn't want to be with Henry anymore. He didn't love me. And somewhere along the way, I'd stopped loving him. In fact, I think pride played a big part in why I'd been so angry with Shandra. Henry had been my man, my property. After I realized he and Shandra were having an affair, I'd fought for him for reasons other than love.

But I had loved him. With every part of me. And knowing that he had probably gotten Shandra pregnant felt as if someone had a hand inside my chest tearing my heart out.

I forced myself to think of Morgan. And finally, despite all the horrible things going on in my life, I smiled.

Henry started when he entered his room, his eyes bulging with alarm.

"Phoebe."

I was sitting cross-legged on his bed. "You never called."

I watched the rise and fall of Henry's Adam's apple, and wondered why he was nervous to find me there.

He looked . . . disheveled. Beneath his leather jacket, I could see that his T-shirt was only partly tucked into his jeans.

My eyes kept moving. Then stopped abruptly on his right hand. It was busted and bloodied.

I practically flew across the room to him. "Henry, what happened to your hand?" I took it in mine, examining it.

Henry pulled it away. "Nothin'."

"That doesn't look like nothing."

"I hurt it, all right?" he said testily, pulling it away. "In practice."

"In practice? I thought you wear gloves—"

"Why are you grilling me?"

"I'm not. I'm just . . ."

Henry groaned loudly. "You want the truth? I punched it through a wall, okay? Satisfied?"

I reached for his injured hand. "Oh, baby." That just slipped out. Old habits died hard. "Why?"

Henry stalked past me toward the room's window. "Why?" His tone was incredulous. "Are you honestly asking me that?"

"Yes. Of course."

He spun around and faced me, the look in his eyes lethal. "How about the fact that everyone's talking about how my girlfriend is a murderer and—"

"I didn't kill her."

"Shut up and let me talk."

I jerked backward from the shock of Henry's tone and words.

"It's not just your life you screwed up, Phoebe. It's *mine*. I couldn't play worth shit tonight, and the coach wants to bench me for a while. He doesn't want me showing up at the games because of the damn reporters. A few of them showed up today, on the field."

"Oh my God. I'm sorry."

"And you wonder why I punched a hole in the wall?"

Henry paced the room like a caged lion. Guilt hit me like a ton of bricks. "I really am sorry. . . ."

As I watched him, it dawned on me that Henry's anger had made me forget why I'd wanted to talk to him in the first place. Henry always had a way of making me do that, forget my own priorities.

"Henry . . ."

He gave me a sideways glance as he marched across the room.

"Shandra was pregnant." I said the words quickly, or I knew I might never do it. "Was it your baby?"

Henry yanked open his closet door and pulled out a duffel bag.

"W-what are you doing?" I asked.

"I've gotta get out of here. I'm heading home."

"Answer me. Was it your baby?"

"I'm sure you think it was. It won't matter what I say."

I wrestled the duffel bag from him and threw it onto the floor. "You owe me some answers."

Henry's eyes were cold and hard as he stared down at me. "What kind of answers do you think I have for you?"

"Was it your baby?"

"I don't know! Shandra was a whore, Phoebe. Anyone here could be the father of that bitch's baby."

And there it was. The truth.

I already knew, but still my head started to swim. I lowered myself onto the bed. I watched as Henry picked up the duffel bag, watched him head to his drawers and start taking out clothes.

"It's over, isn't it?" I asked. I'm not sure why I wanted him to be the one to say it. Why I couldn't tell him the truth myself.

Henry dumped clothes into his duffel and went back for more. "I got a call earlier. My mother fell down the stairs and hurt her back."

"Henry, no. Is it serious?"

"She'll live, but she's hurt pretty bad. I want to make sure she's okay."

Henry seemed to be packing all his clothes. "Maybe I can go with you," I offered, testing him.

"Are you allowed to leave the state?"

"I don't care. Who's gonna know?"

"Don't be stupid," Henry said. "You have to stay here."

"When will you be back?" I started to wonder if he would ever return. If he was really headed home, or running away.

"I don't know. Early next week."

"That long?"

"And I may as well tell you now, I'm heading to Berkley for medical school."

"What?" I shrieked. "But you said . . . we'd planned on Harvard . . ."

"I changed my mind."

Henry didn't look at me as he continued to fill his duffel bag. "I don't understand."

"Phoebe, I swear. You're gonna have to give me some space."

I realized in an instant what I was doing. Hanging on, when I really wanted to let go. Hanging on because of my pride.

"I need time to think," he went on. "I can't go anywhere without people looking at me. And everyone's talking."

"You don't care, do you? You don't care how you fucked me over."

He didn't answer. Just zipped up the duffel bag.

I walked toward him, grabbed his arm. "You cheated on me with Shandra, and all along I blamed her. I hated her. But this was your fault. I should have been angry with you."

"So you killed her?"

"You think that? You really think that? Or do you know I didn't . . . because you did?"

"Now you're tripping."

"Was it your baby?"

Henry shoved me aside. "Get out of my way."

I charged after him. "Did you fucking kill her? Kill her because you got her pregnant?"

Henry spun around and backhanded me. Crying out, I flew backward. I landed hard on the floor.

My eyes flew to Henry's. I expected him to gather me in his arms, apologize profusely for snapping. But he just stood there, his eyes enraged.

The taste of copper filled my mouth. I ran my fingertips over my lips, then looked at them.

They were covered in blood.

"Oh, my God, Henry. What are you doing?"

"Fuck, Phoebe. I told you. . . ." He didn't finish his statement. Instead, he grabbed the duffel bag, opened the door, and took off.

Morgan's question sounded in my brain: *How well do you know Henry?*

Apparently not at all.

45

A CROWD OF guys started to form outside Henry's door in the hallway. Sprawled out on the floor, being seen like this, I was humiliated and hurt.

Tears spilled from my eyes.

Part of me wanted to die. That was what I was reduced to. Because of Henry. Public humiliation, and people thinking I was capable of murder.

"Holy shit! Phoebe!"

I didn't look up at the sound of Morgan's voice. I was too ashamed.

Next thing I knew, he was beside me, gathering me into his arms. "Are you okay?"

I nodded jerkily.

"That son of a bitch."

Morgan lifted me to my feet. I stole a quick glance at the door and saw that even more guys had congregated in the hallway. I buried my face against Morgan's chest.

"Everybody's staring," I moaned.

Morgan released me and made his way toward the

crowd. "She's all right," he told the spectators, then shut the door. He hurried back to me, taking both my hands in his. "That fucking bastard. He hit you?"

"It's okay," I said. But it wasn't. How could it be? In all likelihood, Henry was a killer.

"Okay? It's fucking *not* okay! You need to call the police."

"No!" I shrieked.

"Henry hit you—"

"I know. But the last people I want to talk to right now are the police. You have to understand that."

"Phoebe . . ."

"No."

Morgan placed his hands on my shoulders. "Look at me." I lifted my gaze, looked into his eyes full of concern. "There's something you need to know. The police are gonna want to take Henry in for questioning regarding Shandra's murder."

"Because she was pregnant. I know."

"Yeah, I found that out today. Fucking pig." He gripped me harder. "But that's not what I was going to say. I heard something else today. And it's the reason you've got to call the police."

"Okay, you're scaring me. More than I was already."

"Another girl—I don't know who—said he roughed her up this morning." I felt the same brutal shock I'd felt when Henry backhanded me. "W-what?"

"It gets worse." Morgan blew out a heavy breath as he glanced away. "This woman—she apparently said that she was with Henry the night Shandra was killed. That he kicked her out of his room in the middle of the night after getting a phone call and was acting all strange. She said she hung out in the common room downstairs and saw him leaving a short time later."

My legs faltered.

Morgan threw his arms around me, cuddled me against him. "I know, and I'm sorry. This has got to be awful for you."

"*Awful* doesn't begin to describe what I'm feeling." No wonder Henry had quickly thrown some clothes together. He was trying to evade the law.

Morgan softly kissed my temple. "I'm here for you."

I managed a small smile as I gazed up at him. "I know."

"You want to head to my room?"

I nodded. "Yeah. At least for a little while."

Guys were still hanging out in the hallway. They tried to look casual, as though they hadn't had their ears to the door, trying to eavesdrop.

I knew that was bullshit.

Morgan held me closely to his side, and I didn't pull away from him. His arms were a safe haven.

Maybe it was the stress of what I was going through, but I was seeing Morgan in a whole new light.

I was seeing him as a potential boyfriend.

A short while later I sat cross-legged on Morgan's bed. My hands were wrapped around a mug of hot tea he'd prepared for me.

I was feeling . . . I'm not sure what I was feeling. Numb, I'd say. The day's events were overwhelming, too hard to comprehend. The news that Shandra was pregnant. The media swarming me and my friends. Henry hitting me.

My God, was he really capable of murder?

Morgan was sitting beside me, an arm casually draped around my waist. His fingers were on my flesh, softly stroking my side. He didn't say a word. He didn't have to. His presence said everything.

"Henry once asked me if I'd be in a threesome with him," I said, breaking the silence. "With another woman."

"Oh . . ."

I turned to look at Morgan then. "Don't get your hopes up. I told him no."

"I wouldn't want to share you with anyone." He brushed his lips across my forehead. "I want you all to myself." He moved his mouth to my jaw.

I sipped my tea. "I loved Henry so much."

Morgan stilled.

"No, you don't understand. I'm trying to say that I loved him so much, I would do almost anything for him. I really considered his threesome idea, to make him happy." I sighed softly. "It's something I would never ever want to do. But he asked me when I first sensed he was slipping away from me, and I actually considered it. It's so obvious now, I lost myself. I didn't know who I was with Henry."

Morgan pulled back from me. He didn't have to say it. I sensed his disappointment.

I leaned over and put the mug onto the floor. "Don't do that." I snaked my arms around his waist. "Don't pull away from me."

"I can't compete with Henry, can I?"

I nuzzled my nose against his neck. "I can't erase my relationship with him. But I'm ready to move forward." I breathed in deeply, inhaled the masculine scent of him. "With you."

"Oh yeah?"

Moaning softly, I nipped his chin. "Oh yeah."

A deep rumbling sounded in Morgan's throat. I planted my lips on his and urged him backward on the bed.

Right then I needed to forget all the drama, to feel alive again. To feel normal.

With Morgan, if only for a short time, I would feel whole.

46

AFTER MAKING LOVE with Morgan, I went back to the sorority house. I wanted to check on Miranda, make sure she was okay.

As I made my way up the walkway to the house, I heard, "There she is!" Then a group of people charged me. I jumped back in fright, not realizing they were reporters until I saw the camera flashes going off.

In my confusion I'd hesitated, but now I forged ahead. What the hell were reporters doing there at eight o'clock at night? Lord only knew how they'd recognized me in the dark. They threw the same questions at me they had earlier that day, and I kept repeating, "No comment," as I fought my way to the front door.

Paying no attention to my sorors and the pledges, I didn't stop hustling until I was upstairs at the door to my room. It was my only place of escape in that house.

The hand on my shoulder scared the crap out of me. I screamed, whirled around. Katrina stood beside me, scowling at me. She must have followed me upstairs.

"Effective immediately," she said, "you and Camille and Miranda will no longer be involved in any chapter activities. There's going to be a hearing, and you may very well lose your sorority pins."

"Yeah. Whatever." I loved the sorority with all my heart and soul, just as my mother had, but I couldn't muster enough emotion even to feel sad at Katrina's words. Right then, I just didn't care. Not after the day I'd had.

I guess my response surprised Katrina, because she turned and marched down the hall. Some of my sorors hung in the hallway. They watched me but didn't say hi. I opened my door and slipped inside.

I stopped short when I saw Miranda sitting cross-legged on Camille's bed. "Miranda." A relieved breath oozed out of me. "Hi."

"I didn't want to stay in my room. Not with the Wicked Witch of Buffalo hanging around."

I nodded as I slipped the tote bag off my shoulder. "No problem." That's when I noticed the bottle of vodka in Miranda's lap. I lifted my gaze to her eyes, saw that they were red and swollen, as if she'd been crying.

"Miranda . . ." I walked toward her, shaking my head sadly. "What are you doing?"

"Getting shitfaced." She burped and laughed at the same time.

"I feel so bad, seeing you like this. If I could take this back, I would. I'm the one who deserves to be going through this pain, not you and Camille." As I lowered myself onto the edge of the bed, an image of Camille earlier, distraught and barely functional, zapped into my mind. I had destroyed my friends' lives. "I don't care what happens to me. I wish I could turn back the clock and that Shandra was still alive. Even if she was pregnant with Henry's baby. Even if he publicly dumped me for her. I never wanted her dead."

"Was it his baby?"

"I don't know. But he admitted it could have been."

"Ouch." Miranda raised the bottle. "Have a drink."

"I guess I could use one." That was the understatement of the year. I wanted to numb my feelings as much as possible.

It had been devastating enough to deal with the realization that Shandra was pregnant. But how could I ever admit to Miranda that Henry had hit me when I'd tried to talk to him about it? How could I admit that I now wondered if he was the one who'd murdered Shandra?

I took the bottle of Smirnoff from Miranda and sucked back a liberal amount of vodka. I closed my eyes as it burned a path down to my stomach.

"Everyone said I was the most gullible girl in the history of the world, but I didn't want to believe it." Miranda's smile didn't reach her sad eyes. "Damon . . . I thought he wanted to be with me again. He's been so sweet the past couple of days. Then just about an hour ago we were getting hot and heavy, and he stops to ask me if we . . ." Her voice trailed off as she winced.

"What?" I all but shouted in alarm.

"I'm sorry. It's just so hard for me to repeat. He asked . . . he asked if we *raped Shandra with a stick!*"

I gasped in shock.

"Do you believe it? He's got his hands down my pants, and he asks me if we raped Shandra! I realized then and there, Damon isn't into me. He's into this story. And the sex, of course. I should have known from the beginning that he was an asshole."

"But where'd he hear that? Who would make up such a vile rumor?"

"I don't know, but I had to get out of there. He may

never publish our side of the story in the paper, and I don't care. I never want to see him again."

"I can't blame you."

"And Cheryl—that fucking bitch—she said I had a lot of nerve showing my face in the room after what I'd done. That room is partly mine, too."

"I'm sorry, Miranda."

"Don't apologize. We've been over this. It's not your fault."

I nodded. Then we fell silent. Miranda drinking, me thinking about Damon's words.

Had someone actually told him about this "rape," or was he being a complete asshole? With my father a defense attorney, I knew there were often facts of the case that weren't disclosed to the public. Was this one of those facts, and if so, did Damon have some kind of police contact who would have told him that?

"The icing on the cake is that I lost my job. They fired me after seeing me on the news."

"Oh, Miranda." I squeezed her hand.

"*Don't* apologize!"

I wanted to, but I didn't. Instead, I gave her a small smile. "No wonder you're drinking."

"You got it." She put the bottle to her lips and tipped her head back.

I was still pondering what Damon had asked her. "I know you're angry with Damon—and I would be, too—but you might have to talk to him again—"

"Phoebe—"

"No, hear me out. You have to find out if what he asked you—if someone told him that from a credible source."

"What are you thinking?" Miranda asked me.

"That there's something there, maybe. Something important."

"Like what?"

I took the bottle from Miranda's fingers and chugged back another swig of vodka. "I don't know, Miranda. I don't know."

47

AFTER MIRANDA PASSED out in an alcohol-induced stupor, I put on a UB baseball cap and went down the back staircase. I made my way around to the front of the building, then across the street, headed to the Zeta house.

But I stopped abruptly when I saw the people hanging out on the lawn. An instant later I heard the pulsating music.

No wonder I hadn't heard any sound in my sorority house as I'd crept down the back stairs. My sorors were at the Zeta party I'd forgotten all about.

I pivoted on my heel. Glancing back in the direction of the Alpha house, I saw a small group of people.

Reporters.

Friggin' vultures.

I wanted to see Morgan, but he'd probably be busy guzzling beer. Obviously I couldn't see him right now. I didn't want to skulk into the party and tell him that I needed to cuddle and make love again.

My head was buzzing from having vodka on an empty

stomach, and I decided to take a walk to clear my head. I headed the way most familiar to me—toward Frontier Road, where I turned to the right. If I continued that way, I would soon be at the Letchworth Woods.

I thought about Angelina, the path she had taken the night she'd been attacked. I remembered the night I'd been walking in the woods and thought someone was following me.

And yet I kept walking toward the woods, knowing it was foolish. But I was angry. Angry enough to be irrational and think I could draw the creep out from the shadows.

Was he watching me now?

Had he killed Shandra? Or had Henry killed her?

I got to the entrance to the bike path. I wanted to scream at the top of my lungs, dare a killer to come out of the shadows.

But I didn't. Try as I might, I couldn't step onto the path. I couldn't put myself in danger, not alone. Not at this time of night. I wasn't some kick-ass movie heroine with a gun.

The wind swirled around me, whistling through the trees as it made the leaves rustle. I shivered, but not from the cold. I was afraid.

There really was something out here—something evil. Was it the evil Shandra had faced on the night she'd lost her life?

I turned and started to run back toward Greek Row. Fear fueled me, making me run as fast as I could. I thought I heard something. Was someone behind me? Oh, God— was that creep going to murder me the way he'd murdered Shandra?

My chest burned and my sides hurt by the time I got to the Zeta house. I doubled over in relief and pain, gripping the stair's wrought-iron railing to catch my breath.

I'm not sure how long I was in that position, but after a while a thought struck me.

Man, I was stupid!

Why didn't I think of it before?

48

CATCHING MY BREATH, I ran past the few couples making out on the front steps and into the Zeta house. The hip-hop bass was deafening, and it thundered in my head, making my headache worse.

But I needed to talk to Morgan.

From the hallway I scanned the room. Some of my sorors looked at me in surprise. I guess they didn't expect to see me there.

Not seeing Morgan in the immediate area, I moved to the huge common room. Guys and girls were shaking their bodies to the rhythmic beat. Again I got some looks, but I ignored them on my quest to find Morgan.

And then I saw him. On the far edge of the makeshift dance floor. (The common room's furniture had been pushed aside to make room for dancing.) I sucked in a surprised breath when I saw that he was with Katrina and Evelyn.

Something about the way Katrina was standing close to and laughing with him had me thinking the worst. *Don't tell me she's into Morgan,* I thought sourly. Feeling a bad sense of déjà vu, I headed toward them.

Evelyn's eyes caught mine, and the smile on her face morphed into a frown. Then Katrina spotted me, and she glowered. As I neared the three of them, Evelyn said to me, "You know you're not supposed to be here."

"Don't worry, Evelyn. I'm not here to party with you. Morgan—"

"You need to leave, Phoebe," Katrina said. She grabbed my arm. "And now."

I looked at her fingers squeezing into my upper arm, then pulled my arm free. "I need to see Morgan, if you don't mind. What's it to you?" To my surprise, I felt a spurt of jealousy.

"I do mind," she said.

Evelyn pinned me with an ugly glare. "If you want a chance at keeping your sorority pin—"

"You don't scare me, Evelyn. So just shut up, okay?" I couldn't believe what a bitch she was being. One minute she'd been on my side where Shandra was concerned; the next, treating me like a leper.

"What are you gonna do—strangle the life out of me like you did to Shandra?" she challenged. Of course, she said it loud enough that people within immediate earshot could hear.

And then I felt something that surprised me. Rage. The kind of rage that had me wanting to pummel her. How dare she speak to me that way, after having befriended me before Shandra's death?

"Why don't we head outside?" Morgan said. My eyes flew to his. He saved me. He really did. Because I was so close to hitting Evelyn at that moment.

I *had* changed. Just as Morgan had said. I didn't like the person I had become. I didn't want to be that person.

"Fine," I said, backing away. "I'll just leave."

Crushed, I turned to leave. I'd lost too much already. How could I deal with losing Morgan? Sure, he wasn't technically mine, but still.

I nearly jumped out of my skin when I felt a hand clamp down on my shoulder. Then Morgan was moving in front of me, looking down at me with concern.

"What's going on?" he asked.

"I just . . ." I sniffled. "It's all right."

"No, it's not all right. Let's go outside where we can talk, okay?"

I nodded, and Morgan led me through the crowd to the door. Cold air enveloped us the moment we stepped onto the front steps. I needed that cold blast. It was sobering.

"What's going on?" Morgan asked me.

I should have asked him what I was most concerned about, but instead I blurted out, "What's up with you and Katrina? Or is it you and Evelyn? Or you and both of them?"

He shot me a surprised look. "Nothing."

"Nothing? Katrina didn't bite my head off because there's nothing going on between you two."

Morgan shrugged. "I don't know. She's been talking to me a lot lately. I guess she likes me."

Great. Just great. And what had happened to her boyfriend?

"So you . . . you're not interested in her?"

"Phoebe, why are you asking me that?"

"Because I don't want to be a fool for another guy who thinks it's okay to date me and screw other girls behind my back. So if you're interested in Katrina—"

Morgan put a finger on my mouth to quiet me. "Phoebe, stop. I'm not interested in Katrina. You know that. Maybe she likes me, but she's just a friend. How could I be interested in her when I'm crazy about you?"

Something inside me ignited, spreading warmth through my body. "I thought Henry was crazy about me."

"Please. Don't compare me with Henry. Okay?"

Slowly raising my eyes to his, I nodded. "Okay."

"Hey," he said. Putting a finger beneath my chin, he tilted my face upward. "I'm totally crazy about you. You do know that, right?"

"I think so."

"You think so? Oh, I'm wounded," he joked. Then he grew serious again as he trailed a finger along my cheek. "Maybe I haven't done a good enough job of showing you how I feel."

Butterflies fluttered in my stomach as Morgan lowered his mouth onto mine. He kissed me, a tender kiss that made me feel better.

When he pulled away, I moaned softly in protest. "I can show you more," he whispered, "if you want to go upstairs."

"Oh, don't tempt me."

He raised an eyebrow. "You have a better offer?"

I thought about Miranda passed out on Camille's bed. "No, not really."

"Not really?" he repeated, surprised.

"What I mean is, Miranda had too much to drink, she's passed out in my room, and I figured I should be there for her. If everyone's treating her the way they are me . . ."

Morgan linked his fingers with mine, and I went silent. Every time he touched me, kissed me, my body came alive in a way it never had with Henry. Maybe that's because Morgan had a way of making me feel cherished, even with the simple brush of his hand against mine.

"You can be there for her in the morning," Morgan said softly. "But tonight I need you with me."

My insides turned to mush. I tipped onto my toes to kiss his chin. "That's an offer I can't refuse."

"Good." He kissed me again, deeply this time. The kind of kiss that had me getting wet right there on that step, with a dozen people milling about on the lawn.

Aware that we needed privacy, I broke the kiss and whispered, "Let's go."

I was blushing as we went back into the Zeta house. I held on to Morgan's hand tightly, figuring everyone could read on my face what we were about to do. I stayed close to his side, not looking up for the most part. But as we hit the stairs, I felt a hand on my arm.

Gasping softly, I whirled around. Katrina snarled at me.

"I know you're a filthy killer," she spat out.

I rolled my eyes. "Do you mind? I've had about enough bullshit from you tonight. I'm about to get laid here."

Her lips tightened. "You might think you're smart because you haven't been arrested yet, but it's only a matter of time. Evelyn told me what you discussed, okay?" she added in a lowered voice. "She thinks you killed Shandra, and so do I."

I felt the familiar rage again, and this time I couldn't ignore it. I'd had enough of Katrina. I pushed her with all my might, shoving her backward onto the floor.

Her eyes narrowed into lethal slits. "You—"

"Fuck off," I told her, then turned back to Morgan. "I'm sorry, baby," I said sweetly. "You ready?"

He pulled me close to him, something Henry probably would not have done after a fight like that. "Let's go."

49

AFTER MORGAN AND I made love, I fell asleep in his arms. I didn't bother to bring up the question I had about Henry, because I knew it wasn't the time.

But as the bright morning sunlight spilled into the room, covering our naked bodies, I could no longer hold off on asking the question, because it was important.

"Morgan," I whispered, moving my head from his shoulder to look at his face. His eyes were closed, but still I asked, "You awake?"

"Mmm."

"Look, I know you're tired, but I have something to ask you."

He yawned. Wrapped his arms around me tighter. "Can't it wait?"

"Not really. I'm gonna head out soon, see how Miranda's doing."

Morgan rolled onto his back, opened his eyes, and looked at me. "It's not about Katrina, is it?"

"No. It's about Henry."

"Great." He rolled his eyes. "You know, I'm getting tired of hearing his name."

"Just hear me out." I placed a hand on his warm chest. "It's not what you think."

"All right."

"That night—when everything happened—you said you thought you saw Henry's car. I can't believe I didn't ask this before, but *when* did you see it? When you were heading *to* the scene, or *leaving* the scene?"

Morgan thought for a moment. "I was leaving," he said.

"So you saw Henry's car when you were heading back to UB," I stated.

"Yeah."

"Which means he was *on his way there*," I said excitedly. "And if you saw no sign of her, Henry wouldn't have, either."

"I was at the gas station, Phoebe. Henry could have easily already finished his dirty work and just been leaving the scene."

"When did you get gas—before or after you looked for Shandra?"

"After," he said slowly.

"Well, if it was after—what does that tell you? For you to have seen Henry leaving the scene afterward means when you first got to the scene he should have been in the middle of killing Shandra."

Morgan was silent, as though trying to figure out my time line. "Not if he took her somewhere else," he finally offered. "She could have been hiding somewhere else, which is why I didn't see her. Waiting for Henry to get there."

I sat up, facing Morgan. It was possible, but I didn't believe it. "You looked all around, didn't you? You would have found Shandra if she was there."

Morgan nodded. "Yeah, I guess."

"Then Henry didn't do it. He didn't kill Shandra." I actually giggled with relief.

How Shandra had gotten ahold of Henry to have him go pick her up that night, I had no clue, since she didn't have a cell phone with her. But maybe she'd put her pajamas back on, found her way to a pay phone, and had made a collect call. She'd obviously gotten a call in to Henry, and he'd agreed to go get her.

Had she stepped out of the phone booth and immediately been surprised by her murderer? The thought had me shuddering.

"So what are you thinking?" Morgan asked. "That you're gonna run back to Henry now? Was I just something to pass the time till he came back?"

I stared at him in shock. "No! Of course not."

"You sure about that?"

"Yes. I'm sure."

Morgan glanced away, unconvinced.

"Henry and I are through," I continued. "But that doesn't mean I'm not relieved to know he's not capable of murder."

"Hmm."

"What—you don't believe me?"

A slight frown marred Morgan's gorgeous face. "I don't know what to believe. You two were engaged."

"Yeah, and he didn't know how to keep his dick in his pants. I get it now. It took me a long time, but I get it." I shook my head, thinking of how Henry had betrayed me. "You know what the worst thing is—I thought he was just fucking Shandra. But like you said, he was obviously involved with at least one other girl. Hell, she said she was with him the night Shandra went missing. . . ."

My voice trailed off as an idea hit me. I really was determined to do my own investigation. "I have to talk to her," I said. "Do you know who she is?"

"Phoebe, for God's sake, let the police handle this."

"So I can be railroaded for a crime I didn't commit? I want to talk to this girl—"

Morgan groaned softly. "You know what, I don't think you're over Henry."

"You don't think I'm over Henry?"

"You heard me," Morgan retorted.

"You're wrong," I told him.

"Am I?" Morgan stared at me, a look of doubt in his eyes. "What do you think talking to this girl is going to accomplish? I mean, you've already figured out he didn't kill her, right?"

"I . . ." I didn't have an answer for him. The hell of it was, I couldn't deny what he'd said. I wanted to, but how did you erase five years overnight? Even when you wanted to?

"That's what I thought." Huffing, he lay down and turned his back to me.

"Morgan—"

"Not right now, Phoebe."

I sat there stupidly for a moment. But as much as I wanted to work things out with Morgan, that would have to wait. First, I had to head back to the Alpha house and check on Miranda. Then I had to see if I could find out who this girl was Henry had been with the night Shandra went missing.

I wanted to have a chat with her.

50

MY DOOR WAS unlocked. I opened it to find Miranda gone. That surprised me. With all the alcohol she'd consumed, I didn't figure she would be up and out of the room before eight.

I stepped into the room, closing the door behind me. Then I saw my bed—and drew up short.

Could it be?

Drawing in a shaky breath, I started across the room.

Good God in heaven, help me—it *was*.

My head started to spin out of control. I didn't understand how it could be possible.

But there was a belt on my bed. The rhinestone-studded belt I'd used on Shandra.

I stared at it, my insides churning. "What the fuck?"

My bed was neatly made—something I hadn't done the morning before—and the belt was laid out flat on top of the pale pink comforter.

My belt had been missing since that night. In fact, I was

sure I'd foolishly left it at the scene. *Maybe Miranda found it in her car,* I thought, my heart lifting. But to lay it out on my bed like that? It was a bit creepy.

Unless Miranda . . .

Unless she put it there deliberately to freak me out? I wondered.

Why the hell would she do that?

My mind started to work overtime. We'd all returned to the Alpha house that night, but what if Miranda had gone back out? Maybe her conscience had gotten the better of her and she'd planned to bring Shandra back. Only what if she and Shandra had minced words and things got ugly? Was it possible Miranda could have killed her?

Groaning with frustration, I fell onto my bed and gripped my head in both hands. What on earth was I thinking, suspecting Miranda of something so foul?

The whole situation had messed up my head, my thinking. Miranda was my girl. One of my best friends. She would never do anything to hurt me.

She must have found the belt in her car and put it on my bed. Simple as that. No big deal.

I didn't remember lying down to sleep, but when I heard the phone ring, I jumped up in fright. My eyes flew to the clock. Ten twenty-eight.

I reached for the phone on the night table beside my bed and dragged it to my ear. "Hello?"

"Phoebe, it's me."

"Oh, hi, Miranda."

"Something's going on, Phoebe."

Every call these days was some sort of bad news. My nerves were frayed, and the possibility of a nervous breakdown was very real. I didn't know how much more I could take.

I sat up slowly. "What is it?"

"Cops are all over Shandra's room."

"Her *room?*"

"Uh-huh. Apparently searching for evidence."

"Evidence?" I asked, shocked. "When her body was found downtown?"

"Apparently."

"I wonder what's going on."

"All I know is, they're downstairs right now."

"Why would they be *here*—and why now?" I wondered aloud. "Have you heard from that detective again?"

"No."

I wondered what that meant. If it was good news or bad.

"Have you?" she asked.

"No."

"They'll find our fingerprints," Miranda said. She sounded defeated—way past worried. As though she was just going to accept what happened next, no matter how awful.

I, on the other hand, didn't know what to feel. Scared out of my mind. Relieved. I had no clue. I guessed that would depend on what they found.

But I said, "Our fingerprints can be explained. We all live in this house. And Shandra was a pledge. It's not like there's some sinister reason for our prints to be in her room."

Miranda sighed. "I guess."

"I know it's easier said than done, but try not to worry. Somehow this will all work out." I really wanted to believe my words but wasn't sure I could. I wasn't that naive anymore.

"I'm trying."

A moment of silence. I broke it by saying, "I was surprised to find you gone when I got back to the room."

"I woke up about four, puked my guts out in the bathroom, then decided to head back to my room. Screw Cheryl. It's my room, too. She can't keep me out."

"How are you feeling now?"

"*Much* better. Once I got all that alcohol out of my system. Ugh," Miranda groaned. "I swear, I'm *never* drinking again. I don't care how bad I feel."

"Take some aspirin."

"I already did."

"Good," I said. And then I remembered. The belt. My stomach spasmed.

I blew out a frazzled breath. "Miranda, did you find my belt in your car? Did you put it on my bed?"

"What belt?"

"You know . . . the one that night. With Shandra."

"No, I didn't find it."

"It was on my bed when I came back to my room this morning. Laid out neatly on the sheets. My bed was also made. . . . You didn't do this?"

"Well, you saw me last night. I was a mess. Between then and now I didn't find your belt, and if I'd found it before that, I would have told you."

"Yeah," I said softly. "I know. But I was hoping . . ." My stomach sank as the worse option became clear.

"You're sure it's the same belt?"

"Absolutely sure. Remember my cute rhinestone-studded belt I got on sale last spring when we were at the mall?"

"Right, right. Damn, you think someone—"

"I don't know what to think," I admitted. "But I'm starting to believe that something's up, Miranda. Something bigger than we know."

51

MY PARENTS HAD left messages on my cell and room phones after my visit to the dean's office, but I'd been putting off calling them back. I wanted to do the chickenshit option and wait till that night and leave a voice-mail message for them, but in my heart I knew that wouldn't suffice. I could leave them a message assuring them that I was okay and totally innocent, but they would be freaked out nonetheless. No, I had to gather the courage to call them. At least my father. Right then, I needed his help.

Sighing deeply, I reached for the phone. I punched in the digits to his office number. Moments later his secretary answered and put me through to his office.

"Phoebe," he said in a long-suffering way.

"I know, Daddy. I've been meaning to call."

"What is going on with you?" His tone said he was exasperated from worry. "Do you know how out of our minds with worry your mother and I have been? My God, Phoebe, a *murder* charge—"

"I didn't do it."

"I know you didn't but, my God, how did you even get yourself mixed up in something like this? I've heard from the dean. Sorority hazing? You left that girl downtown alone?"

"Believe me, I know." Tears welled up in my eyes. Sure, I deserved some scolding from my father but, emotionally, I wasn't ready to hear it. "I'm sorry about all of this, Daddy. I was stupid, and things went horribly wrong."

"You know I love you," he said, sounding softer. "No matter what happened, I'll always love you."

"I know. And thanks. I needed to hear that right now." I blew out a ragged breath. "Daddy, I need your help. I'm starting to wonder if more isn't going on than what I thought."

"Meaning?"

"The cops are apparently here right now. Downstairs, searching that pledge's room. But the thing is, she was murdered miles from here. So why would they be here, days later, searching her room?"

"Could be a number of reasons. Want me to make some calls?"

"Would you, Daddy? I've got the detective's card. Can you call him and find out what's going on?" Not only was I afraid to call Detective Longhorne, I figured a call from my father the lawyer would persuade the cop to give out more information.

"You know I'll do anything to help you."

My heart lifted. "Thank you. Let me get his card."

I found Detective Longhorne's card and rattled off the number.

"One of my fraternity brothers is a lawyer in Buffalo. Let me make some calls, and I'll get back to you soon."

* * *

Twenty minutes later my father gave me a quick call to tell me he'd retained his friend, George Theron, as my attorney. He would be calling me shortly.

"Shortly" turned out to be close to an hour later. "Phoebe?" he said when I answered my room phone.

"Yes."

"I'm George Theron. Your father has retained me on your behalf."

"Yes, he told me to expect your call."

"I have interesting news for you."

"You do?" I said hesitantly. "Interesting good, or interesting bad?"

"Time will tell. I spoke with Detective Longhorne a short while ago, and he gave me a quick rundown of the case and why he questioned you. Why don't you tell me your side of things?"

I spent the next few minutes doing just that.

"So you and your friends left Shandra downtown because you had a flat tire, then you returned to your dorm."

"Yes, but like I said, I'd called my friend Morgan, who was on his way to get her. Only by the time he got there, he couldn't find her."

"Well," George began. "This is where it gets interesting. It looks like Shandra James returned to the dorm that night."

"No," I said, shaking my head. "That can't be right. How could she have gotten back here? She had no phone, no money. She was in her pajamas. Well . . . truth be told, she was naked when we left her, but the pajamas were still there, so I assume she put them back on."

"What did the pajamas look like?"

"Pink flannel. With—"

"White and blue polka dots?"

"Yes," I said slowly. Then realized that George would know that because they would have been found at the scene of Shandra's murder.

"Those pajamas were just found in a laundry bag in Shandra's closet."

His words hit me like a slug in the chest. "In her closet? But she died . . . she was found downtown."

"Behind a Dumpster."

"Naked, right?"

"Partially. Shandra was naked from the waist up, but she was wearing jeans. The jeans were pulled partway down her thighs, and there was evidence of sexual assault."

"Someone raped her."

"Yes." George paused. "But with an object."

I gasped in horror. And then I remembered what Miranda said Damon had asked her. *Did you rape Shandra with a stick?*

I almost asked George that, but something stopped me. I guess I didn't want him to think I knew too much, or it would make me appear guilty. Instead, I asked, "You said she was in *jeans?*"

"Yes."

"But we took her out in pajamas."

"Exactly. Pajamas that were just found two hours ago, discovered in her closet."

"But . . . how?"

"Apparently her mother was going through her things. There was a bag in the closet with discarded duct tape and pajamas inside. The duct tape made her suspicious, and she called police."

"I don't understand," I said softly.

"I know you didn't do this, and the fact that the deceased was found wearing different clothes—"

"Means she came back here, then was killed later—on the same night?"

"It would appear so."

My breath caught in my throat.

"I also get the impression—though the detective did say he might still want to question you in the future—that he doesn't believe you had anything to do with Shandra's murder."

"What?" Tears filled my eyes, and I moaned in relief.

"Listen, I'll keep digging. See what I can find out. See if there's someone else they're considering as a suspect. And I'll get back to you. Of course, if you hear from the police and they want to question you, call me."

"Yes. Definitely." I blew out a shaky breath. "I'm so . . . I'm in shock right now."

"I'm sure," George told me. "We'll be in touch, okay?"

I nodded. "Okay."

52

IT TOOK ME a good forty minutes to get over the shock.

Shandra had returned that night! Then she went back out later and was killed. . . .

It didn't make sense. How could that make sense?

Yet, if the lawyer was right about the clothes Shandra was wearing, that meant everything I'd believed was a lie. Somehow she *did* make it back to campus. She tossed her pajamas and duct tape into a bag—possibly for evidence?—then for some reason went back downtown.

I didn't understand. But I knew I had to talk to Shandra's roommate, Cassie. There was a good possibility that she'd been there when Mrs. James found this bag. Cassie could have some answers for me.

Unfortunately, when I went down to Cassie's room, she wasn't there. She was no doubt in one of her classes. If not off getting therapy to deal with all this trauma. I went back up to my room, and no sooner was I there than the phone rang.

I started for it, thinking it had to be the lawyer calling back. But when I answered the phone, I got the shock of my life.

"Hello?"

"Phoebe."

Oh my God. Henry!

Despite everything I had told myself over the past twenty-four hours, my insides warmed at the sound of his voice. I wrote the reaction off as relief. Relief because I didn't want to believe he had murdered Shandra. If he had, would he be calling me?

"Henry—"

"Phoebe, I'm sorry." Henry exhaled harshly. "I've messed up. God."

I gripped the receiver until my fingers hurt. That wasn't what I had expected him to say. Wasn't what I wanted to hear him say.

"Where are you?" I asked.

"Somewhere safe. For now. I'm in trouble, Phoebe."

I sank to the floor in front of the night table where the phone sat, another realization hitting me. If Shandra had somehow returned to campus, then she could have gone to see Henry—her lover. Despite the theory I'd tossed around with Morgan, there was still a possibility that he'd killed her.

God, no. Please, no.

"I know I hurt you, and I'm sorry."

I squeezed my eyes shut. I didn't care about how he'd hurt me. Not when Shandra had been killed and one of his fuck buddies assaulted. I blew out a deep breath and said, "Did you do what they're saying you did?"

"Baby, I'm sorry."

Tears spilled onto my cheeks, and I brushed them away with the heel of my hand. "You're sorry? That's all you have to say?"

"I know I shouldn't have called. But I needed to hear your voice."

"Why? You don't love me. You were screwing Shandra, and God only knows who else. Why did you kill her? Because she was pregnant?"

"Whoa, wait a second. *Kill* her? You think I killed her?"

"I know she called you that night. I know you went to get her."

"Yeah, I did. But I didn't kill her. I didn't even find her. Next thing I know, she shows up at my door. She's pissed because of what you did. And she was talking about the baby, how she was scared she might lose it. Suddenly she's talking about us moving in together, getting married . . . it was freaky. Especially when I knew that baby wasn't mine. Shandra slept with everybody."

So my theory was true. Shandra *had* gone to see Henry when she made it back to UB.

"So suddenly she wanted more from you and you killed her—didn't you?"

"Why would I kill her because of the baby? I'd bet money that a paternity test would prove she was a liar."

"Then why are you on the run? Why are you in trouble?"

"Because it's obvious someone's trying to set me up. I'm thinking Morgan."

"Morgan?" I asked disbelievingly.

"He's got the most to gain."

"That's crazy."

"Is it? He wants you, Phoebe. With me gone, he's finally got his chance."

Henry's words gave me pause. But I said, "This is not about me."

"Isn't it?"

My mouth fell open, but I couldn't form a word. I wasn't sure of anything anymore.

"Trust me, Phoebe. For once in your life, trust me. It's Morgan who's behind this."

"You're trying to tell me he murdered Shandra?"

"I'd bet money that he did, yeah."

I simply couldn't believe it. He didn't have a motive. And I couldn't imagine him setting Henry up.

"What about this woman who says you—"

"Oh, shit," Henry muttered.

"What?"

"I've gotta go. But Phoebe, watch your back."

"Hen—"

The dial tone sounded in my ear. After a moment I dropped the receiver to my chest and held it there as I sat, stunned.

Fuck!

Henry's call had given me more questions, but no answers.

53

HENRY'S PHONE CALL left me more confused than ever.

Watch your back. What the hell had he meant by that?

Clearly, as I'd suspected when I last chatted with Miranda, something else was going on. Something I didn't understand.

Or did I?

Watch your back.

It wasn't that I understood what was going on—how could I?—but I started to wonder if I had an inkling of what was actually happening.

Henry thought someone was setting him up. Was someone setting me up as well?

The rational side of me wanted to believe that was ridiculous, but the more I thought about it, the more it seemed possible. Why the belt on my bed? Why the clothes and duct tape in Shandra's room? Was any of this coincidence?

I sat thinking for five minutes, still holding the receiver

to my chest. Henry had all but accused Morgan of murder, but what if he was lying? What if that was what his call had been about—to rattle me, shake me even more than I already was?

If so, his plan had worked.

Until ten minutes earlier, Henry had never once said that he'd seen Shandra on the night she'd been killed. Why not, if he hadn't killed her? What did he have to hide?

I didn't want to think Henry could be responsible for Shandra's death, but the pieces seemed to fit.

Watch your back.

A chill ran down my spine.

Henry's words scared me. They scared me so much that I crawled under the covers and wasn't sure I'd come out until the police had announced that Shandra's killer had been arrested.

I was starving, but I didn't dare leave my room to eat. Worse than my hunger was my throbbing headache and aching heart.

Once and for all, I wanted this situation to end. I wanted my life to return to normal. If that was possible.

When my room phone rang again, less than an hour later, I quickly snatched it up. "Henry?"

Click.

I stared at the receiver in shock, but fear started to grow in the pit of my belly. Had that been an innocent call, or something worse?

Lying back down, I closed my eyes. But I knew there was no chance of getting any sleep.

Some time later there was a knock on my door. I nearly jumped out of my skin.

"What are you doing?" I asked aloud. "You can't start freaking out like this." I couldn't let paranoia kill me.

I threw off the covers and headed for the door. There was another brisk knock, and I edged it open a crack.

My heart slammed hard in my chest when I saw Morgan. "Morgan . . . what are you . . ."

"Are you all right, Phoebe?"

"Uh, yeah."

"I don't like how things ended with us earlier." He narrowed his eyes as he stared down at me. He had to be wondering why I hadn't opened the door for him. "Can I come in?"

Henry's words sounded in my head: *Someone's trying to set me up. I'm thinking Morgan.*

"Right now?" I asked lamely.

"I love you, Phoebe. Let's work this out."

Just the night before, I would have been elated to hear his proclamation of love. Now I was wary. Suspicious.

"Come on, Phoebe."

"I . . ." I what? What could I say to justify keeping Morgan out of my room, other than to say I was afraid of him? And I'd be basing my fear solely on Henry's speculation, which all of a sudden seemed pretty damn foolish.

I swung the door open. "C-come in."

He did. And when he leaned down to kiss me, my back stiffened.

"What's going on, Phoebe?" Morgan asked me pointedly.

"Nothing," I lied.

"You've heard from Henry, haven't you?"

That floored me, that he knew. But in a way I was relieved. I didn't want to lie anymore. "Yeah. He called about an hour ago."

"And? He begged you to take him back and you said yes?"

Looking into Morgan's eyes, I blew out a soft breath. I

saw, as I often did, gentleness. Concern. Vulnerability. How could I be afraid of him?

"No." I shook my head. "But he did say . . ." I stopped myself.

"What?"

"I don't want to talk about Henry."

"You don't want to talk about him," Morgan repeated in a deadpan voice.

"I am so confused right now, I feel like my head's gonna explode."

"You're confused about me?" Morgan asked in disbelief.

"Yeah, I guess I am. I'm confused about everything. One minute I'm engaged to Henry, the next I'm suspected of murder, and then I'm with you. Too much is going on, Morgan. I need a break."

"From me?"

"Yes," I replied, exasperated. "From you, from—"

I stopped short when Morgan gripped both my arms. Gasping, my eyes flew to his.

I tried to pull free, but he held me tight. "Morgan! What are you—"

"Don't do this," he said. "Don't break up with me now, not when we're finally getting our act together."

Terror took hold of my body, and my heart pounded out of control. "Let go of me!"

I wriggled and twisted until I broke free of his grip. I panted from the effort—and the fear. "What's going on with you?" I asked. "You're acting—"

"Did he tell you there's a warrant out for his arrest?"

"What?"

"I didn't think so."

"For murder?" I asked.

"For starters, assault. I'm sure murder will be next."

Morgan's words left me speechless.

"I love you, Phoebe. If I'm frustrated now, it's because I've waited so long to be with you. This is our chance. Why can't you see that?"

Morgan started for me again, and I jumped backward. What Henry had said a short while before finally clicked—that Morgan was probably setting him up so that he could have me.

Was it true? *Could* it be?

"Why are you acting like . . . like you're afraid of me?" Morgan asked.

I was saved from answering by the ring of the telephone. I darted for my night table and picked it up. "Hello?" To my own ears, I sounded like a scared kitten.

"Phoebe, are you all right?"

At first I didn't recognize the voice, then I realized it belonged to Evelyn. "Well . . ."

"Someone's there with you."

"Yeah, sure."

"Should I come to your room?"

"Oh, that'd be great," I said, relieved.

"Give me ten seconds."

I hung up but didn't face Morgan. I felt him moving closer to me. "Who was that?"

I turned to meet his gaze. "Morgan, I've got some sorority stuff to take care of. Can we talk later?"

Something sad passed through his eyes, and despite myself, the look broke my heart. "There isn't gonna be a later, is there?"

I didn't get to answer him, because the door flew open, and Evelyn rushed into the room. "Phoebe."

I whipped my head around to look at her. She wore a harried expression and eyed me and Morgan curiously.

"That was fast," I said. "But I'm ready to go. Just let me grab my jacket and my purse. . . ."

"Right," Evelyn agreed.

I scooped up my purse and grabbed my leather jacket off the back of a chair. Then I faced Morgan. He was staring at me with a helpless expression.

"Later, okay?" I said to him. I headed to the door, and he followed me. He stepped into the hallway and walked toward the stairs, not looking back.

"Are you okay?" Evelyn asked when he was out of earshot.

I nodded. "Yeah, I think I am." *As okay as I can be right now.*

A loud breath oozed out of me. I was thankful that Evelyn had called when she did, even though she wasn't my favorite person at the moment. "What did you want?" I asked her.

"You probably hate me, but we need to talk."

"We do?" I asked skeptically.

"Yeah."

She didn't elaborate, so I prompted, "About?"

Evelyn glanced around. "I don't want to talk about it here."

"What about my room or yours?"

"No offense, but I don't trust the walls. I'm starting to worry about who might be listening."

At that moment a memory zapped into my brain. I remembered Angelina's words just hours before she was attacked.

I'm starting to wonder who I can trust.

Alarm gripped me. In a whisper, I asked Evelyn, "What's going on?"

She sighed softly. "Look, can we just go for a ride and talk?"

"A ride?"

"Yeah. Away from this place. Somewhere safe."

"Safe?" The word was almost laughable. Was anywhere safe anymore?

"If you haven't figured it out, what I have to say is about Shandra."

"Shandra?" I felt like a broken record, repeating everything Evelyn said.

"I know you didn't kill her," Evelyn said, sounding sincere. "But I think I know who did."

That got my attention. Got it good.

"Someone close to you has an agenda. That's why we can't talk here."

"Don't tell me it's Rowena," I blurted out, and was surprised at my own words. But in my heart, I knew why I'd said it. Ever since Rowena had been suspiciously absent the night Angelina was attacked—and after seeing the two of them in some sort of heated discussion only a couple of hours before—I guess I'd been subconsciously wondering about the possibility of Rowena's having hurt Angelina. That and the fact that other girls from our sorority had clearly been targeted had me wondering if the killer wasn't some freak lurking in the woods, but someone closer to home.

But Henry was also someone closer to home.

So was Morgan.

"Do you know something?" I asked Evelyn.

She glanced around, as though she feared someone was listening. "Please, will you just go for a ride with me?"

I saw fear in Evelyn's eyes, and I knew I had no choice. I didn't want her dropping out of UB the way Angelina did before I could get any answers.

"Of course," I told her.

If Evelyn knew something, I wanted to know what it was. Even if it meant finding out a truth I wasn't prepared for.

54

I WINCED AT the cold as I stepped out of the sorority house with Evelyn. Cold fall days depressed me. They promised winter—and winter in Buffalo was tough to endure.

I had a feeling that would be the hardest winter of my life.

"You don't look so good," Evelyn said when I was buckled in her passenger seat. "Have you even eaten?"

I pulled down the visor and glanced at my reflection in the small mirror. Evelyn was right. I looked wretched. My hair was disheveled, and there were dark circles under my eyes. I had to have dropped five pounds in the last two days alone.

"No, I haven't eaten. I've been hanging out in my room. I'm totally stressed out."

"You want to go somewhere, get something to eat?"

"I don't really care," I answered glumly. "I'm not even sure I can keep anything down."

"You need to eat," Evelyn told me.

"I want to know what's going on more than I want food," I said.

"I'm sure you do." Evelyn shot me a quick glance before starting her car.

She started off, and neither of us spoke for a few minutes. I stared out the passenger-side window, looking at the landscape of large maple and oak trees with sprawling branches. At night, the way the moon illuminated them, the trees almost looked eerie.

A shiver danced across the nape of my neck. I didn't want to think about eerie. I didn't want to think about Shandra. I didn't want to think about what Henry or Morgan or God knew who else had done to her.

But I had to. That's why I was with Evelyn.

I closed my eyes briefly, then reopened them and faced her. "I have to admit," I said to her, "you have me pretty freaked out right about now."

"About as freaked out as I was when I realized that *Morgan* was in your room with you! You sounded really scared, and I knew something awful was going to happen if I didn't get to you right away."

"You—" My stomach sank. "You did?"

She flashed me a look that screamed, "Of course!" Then she said, "I guess you've probably figured things out."

My stomach curdled. "Morgan?"

"Some guys, Phoebe—they're just too good to be true."

Her words hit me like a Mack truck. Yes, Henry had warned me about Morgan, but something in my brain—or my heart—didn't want to believe he could hurt anyone. I didn't want to believe Henry could hurt anyone, either, and he'd apparently assaulted a woman and he'd definitely assaulted me. What did all this say about me? That I was too stupid to trust my judgment when it came to men?

"I don't want to sound stupid here, but are you saying that Morgan—"

"He has an agenda, Phoebe. He's told you some stuff about Henry, but I wouldn't believe what he's said."

"Like what?"

"You know what. About that girl he beat up."

"How do you know that?"

"I just do."

"And you're saying that's a lie?"

"I'm saying you have to question what Morgan said. Did it ever occur to you he was just trying to bad-mouth Henry?"

"Then why is Henry on the run? I'm so fucking confused!"

Evelyn didn't answer, and I sulked in my seat beside her. My head began to pound. I felt as if I were in some sort of psychotic maze, trying to work my way out.

"So you think," I began after a moment, "you think Morgan killed Shandra?"

"I think so, yeah."

"Oh, God." I slapped a hand to my forehead. Hearing her finally voice her opinion suddenly made it real. I thought of how Morgan and I had made love, how his tongue had caressed the most sensitive parts of my body. How I had connected with him in a way I never had with Henry. Had I given myself to a killer?

That day on the path, when he grabbed me . . .

"I can't believe it, either," Evelyn said, interrupting my thoughts. "I'd never have figured him the type to do something like this."

The sound of my labored breathing filled the car. God, I sounded like a wounded dog. I drew in slow and steady breaths to calm myself and willed my brain to work.

Obviously, Evelyn was guessing. I mean, she couldn't know for sure that Morgan was guilty—unless she'd seen him do the deed. So I asked, "How do you know? Or rather, why do you *think* that? It's important."

"Because of a chat I had with Katrina earlier."

"Katrina? What does she have to do with this?"

"We talked earlier and . . . she's worried, too. She wanted to talk to you quite frankly, but she didn't figure you'd listen to her. So I volunteered. We're both really concerned."

"So what you're saying to me has come from Katrina's mouth—nothing you know specifically."

"I trust Katrina," Evelyn said. "And she was really scared. Scared for herself—and for you."

Skeptical, I folded my arms across my chest. "Since when does Katrina give a shit about me?"

"She may not like you, but she doesn't want you murdered. Because that's the threat here, Phoebe, whether you realize it or not. In fact, she's at a restaurant waiting for us. She's hoping you'll agree to meet her there and talk."

I took a moment to let her words register. "So this is some sort of setup?"

"Don't make it sound so morbid. Like I said, she was worried you wouldn't want to talk to her. Can we go to the restaurant to meet her? Hear what she has to say?"

"She's right. I don't want to see her. And anything she said, I don't believe a word of it."

"I'm just telling you what she told me," Evelyn pointed out.

"And I'm telling you it's a load of bull. I don't want to see her. I want to go back to campus."

"Okay, okay," Evelyn said. "She figured you might not want to see her. So she asked me to bring something to show you. Something to prove her theory to you. But maybe I ought to call her first, see if it's okay."

This whole thing was one giant riddle and getting on my nerves. My frustration was mounting as Evelyn dug her cell phone out of her jacket pocket. Sighing, I closed my eyes. What the hell was going on?

"Hey, Katrina. I'm with Phoebe right now. Yeah, I got her away from Morgan, thank God. But she's not sure about your suspicions—I guess she doesn't entirely trust you, which you figured might happen. So I just wanted to know—should I show her the thing now?"

As I listened to Evelyn's end of the conversation, I was more confused than ever.

"I should?" Evelyn asked. "Okay."

"Let me talk to her," I said.

Evelyn lowered the phone. "She just hung up."

"Fine. What is this *thing* that you want to show me—what kind of *proof?*"

"Something Morgan had," Evelyn told me. While holding the steering wheel with one hand, she reached into her jacket pocket with the other. She produced a necklace.

I recognized it immediately. The pink and white heart-shaped diamond necklace.

The same one I'd seen on Shandra the night we took her out for that initiation.

55

"MORGAN . . . HAD . . . THAT?" I barely got the question out.

Evelyn nodded. "Apparently, he had the nerve to give it to Katrina earlier today. He didn't realize that she'd seen it before. According to her, she played cool, but she suspected that if he had this necklace, he had to have taken it from Shandra. Shandra was so proud of it, she never took it off her neck."

I wasn't sure what was more shocking—that Evelyn was practically saying Katrina and Morgan had a relationship or that Morgan had had Shandra's necklace in his possession.

Then my brain started to work. "Has it occurred to you," I began, "that Katrina is lying? That if she had that necklace, *she's* the one who killed Shandra?"

"You think?" Evelyn spoke lowly in a voice filled with horror.

"It's a definite possibility," I said. "I wouldn't trust her."

"Truthfully, the thought *did* cross my mind," Evelyn admitted.

"And what are you supposed to do when you've brought me to her? Leave us alone to chat?" I was more wary with each growing second.

"Yeah . . ."

"Wow. That's a surprise."

"Why—you think she wants to hurt you?"

"I'm more than starting to wonder, yeah."

"But if you meet at a restaurant, what can she do to you there? Maybe you're jumping to conclusions. I know we're all searching for answers here. And you're smart to question Katrina's suspicions. I did, too. But then I thought about it—and the more I thought about it, the more I started to see her point. I know for a fact that Morgan isn't the man you think he is."

"How do you know that?" I asked. An idea was taking shape in my mind—an awful one regarding Shandra and Katrina. I could see Shandra heading back to the sorority house after we'd left her downtown and heading straight to the sorority's president to tell her what we did. Then, in a shocking twist for a reason I might never understand, Katrina had taken the opportunity to murder Shandra.

"He fooled all of us, Phoebe. No, I think Katrina's right. When I found out that Morgan had screwed Shandra, too—I think he thought the baby was his."

"What?" I shrieked.

"I know. You think you know someone. . . ."

Shandra and Morgan. *Katrina* and Morgan. *"Morgan was sleeping with Shandra?"*

"What guy wasn't?" Evelyn asked sourly.

I was stunned. And horrified. Why wouldn't Morgan tell me that?

And then Katrina, a girl I could barely stand. "So

Katrina . . ." I swallowed hard. "She and Morgan . . . they were dating?"

"If you want to call it that. I think a better description is fucking."

"But he gave her a necklace—"

"He was upset this morning, thinking you were going back to Henry."

"Holy shit," I whispered. Any doubts I had were just erased.

"I don't think he ever truly cared for me," Evelyn went on. "I was just a distraction for him."

My stomach sank. Lord, I'd been hoping that Evelyn was wrong, but she knew too much. And the timing of our disagreement that morning . . .

"Wait a minute," I suddenly said. "What do you mean you don't think he ever really cared for *you?* That *you* were just a distraction for him? You just said he was involved with Katrina."

Evelyn looked at me long and hard. I thought she wasn't going to answer, then she said, "I slept with him, too."

My head started to spin. "You . . . you what?"

"If we're being completely honest here. It hasn't been going on long. Most recently, it was a couple of nights ago."

"Oh my . . . oh . . ."

"Like I said, you think you know someone. . . . You can't trust men, Phoebe."

"I don't understand."

"What's to understand? Morgan's a guy. He likes to fuck. Anything."

No, not Morgan. *Please,* not Morgan.

I needed more answers. "You said Katrina wants to talk to me?"

Evelyn nodded. "She's waiting at the restaurant right now. Do you want to go there?"

I nodded grimly.

For the first time I noticed that we were driving along the 33 Expressway toward downtown Buffalo. Hard to believe, I know, but I was so wrapped up in what we were discussing that I wasn't even thinking of anything else.

Now, however, I glanced around and asked, "Where are we going?"

"The restaurant's downtown. Sorry. It was Katrina's decision. She didn't want to go anywhere on campus. And there's this Italian spot downtown that she loves."

"Oh."

"That's not a problem, is it?"

"No." Shivering, I wrapped my arms around my torso, but I didn't get warm.

"Have you heard from Henry?" Evelyn asked me after a moment.

"I . . ." I paused, debating whether or not to share that with Evelyn. But we'd just discussed something far more serious—Shandra's murder. "Yeah. Yeah, I did."

"Is he going to turn himself in?"

It's weird how your subconscious can throw you a piece of information at the oddest time. And that's what happened to me right at that moment.

"Phoebe?"

"Oh, um, I don't know. We didn't talk for long. Ev—"

"Where is he?"

"He didn't say."

"Oh?"

"Evelyn, watch out!" I yelled as her car swerved dangerously close to the sidewalk.

"Shit!" she exclaimed, and the car hit the curb. I screamed, as though I thought we'd plow into a building. Mostly it was my nerves. I closed my eyes and counted to five.

Beside me, Evelyn was cussing in a steady stream. My

mind jerked back to my earlier thought. The thing that had struck me as odd.

If Evelyn and Morgan had been sleeping together, why hadn't he even given her a second glance when she came to the room? With Henry, that's what had pretty much given away his infidelity—I could always sense he was trying to avoid Shandra if she was around us, other than at the party and in the cafeteria when she'd been all over him. Guys just aren't that slick when it comes to cheating.

If, according to Evelyn, she and Morgan had been together just a couple of nights before—at a point when my relationship with him had heated up significantly—wouldn't Morgan have felt uncomfortable seeing her come to my room? At the very least, considering he'd been saying that he loved me, he would have to be worried that Evelyn would spill the beans. Yet his attention had been fully on me, not on Evelyn at all.

Which meant Evelyn was lying. So, what was this—one big fishing expedition for Katrina's benefit? For hers? Was she really lying about Morgan in hopes that I'd give him up?

"People are saying that Henry beat up some girl, that the police want to arrest him for that. I'm sure you've heard." She'd apparently heard everything else. "Do you know who this girl is?"

"Yeah, I do."

My eyes flew to hers. "Who is she? I have to talk to her!"

A few beats passed as I waited for her to answer. I don't even think I took a breath.

Then an eerie feeling passed over me. Evelyn's lips turned in the slightest of smiles.

"You're talking to her right now," she said coolly.

56

I STARED AT her, not understanding.

"Oh, don't give me such a clueless look. You know what I'm saying. I'm the woman, Phoebe. I was with Henry the night Shandra called and asked him to pick her up from downtown."

That was a lie. Some sort of sick, disgusting lie. Yet Evelyn's expression was too smug. My God, she was telling the truth.

"You what?"

"You heard me."

My mind struggled to make sense of her bombshell. To understand why she was telling me this.

"But . . ."

"But what?"

"B-but," I sputtered. I took a moment to try to calm myself. "You were the one who told me I had to watch out for Shandra, that she was after my man. You understood what I was going through. And all this time, you and Henry . . ."

"Oh, you think that I've been fucking him for months?

I haven't. That happened only after you refused to let me help you take care of that slut who stole the love of my life."

I was too confused to understand any of this. I couldn't say a word.

"I tried to help you," Evelyn went on. "And you straight-up dissed me. Then you acted all high and mighty, like you were better than me. I thought that was deserving of a little payback."

"I have no clue what you're talking about."

"That's because you think the world revolves around you."

I didn't even bother to deny that accusation, considering it was completely ridiculous. I may have been a little preoccupied with my love life, but I did *not* think the world revolved around me.

Evelyn hit the power button on the car's stereo, and the soulful sounds of the late Luther Vandross filled the car. I gaped at her. Slow jams at a time like that? Maybe she was schizophrenic.

"You know, Evelyn, I'm sorry if I hurt your feelings—"

"Hurt my feelings?" She laughed without mirth. "Hurt my feelings? Bitch, what you did was disrespect me, when I was looking out for you."

"So you started fucking my man. Makes a lot of sense to me."

"Fuck you, Phoebe."

"What is this about?" I demanded. "Are you and Katrina trying to ruin my life?"

"You want to know what this is about?" Evelyn hit the gas, sending my body backward with the initial burst of speed. She whizzed around the bend at the end of the expressway, and I gripped the sides of the seat for leverage. Evelyn took the corner at such a high rate of speed, I feared the car would spin.

But it didn't. I wanted to throw the door open and jump out, but I knew that was a crazy idea. When we got to the restaurant to meet Katrina, I'd just catch a cab back. Then cut the psycho off for good.

"In case you haven't figured it out, we're not meeting Katrina at her favorite Italian restaurant."

The car slowed. Panic kicked me in the gut when I realized that Evelyn was turning into the driveway behind the building where I'd taken Shandra after midnight on October 3.

"Oh my God," Evelyn said with a laugh. "You should see the look on your face. It's like you've seen a ghost!"

"W-what are we . . . what's going on?"

"I for one think this is fitting. It's where it began, and it's where it will end."

Where it will end. . . . The words sounded ominous.

"So where's Katrina?" I demanded. "You had her on the phone. Is she waiting for us or not?"

Evelyn spit in my face. I reeled backward, gasping in disgust. If I had any questions as to her mental state, I no longer did.

Grimacing, I wiped the gross glob off my cheek with the sleeve of my jacket.

"And if you think I really had Katrina on the phone, then I've got some swampland to sell you in Florida."

Slowly my eyes widened in horror. I finally *understood*. Holy shit. Evelyn had killed Shandra!

Worse than that, I had a pretty good idea that she hadn't taken me out to shoot the shit or to gloat. I had no clue why, but she wanted me dead, too.

"You're psychotic," I told her, and turned in my seat. I undid my seat belt. Then I reached for the door handle with my left hand, because I was secretly digging into my right pocket with the other hand. My cell phone was in there, and I knew it would be my only hope.

"Oh, no no no. You're not going anywhere." She snagged my arm in a viselike grip, jerking on me. As I faced her, I saw she had produced a gun seemingly out of nowhere.

"Evelyn, *what* are you doing?"

"I bet your whole life you've been spoiled. Getting everything you wanted with just the snap of a finger. I wanted that. Wanted that life. And I thought I had it with Jonah. I gave him everything. And then Shandra stole him from me."

"Exactly. *Shandra*. Not me." I pressed a button on my phone—and held. *God, please let this work,* I prayed. *Please let it work.*

I didn't know who I'd reach with my one-touch dialing. I prayed it was Miranda or Morgan.

"Which is why I thought you'd understand, that you'd appreciate my wanting to help. But no, you didn't. You looked at me like I was lower than dirt."

"That's not true."

"My whole life, people like you have been looking at me like that. People from privilege. Like that tramp, Shandra."

I knew Evelyn had to be crazy. Seriously. "If you felt that, I'm sorry." I couldn't tell if my phone was ringing, if someone had picked up on the other end, or what. But I did something brazen—because if someone had picked up, I needed to be heard. I reached for the car stereo and shut it off.

A look of evil on her face, Evelyn raised her eyebrows in surprise but otherwise said nothing about my bold move. "I think we both need to hear what we each have to say," I told her by way of explanation.

"Whatever."

"I've never thought that about you, Evelyn. That I was better than you. Honestly. We haven't been best friends, but I never thought that, not even once. And to bring me here, where Shandra was killed . . . I don't understand."

"I didn't realize how much I hated you until after Shandra was dead, and suddenly you and Henry were all kissy-face again, and you never once even tried to talk to me. And I thought, bitches like you have always had it easy. I made things easy for you. And I thought, I want what you have."

"Meaning Henry."

"Or maybe I wanted to see you flustered for once in your fucking privileged life. But the moment Henry stepped out of line, you went right to Morgan. How do you do that? Get everything you friggin' want whenever you want it?"

Part of me wanted to answer her ridiculous questions by telling her she was delusional and needed help. Because, honestly, I couldn't make sense of any of the shit she was spewing. Was she jealous of me, angry with me, angry with men? I couldn't figure it out.

But that made things much worse, because it meant Evelyn was unpredictable. If she *was* crazy—and I had no doubt that she was—then that meant she couldn't be reasoned with.

My only hope was to keep her talking so that hopefully the person on the other end of the line would be able to figure out where I was and that my life was in danger.

"So you want to kill me, Evelyn?" I asked, making sure to say her name. "You're going to kill me the way you killed Shandra?"

"You're not too dumb after all," she replied, chuckling as though it all was a sick game.

"Okay," I said. "I get it now. I know why you're doing this."

"Do you?" she asked. "Do you get the point?"

"You wanted some revenge on Shandra, just like I did, and you came to me, wanting to help me. I should have included you in my plans. But I didn't. And that hurt you. I can . . . I can see why." I was scrambling, hoping I'd get through to a madwoman.

"That is *not* the point!"

Oh, shit. I drew in a shaky breath.

"Did you not hear a word of what I said earlier? You were never *grateful,* get it? I cleared the way for you and Henry to work things out, and you didn't even look twice at me after that."

"But I didn't—I didn't know—what you'd—done."

"Ugh, it doesn't matter."

"Yes!" I cried out, fearing Evelyn would pull the trigger any second. "It does matter. Tell me what I can do to make this better."

"Phoebe, are you afraid of me?" Evelyn asked calmly.

I wanted to lie and say no but couldn't form the word.

Evelyn chuckled without mirth. "Ah, life. Sometimes it just doesn't turn out to be what you expect, does it?"

I started to snivel. "Please don't kill me, Evelyn. You want me to beg? Because I will. I don't want to die, okay? Evelyn, I'm sorry I hurt you in whatever way I did, but I don't want to die. So please, let's just head back to the Alpha house and forget this ever happened. Evelyn, I promise I won't say a word of this to anyone."

With each word, I'd been silently praying that I would have some effect on her. That the crying, defeated act would work. Now I didn't breathe as I looked at her, waiting for her response.

Her lips curled in a creepy grin. "Oh, Phoebe. If only it were so simple. But I'm not stupid enough for that. No siree, wouldn't find me buying any swampland. And you won't be returning to the Alpha house. Except perhaps in a body bag."

57

EVELYN HELD THE gun between us. I pressed my back against the seat as far as I could, but it was a futile attempt to escape Evelyn, whose threatening presence seemed to fill the entire car.

"Just tell me why," I said. "Why Shandra. Why me."

"Well . . ." She angled the gun, looking at it admiringly. "Shandra was a worthless bitch who deserved what she got for ruining my life. You—you're just a worthless bitch."

I gulped at the insult but told myself to forget it. Evelyn was deranged, her words meant nothing.

She moved the gun, and I gasped in alarm. A smirk spread over her face. "You really are jumpy."

What do you expect, for God's sake! But I said, "I don't understand how it happened. How'd you get to the scene? I mean, I was shocked to hear that Shandra made it back to campus on her own."

"Shandra did what she does best—used her sexuality to get what she wanted. Apparently hitched a ride. And I was ready for her, Phoebe."

"I still don't understand. What does that mean?"

"Oh, do you think I was lying when I said I was with Henry that night? Well, we were together. And he kicked me out of his bed as soon as Shandra called. I was pissed—so I left. But I realized you must have done something. I knew this was my night to strike. I went back to my room and waited."

"And then what—you killed her in her room and managed to get her out of the building yourself?"

"Nothing so . . . careless. After I'd talked to you about Shandra that day in the cafeteria, I knew it was only a matter of time before you went after her. So guess what—I talked to Shandra, told her I was 'worried' that you were planning some sort of illegal initiation for her, and told her that the moment you did anything out of line, she should tell me. I knew you'd plan it when you thought you'd get away with it. I told Shandra to come to me the moment you did it, no matter how late. I didn't know if she would, of course, but I assumed she'd want to. So when she came to my door all irate, telling me about what you'd done, I just had to have her show me the location so we could build a case against you with the police. I almost feel bad, it worked out so well. She was showing me where you'd had her barking like a dog and I smashed a rock against her head. It didn't kill her, just knocked her to her knees, and I was able to strangle her."

I listened to this macabre story in a state of horrific disbelief. That Evelyn could relate it so calmly was chilling—as though she'd do it again if she had the chance.

She *would*—with me.

"And news flash," she went on. "The real reason Henry's on the run is because I threatened to say he's been beating me and that I saw him leave with Shandra when she returned to the sorority house that night. The bitch was pregnant and he was likely the father. Henry knew how it would look if I came forward as a witness."

"Why would you do that?" Although I wasn't sure I wanted to know.

"Because it was fun, that's why. And I wanted him away from you. He couldn't just fuck me and push me aside like that, go crawling back to you like I was nothing. And, hey, it's not like I didn't do you a favor. Henry's scum." Evelyn chuckled like a hyena. "The poor fool thinks the cops are looking for him right now. Wuss."

So Henry was running like a scared chicken. I wasn't surprised.

But there were more important things for me to deal with right then, like Evelyn's confession. There was something else I wanted to know, and somehow I managed to ask, "I heard . . . something . . . that Shandra was raped? Did you . . ." Maybe some vagrant had found Shandra's body and violated her. Surely Evelyn couldn't stoop so low.

"That bitch was used to all kinds of dicks inside her. I thought it was a fitting way for her to be discovered."

My stomach lurched. I wanted to puke.

"Evelyn, I promise"—I made the sign of a cross over my heart—"I promise I'll never repeat a word of this. You and me, we can work past our differences, but—"

"Duh, I know you won't repeat a word of this. Corpses can't talk."

I whimpered. Had anyone heard me speaking on the phone? Was there any help on the way?

"Now this is what you're gonna do," Evelyn began. "You're gonna write a suicide note."

My heart pounded out of control. "Nooo . . ."

"You don't have a fucking choice here, Phoebe. If you do this my way, I promise I'll give you a quick shot to the

heart so you won't suffer. But if you do this the hard way—
then you're gonna die the hard way. And before you think
about fighting me, think about how it must feel to get shot
in the knees—something that won't kill you but will cause
you a lot of pain. Think of all the ways I can torture you."

"If you shoot me in the knees, no one will believe I
committed suicide," I said.

She pressed the gun to my forehead, an act meant to
terrify me. Which it did. Right then and there, I made my
split-second decision. There was no way in hell I would
play this game her way. If she was going to kill me, she'd
have to fight me to do it. A messy fight.

The moment she pulled the gun back, I reached for the
power lock with my right hand and hit the button. When
the click sounded in the car, Evelyn's eyes widened in
surprise.

I acted fast, ramming the heel of my hand into her nose.
I caught her off guard, and in those precious seconds I
twisted my body around, yanked on the door, and lunged
forward.

"Bitch!" Evelyn yelled.

Then a gunshot exploded, and I felt a blast of heat in
my calf. I screamed and tumbled out of the car.

I started moving, blocking the pain from my mind. I
couldn't allow myself that distraction. I scrambled to my
feet as best I could and began a frantic hobble toward the
street.

It was then that I heard the sirens.

Excitement spread through me like wildfire, giving me
more energy. I threw a quick glance over my shoulder and
saw that Evelyn was charging after me. She aimed the gun,
and I ducked.

A bullet whizzed past me.

Adrenaline made me pick up speed. Panting, I charged
ahead, trying to keep low as I ran. I couldn't resist another

look over my shoulder, and my entire body froze as I saw
Evelyn point the gun low in my direction.

I was out in the open with no place to hide. Instinctively,
I closed my eyes and braced for the hit.

But nothing happened. I opened my eyes to see Evelyn
throwing the gun with an angry toss.

Relief rolled over me in waves. Sweet Jesus in heaven,
had the gun jammed?

Evelyn started after me, and I bolted into action. The
sound of sirens was louder now, and the road was in sight,
but I didn't see any cruisers. Grunting, I moved as quickly
as my injured leg would allow, darting into the road and
right into the path of an oncoming car.

"Help!" I screamed, waving both arms in the air.

The driver hit the horn and careened around me.

"Oh, God, no." I looked to the left. As more cars drove
by, Evelyn stood on the sidewalk looking at me as though
wondering what to do.

Then she stepped onto the street.

Shit! She wasn't going to give up. Fear kicking in again,
I took off to the right, crossing the street at the same time.
I couldn't see any sort of open business immediately
before me—exactly what I'd liked about the area when
I'd first scoped it out.

But I could see a gas station in the distance, and the
lights were on. And, shit, it was on the side of the street
I'd just crossed from.

"Phoebe! Come back here. We have to talk!"

God, where were the cops?

When I hit the intersection, I finally saw the flashing
lights. I almost cried with relief.

Running into the street, I again waved my hands over
my head and screamed.

The sound of screeching tires, followed by a thud and
a groan, had me spinning around.

I didn't immediately see Evelyn. But then I spotted her in the glare of a car's headlights, her body sprawled out in the middle of the street about twenty feet away.

The car door opened and a screaming woman emerged as the first of three police cruisers came to a screaming halt.

My entire body shuddering, I watched the scene playing out in front of me in a state of numbed disbelief.

Evelyn wasn't moving.

I finally broke down and cried.

58

THE NEXT FEW hours were a blur of insane, surreal activity. First, I was taken to the hospital to have my leg treated. I had what the doctors called a flesh wound—meaning the bullet had broken the skin but hadn't caused any extensive damage. I would be okay, and I didn't have to stay the night.

I was surprised to see Morgan arriving at the hospital as I got there, but I learned that he'd arrived on the scene shortly after the police had. He was the one I'd reached with my cell phone. I guess it was fate.

The police never left the hospital, wanting to take me into the station once I was finished there. That's when the reality of the night's events finally hit me, and I was scared. Scared because I would once and for all have to come clean about my role in Shandra's death. Oh, I hadn't killed her but I'd certainly made it easier for Evelyn to.

Morgan promised to follow me to the police station and wait for me, no matter how long the questioning took. There, the cops questioned me about Evelyn, questioned me about Shandra, about Henry. About everything, really. I spilled information like a woman in a confessional—denying the offer to have my lawyer present.

At first Detective Longhorne hadn't been in, but he arrived about half an hour after I did to take over. I told him the story from the beginning—how I'd been insane with jealousy, how I'd wanted Shandra to pay, but I'd never wanted her dead. I had, as I'd told him in the past, wanted only to humiliate her. This time I told him about whacking her with a belt a few times. I know I didn't have to, but I needed to purge myself and let the chips fall where they might.

"So your boyfriend, Henry—he's on the run somewhere right now?"

My hands wrapped around a Styrofoam cup of coffee, I nodded. "Yeah. But he . . . he isn't my boyfriend anymore."

The detective nodded his understanding. "You don't know where he is?"

I shook my head. "No."

"Guess you can call him. Tell him to come home. Considering there are no charges against him."

"I'll leave a message for him," I said.

"You gonna be okay in here for a few minutes on your own?" Detective Longhorne asked. For the second time since I'd been dealing with him, his eyes held what seemed genuine concern.

"Yes. I guess." *As long as I don't have any more of this awful coffee.*

"But . . . but can my friend come in here and see me?"

The detective smiled. "Yes, he can. You're not under arrest. You're just here for questioning. And I appreciate your being so forthcoming."

Less than a minute later, the door to the interrogation

room opened and in flew Morgan. He gathered me in his arms right away.

I held on to him with all my might, not wanting to let go.

"It's over," I finally said.

Morgan pulled back and kissed me on the forehead. "Tell me everything."

At the hospital I'd been able to give him only sketchy details, and now I filled him in on the evening's sordid events.

"Evelyn." I shook my head with chagrin. "Can you believe it?"

"I can't," Morgan said. "This whole thing's fucked up."

"I guess I should call Henry. And not because I still love him," I quickly added. I offered Morgan a soft smile. "You shouldn't question that, not anymore."

"I don't." He took my hand and squeezed it. "And I agree. You don't want Henry heading for the Mexican border."

A grin tugged at the corners of Morgan's sexy mouth, and we both laughed for a moment, trying to imagine a scared Henry running like a fool.

I could easily imagine the conversation Henry and I would have when I reached him. He'd be so relieved that he'd probably propose all over again. I was pretty damn sure that he'd tell me he still loved me, and beg me to take him back. But this time there would be no going back to him.

Once, I thought that we fit together so well—that we were destined to be together forever. Suddenly that seemed so long ago, like another lifetime.

In a way, it was.

Now I knew that I needed more out of a man. I *deserved* more. It's funny how clear things become when you look back at them. Never again would I settle for less than 100 percent fidelity from a man. Never again would I let anyone drive me to the kind of rage and hatred I'd felt for Shandra. The next man in my life would have to complement me, bring out the best in me.

My heart knew that Morgan was just that kind of man.

As Morgan watched, I slipped the engagement ring Henry had given me off my finger and stuffed it into the pocket of my jeans. We stared at each other for a long moment, the significance of what I'd done requiring no words.

The door creaked open then, and both Morgan and I looked up. Detective Longhorne strolled into the room.

"You're free to go now," he told me.

"Will I have to come back? What about my friends, Miranda and Camille? Will they have to come in and answer questions?"

The detective shook his head. "As far as I'm concerned, the case is closed."

My heart filled with bliss. "You're serious?" I asked excitedly.

The detective smiled. "Yes, I'm serious."

"And the hazing?" The word still sounded harsh to my ears, but it was the only one that fit.

"Shandra James is dead. Unable to testify to any assault. Besides, the crime we're concerned with is murder. Tonight, there was justice for Shandra James."

"Wow." I blew out a long, relieved breath. "It's really over. I can finally get on with my life." It seemed almost too good to be true. "You're sure?" I asked Detective Longhorne. "This is really it?"

"Look, kid—get out of here before I change my mind, okay?" A smile danced in the detective's eyes.

He didn't have to tell me again. I jumped to my feet. I even gave Detective Longhorne an impromptu hug.

Then, grinning from ear to ear, I turned to Morgan. The smile he wore for me melted my heart.

"You heard the detective," he said. "No point in sticking around."

"No, none at all."

Finally it was over. Morgan took my hand and led me out of the police station.

Epilogue

Three months later . . .

IN THE MONTHS following Shandra's murder and Evelyn's subsequent death, life at UB was crazy. The media had dubbed Shandra's killing the "Sorority Girl Murder," a tagline that was salacious and garnered attention all over western New York and beyond. Being Evelyn's last intended victim, I'd been contacted by reporters more times than I could count, everyone wanting to know if I had any clues as to why a young girl such as Evelyn, with so much promise, would snap. I told all the curious that I was as clueless as they, although the truth was, I'd crossed my own moral lines where Shandra was concerned and felt I understood Evelyn's insane actions more than I wanted to.

As I knew he would, Henry had hoped to rekindle our relationship once he returned to UB, but I stood my ground. I was over him. No looking back. Morgan is my man now, and we've been getting along better than I thought possible. We've clicked in a way Henry and I never truly did.

Thanks to Morgan, my life has some semblance of normalcy amid the chaos, in that we go on dates and hang out and make love as if the world around us is normal. He's been my rock. And he's also helped me deal with my guilt. No, I didn't kill Shandra, but maybe things would have turned out differently if I'd never planned that initiation for her in the first place.

For the most part, I had put the ugly incident behind me and was moving on. But the news that another tragedy had struck close to home just after the New Year had me reeling.

Katrina's on-again, off-again boyfriend, Shemar Williams, had been tragically killed in a car accident.

"After everything we Alphas have been through," Camille, now ten pounds lighter, said when we heard the news. "I can't believe it."

"I feel awful for Katrina," Miranda said thoughtfully.

"God, I know. I can only imagine how she'll be hurting over this." I'd known Shemar, and while we weren't buddies or anything, the news of his death hit me hard, given the recent trauma I'd suffered.

If I felt as bad as I did at the news, Katrina had to be a wreck.

Ever since Shandra's disappearance and murder, Katrina and I no longer got along as well as we had in the past. She'd say hi to me if she saw me, but she did her best to avoid engaging in any small talk with me, and if she was more than twenty feet away from me, she ignored me altogether.

I was hurt by how she'd dissed me. I had hoped that with the truth of Shandra's murder public knowledge, the tension between us would dissipate. But it didn't.

The ramifications of what Evelyn had done had affected us in more ways than the obvious.

Still, despite Katrina's lack of affection for me, I felt I should reach out to her after Shemar's death. Which is why I went to her door shortly after she returned from the funeral the third Saturday in January.

But as I raised my hand to knock, I heard laughter coming from within the room. The laughter belonged to her—I recognized the high-pitched squeal-like sound. What I couldn't understand was why, only an hour after returning from her boyfriend's funeral, she was laughing about anything. When my uncle Manny died, I couldn't smile for months, let alone right after he'd been laid to rest.

I stayed at the door, hand poised, but didn't knock. I kept listening—eavesdropping like some sort of snoop.

". . . didn't want to, but for him to threaten . . ."

"Hey . . . did what you had to do . . ."

My eyes narrowed. Was that . . . Rowena's voice?

I glanced around to make sure no one was coming, then pressed my ear to the door.

"Poor Shemar."

More laughter.

Okay, something definitely wasn't right.

". . . run this sorority."

"Just like we planned" came Katrina's reply. It was louder, as if she was moving closer to the door.

My heart sped up, but I didn't step away.

"The only one to worry about now is Angelina," Katrina said.

"She doesn't know anything for sure. Besides, she's scared. If she's smart, she'll stay in Kentucky."

Huh?

Suddenly I heard the sound of the knob turning, and I jumped backward in fright. Then I bolted down the hallway, my heart pounding a mile a minute. I charged down the stairs, losing my footing as I hit the landing.

I twisted my ankle but didn't stop. I threw a quick glance up the stairs to see if anyone was coming.

No one was there.

I prayed they hadn't heard me.

I quickly hurried to my room and, once there, locked the door.

Camille had gone to hang with Kevin (they'd gotten back together before the holidays), so I was thankfully alone. My pulse continued to race as I lowered myself onto my bed.

What I'd just heard had my mind racing—and had me thinking of the one thing about all that had happened that didn't sit right with me.

In the various media stories reporting the conclusion to Shandra's murder, there was speculation as to whether Evelyn had also killed Carmen Young and attacked Angelina. The suggestion could be neither proved nor disproved, but in the Alpha house, a lot of girls believed it, figuring that the likelihood of two killers, given Evelyn's clear insanity, was far-fetched. That Evelyn had tried to kill me so soon after the attack on Angelina made people only more convinced. That and the fact that everyone remembered Evelyn had been missing from the house meeting the night Angelina had been attacked. People speculated that perhaps Evelyn had some sort of grudge against all of us.

And that's exactly what didn't feel right to me. Now, yeah, Evelyn obviously had a few screws loose to go as far as she did, but her justification of murder when she had me in the car—that Shandra had stolen her man and that I'd been an ungrateful bitch—made sense in a twisted sort of way. At least, I understood how she could rationalize her actions in her own mind.

But Carmen? Had Evelyn even known her? And I'd never known her to have any problems with Angelina.

Not that I *had* to know, of course, but still. When Evelyn had me kidnapped, figuring she was going to kill me so I'd never have a chance to talk, she had gloated at how cunning she was in regard to killing Shandra. Told me without qualms how I deserved to die. If she'd attacked Angelina and killed Carmen Young, wouldn't she have gloated about that as well? In a "this is how smart I am and no one has figured it out" way. Especially since, as she'd stated with reference to me, a corpse couldn't talk.

I'd never believed Evelyn responsible, and what I'd just heard . . .

Oh, my God. Could *Katrina* be the one who'd attacked Angelina . . . the one who *killed* Carmen?

Katrina and Rowena?

Angelina and Rowena in a heated discussion on the stairs . . .

Holy shit.

I knew I had to talk to Angelina. But I had no way to reach her. And if I asked our housemother for her number in Kentucky, she'd be damn suspicious.

And then it hit me.

Ned.

Angelina's boyfriend was a graduate student, living in graduate housing. He should know how to reach her.

And I knew just where to find him.

Ten minutes later I was out of my room and on my way to see him. I looked over my shoulder constantly, expecting to see Katrina or Rowena or both on my tail.

I found Ned in his room and, I have to say, he looked more glum than I'd ever known him to be. He was tall and very thin with thick glasses that did nothing for his face.

His eyes narrowed in question as he looked at me, and I could tell he was trying to remember my name.

"Phoebe," I supplied.

"Right. Hi. What's up?"

I shifted from one foot to the other. "I was wondering if I could come in for a minute."

He stepped backward and I entered his room.

"I'll get right to the point. I'm hoping you can give me Angelina's number in Kentucky."

"Why?" he asked, sounding defensive.

"I need to . . . ask her about something."

"What?" he pressed, now eyeing me suspiciously. And I knew then that he must know something.

"It's about who attacked her," I told him.

"Hmm." He nodded, his expression grave. "That changed everything," he said. "Everything between us."

"You broke up?" I asked.

"She's 'working through her feelings,' " Ned said, making air quotes as he spoke.

"I see." I paused. "Does she have any clue who could have done that to her? Please, it's important."

He shrugged. "I can call her. See if she wants to talk to you. She doesn't want anyone to have her new number—especially now that she knows about Shemar's death."

I followed Ned through the small living room to his phone, and looked away as he dialed Angelina's number. I listened while he greeted her, explained that I wanted to talk to her.

"Here," he said, passing me the phone.

"Angelina, hi."

"Before you say anything, Phoebe, I want to warn you that you're embarking on dangerous territory."

I let out a slow, nervous breath. "I hear you. But I have to know. Do you have any idea who attacked you that night when you left Ned's place?"

"Hell, yeah, I have an idea. Why do you think I left for good? But Phoebe—"

"Was it . . ." I lowered my voice. "Was it Rowena?"

There was a pause. "I can't say for sure. But the person was her height, her size. I think so, yeah."

Now I exhaled sharply. "Why?"

"Because I stumbled onto something. And Ned knows this, by the way, but I've sworn him to secrecy. A friend of his knew Carmen Young, knew that she'd applied to our sorority but had her application denied. No one in the house knew this, but apparently Carmen lodged a complaint with the national board, saying our sorority was discriminatory in denying her admittance. Something about how she met the grade-point average, and just because she wasn't 'beautiful' didn't mean she shouldn't be able to be an Alpha."

"Holy . . ."

"Apparently, a large part of her complaint was that Katrina was really nasty to her. She was prepared to take this as far as she could. When this friend of Ned's told me all this, I started to wonder . . . what if? I went to Rowena, thinking she needed to know. If necessary, she could contact the regional director about the issue and go from there. She got pretty upset with me, saying I was attacking our sorority president with an allegation that was ridiculous. That's when you saw us on the landing. I had to get out of there, see Ned. And the next thing you know, I was attacked."

"Oh, God."

"And now Shemar's dead?" Angelina went on. "I don't know the details, but I'd bet anything it wasn't an accident. I bet he knew what Katrina did, and she killed him for it."

I couldn't say a word. What Angelina had just told me fit with the snippets of conversation I'd overheard. Maybe both Rowena and Katrina had attacked Carmen in the woods, both of them snuffed the life out of her. . . .

But they hadn't had the two-person advantage over Angelina. . . .

"Phoebe?"

"Yeah?"

"They're dangerous. I don't know what their motives are, but they're dangerous. Don't even hint that you might suspect them of anything. Don't look at them funny, don't say a word. Unless you want to become their next victim."

A chill ran down my spine. "I won't," I told Angelina. "I swear. Thanks for sharing, and you take care of yourself."

"You, too. Be careful."

All the way back to the Alpha house, I was in a state of shock.

And fear.

Katrina and Rowena—killers.

Was it true, or was it all speculation? Certainly there was no concrete proof. But what I'd overheard . . .

It fit, God help me, *it fit*.

And whatever Shemar knew had probably gotten him killed.

I shivered as I walked past the Letchworth Woods, not daring to go near the bike path. I would never look at it the same way. I'd also never step foot on it again.

I wondered if the police would ever make the connection between Shemar's death and Katrina, but I doubted it. I certainly wasn't about to bring it up to them. I wasn't going to mention what I suspected to anyone. Not even to Camille and Miranda.

But in my heart I would know. Know that living in the Alpha house were two killers.

Killers who would likely never pay for their crimes.

Read on for an excerpt from the next book by

Kayla Perrin

WHAT'S DONE IN DARKNESS

Coming soon from St. Martin's Paperbacks

Prologue

University at Buffalo campus
Five years ago . . .

The night air held a biting chill, and the sky was darker than usual, filled with thick black clouds that looked almost ominous. The dark masses crept toward the moon, finally covering it completely—and providing the much-craved darkness on the street thousands of miles below.

With a final look around to be certain no one was in the vicinity, Katrina Hughes said, "Let's do this."

Going down onto her behind, Katrina lay flat on her back, then quickly slipped beneath the front of the car.

Rowena James blew hot air onto her gloved hands, trying to keep them warm as she glanced from left to right, keeping a lookout. At least there was no snow on the ground, but damn it was cold.

The light from the flashlight came on, illuminating the ground beneath the car. Rowena suddenly felt queasy. Was this truly necessary?

"Are you sure you want to do this, Kat?" she asked. "I mean, it's not too late to change your mind."

"Are you kidding?" came Katrina's reply. "Even the parking-lot light is out—a stroke of luck I couldn't have planned. It's fate. I *have* to do it."

Rowena said nothing, but she wasn't entirely sure that she agreed with Katrina's reasoning. This whole tampering with Shemar's brakes . . . the way Rowena saw it, this was too risky.

"And of course, Shemar had his car checked out earlier today. Got the all clear for his trip." Katrina chuckled. "The jerk won't suspect a thing."

Rowena tried to imagine the moment when Shemar realized his brakes were shot. Maybe it would happen long before he was on the interstate. Maybe the crash wouldn't be fatal. . . .

"Pass me the knife," Katrina instructed her.

Rowena bent low and placed the handle of the knife in Katrina's extended hand. "Are you even sure this will work?"

"Of course it will. I worked on plenty of cars with my dad. I know exactly what to do."

"But how do you know the brakes won't fail while he's driving out of this parking lot?"

"Because it's about putting a tiny hole in the brake line. That way, the fluid will escape gradually—most likely when he's going full speed on the interstate—before he realizes there's a problem."

Rowena stood slowly, glancing anxiously around the parking lot. Earlier that evening, Katrina had gotten Shemar to park in this exact location, under the guise that it was a great area to make out without prying eyes. Not that they didn't have rooms where they could get it on, but she had appealed to his sense of adventure and exhibitionism. And of course, Rowena could imagine that once Katrina had started to give Shemar a blow job in the car he stopped thinking.

Katrina's plan had already been in motion. She'd scoped out this spot and knew that it was a blind spot that the university's security cameras couldn't see.

In the distance, Rowena thought she heard a car, and tingles of fear spread through her. She bent low, saying, "Look, I was thinking . . . maybe we shouldn't. I mean, I don't think he'll ever—"

"That's right. He never will." Katrina peeked her head out from under the car. "And you know why? Because he's going to be fucking dead."

Rowena bit her inner cheek, trying not to let any emotion show on her face. But she wasn't comfortable with this. Not at all. Shemar . . . he hadn't been part of the plan. The others, yes, she could understand why. But Shemar . . .

"But what if it doesn't kill him?" Rowena asked. "He could be injured, sure. Maybe even paralyzed. But he might not die." And the last thing they needed was for Shemar to survive—and point the finger at them. Nothing about what they were doing could be construed as heat of the moment. Any charges would be of the first-degree, pre-meditated variety.

"Shit, will you stop worrying? I know exactly how to do this. He'll crash on the interstate. He won't have a chance."

Rowena stood tall and shifted from foot to foot, trying to keep warm. But the chill she felt was internal, and she knew it had nothing to do with the sub-zero Buffalo temperature on this brutally cold January night.

"I need you to get down here and hold the flashlight," Katrina said.

A quick look around the parking lot confirmed for Rowena that no one was coming. Then she did as Katrina had asked, carefully lying on her stomach. Katrina passed her the flashlight, and Rowena shone it under the car.

"Angle that light a little, will you?"

She turned the flashlight in a few different directions until Katrina said, "Good. Hold it right there."

The seconds seemed to tick by like hours. This was taking too long.

"How much longer?" Rowena asked.

"Just a moment. I want to make sure I hit the right spot. And it can't be obvious; otherwise the police will be able to see that the brake line was tampered with."

As Rowena's eyes went back to scanning the area, she suddenly said, "Oh shit."

"What?"

She quickly shut off the flashlight. "I think it's security or something. A car's coming!"

And in that moment, she found herself hoping that Katrina hadn't had enough time to do the deed. That the brake line remained intact and that Shemar wouldn't die.

"Maybe we should do this another time," Rowena said, unable to hide her anxiety.

"Are you in this with me or not?" Katrina snapped. "Because if Shemar brings me down, you go down, too. Is that what you want?"

Rowena swallowed. "No. Of course not."

"It has to be now. Shemar's leaving for Albany in the morning."

The car sounded like it was getting closer and slowing down. Was it entering the parking lot?

"That car is in the parking lot!" Rowena said in a panicked whisper. "We've got to go!"

Katrina emerged from the car but stayed low, glancing around. Still crouched, she made her way around to the rear of the vehicle. "Okay, then let's go."

Rowena followed her, her heart pounding. Damn it, they couldn't be spotted!

Katrina took the lead, creeping low behind the row of cars at the back of the parking lot to avoid being seen. After about thirty seconds—when they heard a car door slam shut in the distance—Katrina slowly stood to her full height. "Someone just got out of the car," she said. "Walking away from us."

Standing upright, Rowena followed Katrina's line of sight. About fifty feet away, a male was walking briskly toward the nearest residence building.

"We're cool," Katrina whispered. "He's not even looking this way."

Rowena started to jog toward the main path.

"Slow down," Katrina told her. "Walk calmly. No need to draw attention."

"I know. I just want to get out of here."

"We're two friends out for a stroll. Nothing suspicious."

Except for the fact that it was four in the morning and it was too cold for anyone in their right mind to be out on the campus grounds taking a stroll.

How did Katrina remain so calm while Rowena's heart was spazzing out?

"Did you do it?" Rowena asked after several seconds.

Facing her, Katrina's eyes lit up with malicious pleasure. "It's done. This loose end has been tied up. Shemar's as good as dead."

I

Present day

Shawde

Shawde Williams knelt onto the grass beside the tombstone, the tears already blurring her eyes. Five and a half years had passed. Five and a half years and her grief was still strong.

"Hey," she said softly, placing the bouquet of flowers in front of the tombstone. Five and a half years later and the fact that her brother was in a coffin six feet below this spot was still surreal.

Her eyes landed on the etching of her brother. Every time she came here, she was amazed at just how well his essence had been captured on the headstone. His handsome face lit up in a smile, those eyes twinkling, his dimples as charming as they had been live. She fingered the etching, the only way she could touch her brother now.

Then she fell onto her bottom, crying softly. She'd lost

more than her brother on that horrible day in January. She'd lost her mother, who had become a shell of herself as the despair had ripped her apart.

And most recently, Shawde had lost her fiancé because of this tragedy. Maurice had told her that he couldn't take it anymore. Either she let go of her obsession, as he'd called it, or they were done.

Shawde had called the wedding planner the next morning to tell her to cancel all the plans. Then Shawde had met with Maurice to give him back the ring. As long as she lived, she would never forget the look on his face as she'd placed the stunning diamond into his palm. The look of despair had damn near brought her to her knees. But he'd stood his ground, and so had she. If she wasn't over her obsession, then they were over. And she could never be over Shemar's murder—not until the killer was brought to justice.

Maurice didn't understand, and maybe Shawde couldn't expect him to. He hadn't had his family ripped apart because of a murder.

"What proof do you have that it was murder?" Maurice had asked before they'd finally called it quits, exasperated when she'd failed yet again to get the police to reopen the case.

"Shemar knew cars inside out. There's no way he would have missed an issue with his brakes. He would have given his car a complete inspection before a long road trip. I'm one hundred percent certain of that. And it's not that the cops didn't believe the brake line had been faulty. They just can't prove that it was deliberately tampered with. According to them, Shemar could have hit debris in the road."

"Exactly."

"But he didn't. That's not what happened."

"How can you know that?"

"Call it intuition."

"Intuition?" Maurice had thrown his hands into the air. "Do you even hear yourself?"

His patience had been wearing thin, and Shawde couldn't entirely blame him. Perhaps if their situations had been reversed Shawde would feel the same sense of exasperation. But this was her brother, and she could not go on until she got justice for him.

"Why would his girlfriend want him dead?" Maurice demanded.

"Some people are evil at their core. They get off on hurting others. People like you and me can never understand them."

"I don't understand you," Maurice had mumbled.

Shawde figured he hadn't thought she'd heard him, but she had. Loud and clear.

She'd slept alone that night, and a week later Maurice was telling her that she had to either let go of the past or forget about their future together.

"Maurice and I are over," Shawde said now to the tombstone. "He wants me to give up trying to solve your murder. Of course, he doesn't think it *was* murder. Dad's convinced, but thinks it's eating me up. And Mom . . . well, she can hardly talk about it. She's not the same, Shemar. She's . . . cries all the time. She retired, because she's too depressed to work." Shawde wiped at her tears. "Which is one of the reasons I *have* to keep going. Once Katrina pays for what she did, we can all heal. Finally put this past us."

As Shawde so often did, she stayed quiet, listening to see if she could hear the voice of her brother on a whisper of wind. Every fiber of her being believed that he was looking down on her, that he could hear her. That he was with her at this very moment.

It was one of the reasons she couldn't give up her fight. Shemar had been her little brother. She'd protected him in grade school. When that bully in his second-grade class had been beating him up, Shawde had given the little bugger a beatdown. He'd never bothered Shemar again.

A smile touched her lips as she recalled the memory. But it quickly faded.

The time it had mattered most, she hadn't been there to protect him. From that bitch Katrina. The moment she'd met Katrina when she'd visited the university in the fall, Shawde hadn't liked her. There had been no warmth in the smile she'd plastered on her face. In fact, it felt as though all the positive energy had been sucked out of the room when she'd entered, replaced by something cold and unsettling.

Shawde had told her brother that she didn't like Katrina, that something about his girlfriend didn't sit well with her. But Shemar hadn't dumped Katrina. Not that Shawde had expected him to.

Nor had she expected Katrina to kill him.

The last thing Shawde's brother had said to her was that he thought she was right. He'd learned something about Katrina, something upsetting. He hadn't shared with Shawde what that thing was but said he'd update her when he'd gotten to the bottom of it. He was planning to fill her in on all the details in person when he got back home to Albany.

Then his car had lost control on the interstate. For some inexplicable reason, Shemar's car had crossed the center line and collided with a truck. That had sealed his fate.

A fate that Shawde was certain Katrina had maliciously planned for him.

At first, the cops had speculated it was suicide, as the witnesses all said that Shemar hadn't applied the brakes. Further investigation of the burned car had shown that the brakes had failed because the brake line had been ruptured, but there had been no conclusive evidence that the car had been tampered with.

"I know you want me to keep going," Shawde said to Shemar. "And I know you'd do the same for me."

Shawde fell silent again. It was weird how five years could pass and yet a part of you still couldn't quite believe what had happened.

Looking at her brother's name, it was never quite easy to believe.

Shemar Lewis Williams

Then she read the inscription below the dates of his birth and death, even though she knew it by memory.

> Called to be an angel at the age of 21.
> You left a hole in our hearts,
> Where there hadn't been one.
> Our loss is heaven's gain.
> We try to remember that through our pain.
> Oh, how we miss you!
> And wish we never had to part.
> Gone too soon,
> But always in our hearts.

Every time Shawde looked at that inscription, she wanted to scream. She had wanted an inscription that reflected the truth. *You weren't supposed to die* or *Taken before your time* or even *Murdered by a devious bitch* would have indicated the reality of his death.

Shawde's anger was brewing, and she drew in a deliberate breath in an effort to calm herself. She had long ago stopped wearing an elastic band on her wrist, which she was supposed to snap against her skin when her thoughts began to overwhelm her. Such a stupid idea. It simply didn't work.

"One day," she said, smoothing her hand over her brother's face. "One day, Katrina will have to pay for what she's done. She's already killed again. I told you that. Her parents. I didn't realize it was so easy for people to get away with murder." Shawde snorted. "Hell, maybe I should just take her out."

She heaved a weary sigh. "Of course, with my luck, I'd get arrested. No, I'll just wait for her to slip up. Because I'm sure she will. The friggin' psychopath has killed and gotten away with it, so she's even more confident now. She'll kill again, but her luck will run out. And when it does, I'll finally get justice for you. I promise you that."